SUNSET FLAMES

BAYTOWN BOYS SERIES

MARYANN JORDAN

Sunset Flames (Baytown Boys)

Cover Design by: Becky McGraw

Editor: Shannon Brandee Eversoll

Proofreader: Myckel Anne Phillips

ISBN : 978-1-947214-13-2 (print)

Created with Vellum

AUTHOR INFORMATION

USA TODAY BESTSELLING AND AWARD WINNING AUTHOR

I am an avid reader of romance novels, often joking that I cut my teeth on the historical romances. I have been reading and reviewing for years. In 2013, I finally gave into the characters in my head, screaming for their story to be told. From these musings, my first novel, Emma's Home, The Fairfield Series was born.

I was a high school counselor having worked in education for thirty years. I live in Virginia, having also lived in four states and two foreign countries. I have been married to a wonderfully patient man for thirty-five years. When writing, my dog or one of my four cats can generally be found in the same room if not on my lap.

Please take the time to leave a review of this book.

Feel free to contact me, especially if you enjoyed my book. I love to hear from readers!

Facebook

Email
Website

In 2013, a couple set fire to over 80 structures on the Eastern Shore of Virginia. The story is well documented in the news, both before they were caught and during their trial and sentencing. The mostly volunteer fire stations in the rural area were working constantly for months to contain the destruction.

This book, a work of fiction based solely on my imagination, is dedicated to those who put their life on the line, as fire-fighters and emergency medical personnel.

AUTHOR'S NOTES

I have lived in numerous states as well as overseas, but for the last twenty years have called Virginia my home. All my stories take place in this wonderful commonwealth, but I choose to use fictional city names with some geographical accuracies. These fictionally named cities allow me to use my creativity and not feel constricted by attempting to accurately portray the areas. It is my hope that my readers will allow me this creative license and understand my fictional world.

I also do quite a bit of research for my books and try to write on subjects with accuracy. There will always be points where creative license will be used to create scenes or plots.

Four years ago, my husband and I discovered the Eastern Shore of Virginia and fell in love with the area. The mostly rural strip of land forming the peninsula originating from Maryland, has managed to stay non-commercialized. The quiet, private area full of quaint towns captured our hearts and we rushed to buy a little place there. It has become our retreat when we need to leave the hustle and bustle of our lives. I gather ideas, create characters, and spend time writing when not walking on the beach collecting sea glass.

1

Morning came too early. Or maybe the night lasted too long. Zac Hamilton squinted at the sunlight peeking through the blinds, groaning as he pulled the pillow over his head.

Thoughts of the previous evening flitted through his mind, halting any chance of catching a few more minutes of slumber. Rolling over on his back, he replayed the beach party given by some of the volunteers from the fire station. There were a few attractive women in attendance, one in particular he was just beginning to get to know when the call came in, he thought ruefully. Having to leave immediately, he did not even get her number. *God, when was the last time I got laid?*

Thoughts of her were replaced by the memory of flames dancing against the backdrop of the dark night. His crew was on point, being the first to arrive, but soon after two other fire stations came roaring to the scene as well. As the fire in the old garage was finally extinguished and the other stations left, his volunteers stayed to make sure there were no embers left to catch aflame again.

It had been almost two in the morning when they got back to the station from the scene, where he spent another hour writing up the report while the volunteers cleaned and repacked the equipment.

Fully awake now, he climbed out of bed and padded into his small bathroom. Finishing his business, he stood at the sink, his eyes on his reflection, drifting to the tattoos on his shoulders—one an anchor, eagle, waving flag and USN on a banner over it all and, on the other shoulder, the words *Baytown Boys...Never Forget*.

A slow smile crossed his face as he thought of the Baytown Boys. They had received the nickname as kids because where you saw one, you saw them all. The name stuck even when they played ball in high school. A group of friends, growing up in the sleepy town on the coast, itching to get away and see the world, all joining military services when they graduated.

Sighing, he lifted his hand, fingers skimming the surface of his tattoo. *We saw it all right.* He looked over the rest of his body, objectively analyzing taut muscles. As the Fire Chief for the Baytown Fire Department, he kept in shape and busy. *Too busy.*

The nasty taste in his mouth reminded him of the whiskey he drank when he got home. Just something to take the edge off and help him sleep. He knew that might be a reason but it sure as hell was not a good excuse. A memory of his dad flew through his mind, but he shut that down almost as quickly as it had come. *Nope, not going there. I am not my old man.*

Brushing his teeth to rid his mouth of the taste, he plunked the toothbrush into the holder harder than necessary. Blowing out a long, slow breath, he flipped off the light switch, moving back into his bedroom to pull on a pair of clean boxers, deciding to shower after breakfast.

Making his way slowly into the kitchen, he headed straight for the coffee maker. No coffee-pod machine for him. He liked it strong and black enough to chase the cobwebs away. He leaned his hip against the counter as he watched the coffee drip into the pot. It hissed occasionally, making him wonder if it was close to crapping out.

After another moment of mind-numbing staring, he shifted his gaze around the kitchen and adjoining living area. Luckily, he had a dishwasher or he was afraid there might not be a clean dish in the house. The refrigerator was old but kept the beer and groceries cold. The stove was new when he moved in, but he was hardly a gourmet chef so all he really needed was a stove eye for a pot or frying pan. He bought the microwave, it being the most used of anything in the kitchen besides the coffee maker.

The apartment was not large, but it was cheap. Very cheap. As the Fire Chief, he was offered the apartment in the attic of the fire station, at the back of the town's municipal building. Old, but clean, it was a functional place to call home. He snorted...*might be plain, but better than the home I grew up in.* Wondering where these morose thoughts were coming from, he picked up his coffee and took a sip. *Shit!* He jumped as the hot beverage burned his tongue, and shook his head in frustration.

Grabbing the frying pan out of the sink, he dropped a pat of butter into it and cracked a couple of eggs. Popping two slices of bread into the toaster and placing four slices of bacon onto a paper towel before shoving it in to the microwave, he turned back to the stove. Scrambling the eggs with a fork as they cooked, he threw on some cheese as he dumped it all onto a plate.

He carried his mug into the living room, walking to the window that overlooked the back of the property. He had no yard, but the neighbors had a neat, fenced-in back yard with a few trees and flower gardens. It was not much to look at, but at least it gave him a view. Turning around, he set his mug and plate on the scarred, wooden coffee table and sunk into the sofa. Those two pieces, plus the flat-screen TV on a stand, a small bookcase, and an end table with a lamp, were the only furniture in the room. He ate at the kitchen counter or on the sofa, not even having a table.

Sipping his now-cooling coffee, he tried to remember the woman from the party the night before, but figured it was better to forget since his life did not exactly lend itself to a relationship. *Hell, who needs a relationship? I'd take a quick fling!*

After a few minutes, the caffeine and food worked its magic and he dumped the dishes into the dish-washer before moving back into the bathroom to shower. It was one of his few days off from his job and he had some errands to take care of. Grabbing his truck keys, he jogged down the three flights of metal steps on the outside of the building.

An hour later, groceries bought and put away in his apartment, Zac had also paid his cable and internet bill, and hit the post office and bank. Now, he opened the door to Finn's Pub. Entering the cool, dark interior, he gave a chin lift to Brogan behind the bar.

The pub, owned by two of his best friends, Brogan and Aiden MacFarlane, and their sister Katelyn, was a local icon. Their grandfather, the restaurant's original owner, retained the look and appeal of days past. The building had been one of the early structures in the town. While renovated, it retained much of the original brickwork walls and floor. The bar ran the length of the right side with tall, mismatched, padded bar chairs up against the counter. The left held tables already full of patrons.

Aiden walked in from the back, where the kitchens were, and, seeing him, called out his greeting. Walking to the bar, Zac hefted up onto one of the stools.

"What can I get you?" Brogan asked.

"I'd kill for a Pub burger and fries."

"You got it." Brogan called a server over and gave her the order.

Aiden slapped him on the back and said, "You look a little worse for the wear. What the hell were you up to last night?"

"God, don't mention last night." Seeing the amused look passing between the two brothers, he shook his head. "One of my volunteer firefighters is getting ready to head off to Pennsylvania for a full-time job and a bunch of the others threw him a goodbye bash on the north beach last night. Needless to say, there were some vacationing women out there ready to have fun."

"Fuck! You didn't invite me?" Aiden complained.

Brogan popped Aiden on the back of the head and lifted one eyebrow. "What?" Aiden grumbled.

"You," Brogan said, pointing to Aiden, "stop cussing in front of the customers. And you," he pointed to Zac, "you're not going to find anything permanent with someone who's just here for the week."

"First off, not looking for that. And secondly, doesn't matter anyway," he replied. "We got a call before the night barely got started."

"Damn, man," Aiden said, shaking his head. "You're filling too many shoes over there at the station. When are you going to get some help?"

Saved from having to answer, he nodded toward the server as she placed a plate in front of him, the burger piled high with onion rings, tomatoes, lettuce, and cheese. The pub fries were perfectly crispy and the scent made his mouth water. Taking a big bite after dipping it in ketchup, he chewed in appreciation, before looking up to see his friends still staring at him.

Laying the burger down, he sighed. "Look, Brogan, I get that you've found the love of your life. And, so have Mitch and Grant. Not to mention our other friends who're now part of a couple. But some of us," he nodded toward Aiden, "haven't exactly found the *one*."

Aiden nodded in agreement, but Brogan leaned forward, his hands planted on the smooth surface of the bar and threw out, "And you thought you might find the *one* at a party with a bunch of vacationers only here for a week?"

He stopped and heaved another great sigh. "You're right. I went because I thought it might be fun. I'm not looking for anything else. And if I did find it? Let's not even go there. But the night ended fucked anyway. Got home about three a.m. and drank to get to sleep. God, that was stupid," he admitted, shaking his head. "I never do that. I don't know what I was thinking."

Aiden, called to the kitchen by a server, shot him a sympathetic look, leaving him to his lunch while Brogan glowered over him. He ate in silence for a moment then chanced a glance back up, seeing Brogan now staring back thoughtfully.

"You know you're not your old man," Brogan said softly.

His french fry stuck in his throat as he sucked in a breath. Nodding as he swallowed, he said, "I know. I guess sometimes I just wonder how far the apple falls from the tree."

Two weeks later, flames licked the sunset-streaked sky as the firefighters battled the blaze. The small barn sat on the back of an old farm property, about a mile off the main road that cut through the Eastern Shore of Virginia. No other structures were around and, with the barn's size, it did not take long for the blaze to be extinguished.

Zac jogged back to one of the fire trucks as the hose was being rewound. Pulling off his helmet, he nodded at the volunteer firefighters before moving to the truck from Easton. "Greg," he greeted, shaking the other Chief's hand after pushing back his Nomex hood.

"Zac," he acknowledged. "I just gotta say, I'm getting sick and tired of these fires." He looked over his shoulder and yelled instructions toward one of his men before turning back toward Zac.

"Just so you know, Greg, I've called a meeting of the emergency response team for next week."

"I saw that email. Totally agree. This shit has got to stop."

They watched as the county's fire investigator moved in after getting the all-clear from the firefighters.

"You think they'll call in anyone else? State Police? Maybe FBI?"

"I don't know," Zac replied, nodding at a few of the firefighters around. "I wouldn't be surprised if that's what happens."

"Hey, Zac," a call rang out behind him. Turning, he saw one of the new volunteers, Tad, carrying some of the equipment to stow in the truck. "You think they'll find anything? Is this like the others?"

Shaking his head, he replied, "Don't know and we're not going to make any statements until we do."

Greg dropped his chin to his chest and grumbled,

"Some of these damn kids get too fuckin' excited about this."

Slapping him on the back, he grinned, "Yeah, but where would we be without them?"

"Ain't it the truth."

An hour later, Fire Station 24's equipment had been cleaned and stowed and the group was ready to disband, when one of the volunteers called out an invitation to party at his home. His announcement was met with excitement from some of the other younger firefighters and eye-rolls from the older ones.

As Zac was about to exit the building, Tad came running up, his face split into a grin. "Chief, you coming?"

"Nah, not tonight." He watched confusion cross the young man's face and added, "I think my party days have come to an end, Tad. But y'all go have fun."

He stood with his hands on his jean-clad hips and watched the guys jog out to their trucks and SUVs. Shaking his head, he moved to the office to finish logging the call before moving through the station entrance to his apartment.

2

Madelyn Stevens climbed out of her car but instead of closing the door, she stood rooted to the pea-gravel driveway, staring at the house in front of her. The structure sat in the middle of a large, wide yard, the grass scruffy and in need of mowing. A shed was visible to the left, next to the property line, by the fence posts that were leaning almost criss-crossed.

The dull ache in her chest blossomed and she reached her hand up to place over her heart, massaging slightly to relieve the pain. A gust of wind slapped her and she sucked in a great gulp of air before letting it out slowly.

Knowing there was no getting out of what needed to be done, she slammed the car door after bending to retrieve her purse. Her heeled boots crunched over the drive as she made her way toward the front door. Stopping at the bottom of the front porch, she cast her gaze over the entire structure.

The weathered, grey, cedar boards appeared sturdy and she had to admit that the blue painted shutters gave the house a nice appeal. *At least he didn't let the place fall down around him.* Stepping to the front door, she reached inside her purse for the key she had been given. Placing it in the keyhole, she tried to steady the shakiness of her hand. Steeling herself, she swung the door open and hastened inside, immediately struck by a musty scent before the overload of what her eyes were taking in hit her.

"Oh, my God," she breathed. The TV show about hoarders flooded her mind as her back hit the closed door behind her.

Tightly shutting her eyes for a moment, she cast her mind to the last time she was here. Too many memories began to assault her, so she popped her eyes open, refusing to give the conflicting recollections a place to roost. Straightening her spine, she stepped forward, her gaze moving from one side to the other. A pathway led between all the furniture and as she moved into the living room taking up the front of the house, she realized it was not as bad as she had originally feared. There were no piles of trash, uneaten food, old pizza boxes. No rats running around. *Okay...so not like the hoarders on TV.* And, to her surprise, no empty whisky or beer bottles lying about.

But what she was left with was the evidence of her father slowly collecting pieces of furniture over the years without having a place to put them. Chairs balanced on top of tables, some with a precarious perch on wooden chests. The piles of furniture reached six feet high in some places.

She remembered his penchant for scouring yard sells and antique stores. *"Gotta dig deep to find the treasure, Maddie."* Being here, in this place, the words echoed in her ears as if they had been said aloud, causing a shiver to run over her. It had been many years since she last heard his voice and it surprised her how real they sounded.

Blowing out a breath, she walked through the living room and into the kitchen. Even though the living room was free of garbage, who knew what the kitchen would hold. A sigh of relief escaped when,once again, what she found was not disgusting, just crowded with furniture and bits and baubles. The counters were filled with antique glass jars and vases, with a small place carved out where he must have cooked and eaten. She remembered the spotless house her mother kept here. *God, I'm glad Mom didn't see this.*

A peek into the laundry room off the kitchen gave evidence to the same thing. More stuff piled on top of the dryer and the shelves. She walked back through the living room to the stairs and ascended to the second floor. She kept to the side with the railing out of necessity, considering the steps were loaded with boxes piled close to the wall. Bending over to lift the flap of one, she saw more glass and ceramic figurines.

At the top, the narrow landing gave way to three doors. The master bedroom, a smaller bedroom and one bathroom. She stood, perfectly still, as more memories slipped through the steel doors of her heart, days of laughter giving way to days of arguing and tears. Snapping her heart shut, she moved to the open door on the right where her parents used to share a room.

Just like downstairs, the room was piled high with boxes, furniture, antiques. There was a path from the door to the bed and to the closet, whose door stood open so she was able to see it filled with boxes. The old, maple bed was completely clear of rubble, which made her feel a tad better. No matter the state of their relationship, the sight of her father sleeping in squalor would have been too much. Instead, the bed, covered in a rose print quilt, looked very much like when her parents shared the room.

She stepped over a table, her hand reaching out to touch the fabric, desiring to feel something soft in this house filled with hard objects. The material was worn, but clean, which shouldn't surprise her given the state of the rest of the house—cluttered but clean—and yet she still wasn't expecting that.

Her gaze moved to the nightstand and, once more, she blinked in surprise. Three framed pictures stood, easily viewed, with no clutter around. One of her parents on their wedding day. One of her as a baby. And one of the three of them, in better times, their faces smiling at each other, a beach sunset in the background. That last image, of them walking on the town beach at the end of the day and watching the sunsets from the pier, shot another bolt of pain through her chest.

Heaving a great sigh, she swallowed audibly, wondering how many more shocks she could handle.

Turning, she stepped across the hall to the room that she once called her own. Opening the door, she gasped. No mess. No clutter. It was as though she had just left for school that morning and returned at the end of the day.

The weight on her chest squeezed harder and she blinked at the sting hitting her eyes. The oak, twin-sized bed was still draped with the pink and purple bedspread she had been so excited to get when she was ten. The matching oak dresser with the tall mirror lined another wall. The pink, ruffled curtains were still on the window. Her decorating style as an early teen had been pictures of sunsets instead of boy bands and several framed photographs she had taken were still on the wall.

Preserved. That was the only word she could come up with to describe her old room. Preserved. Like the antiques in the rest of the house. *What the hell, Dad?*

Her thoughts were interrupted by the sound of her phone ringing. Jogging carefully down the steps, holding onto the railing so she would not trip over the accumulations, to where she left her purse by the front door, she grabbed it. Answering, she listened before saying, "Yes, I'll be there in about fifteen minutes."

Disconnecting, she opened the front door and looked over her shoulder before stepping outside. Knowing she would be back soon, she sighed at the amount of work that lay ahead.

Sitting at a large, polished, cherry table, in a matching chair with a heavy, brocade cushion, Madelyn felt a sense of foolishness, considering only she and the funeral director were present. She assumed most funeral planning sessions included lots of family members, but with just the two of them the setting was a bit overkill.

Rubbing her head, she noted his sympathetic expression, thinking how practiced it must be.

"Mr. Melburn, let me get this straight. My father had made arrangements to be cremated and already paid for that."

"Yes, ma'am," he nodded, his solemn countenance and deep voice filling the room. "He also had a plot in the Baytown cemetery, already paid for as well."

"So, all I need to do is..."

"Just plan his memorial service."

She nodded, her mind numb, having no idea how to go about taking care of what Mr. Melburn seemed to think was an easy task. "I have to tell you that it's been a number of years since I was back in Baytown," she started slowly, choosing her words carefully. "And, I confess that my father and I were not...uh...very close."

She watched as he nodded in a noncommittal way, leaning back in his chair, steepling his fingers in front of him. Continuing, she said, "So, I really don't know of a minister here in town, or even if my father was...uh... religious..." She hated to flounder, but he leaned forward suddenly, his eyes wide as though hit with a thought.

"Let me make some calls for you," he said, giving off

an uncharacteristic enthusiasm. "I know your father was a member of the local American Legion organization. I'm sure some of their members would be able to come up with a few ideas."

"American Legion?" she asked, her brow knit with question.

"Yes, yes. The organization for veterans."

"Oh...uh...okay. I didn't know..." Now, feeling even more foolish, she wondered what else she did not know about her father. *And whose fault was that, Dad?* Struggling to push the heavy chair back over the plush carpet, she stood, wanting nothing more than to get out of the oppressive room, with its heavy furniture, dark burgundy, velvet curtains that kept out the sunshine, and the funeral director who knew almost nothing about her father but still managed to know more than she did.

"You have my number so you can have someone call me with any ideas," she bit out. "I'll come back tomorrow and we can settle things."

He jumped to his feet, his thin hand whipping out to clasp hers. "Of course, Ms. Stevens. And please accept my humblest condolences for your loss."

With a curt nod, she pulled her hand from his and turned on her heel, stalking out of the funeral parlor into the sunshine. Standing for a moment, she lifted her face to the sky, the warmth finally penetrating, and sighed in relief. Sucking in the fresh air, she told herself she could do this. *I can get this done and be back home in a week.*

Once inside her car, she headed down Main Street

seeing a few familiar shops that had been there since the beginning of time, but mostly quaint, little, new shops and cafes, unfamiliar to her. Passing by Jillian's Coffee Shop and Galleria, she stomped on the brakes. *I'd kill for a coffee!* Parking in the lot across the street, she jogged over, ready to immerse herself in a caffeine fix and spend some quality time alone.

Stepping inside the coffee shop, Madelyn looked around in awe at the exquisite interior. The dark wood paneling and antique glass counters along the sides gave a rich ambiance under the light of the sconces on the walls. Small tables were arranged in the front and she walked toward the counter, located in the middle of the shop. At this time of day, there were only a few patrons and, after placing her order, she sat at one of the small tables along the side.

The server brought her coffee and pastry over and Madelyn gratefully took a sip from the large cup. Closing her eyes for a moment, she savored the rich brew. She allowed her thoughts to wander away from her father's house, his funeral, and the fact that she was all alone.

"Hello," a female voice spoke nearby.

Startled, she opened her eyes, viewing a pretty blonde dressed in vibrant colors standing nearby, blue eyes staring at her, a wide smile sent her way. She immediately recognized Jillian Evans, the homecoming queen from when she was only a lowly freshman.

Sitting up straighter, she could not help but look to each side to see if there was someone else behind her that the greeting was aimed at, before smiling in return. “Um…hello.”

“I’m Jillian. Jillian Wilder,” the young woman introduced, her hand extended.

Her eyes widened as they landed on the wedding ring and she remembered the former quarterback, Grant Wilder. She extended her hand in return. “Is this your coffee shop?”

“Yes,” Jillian enthused. “I haven’t seen you in here before.”

“No, I’m new…uh…well, sort of new.” She observed the curiosity flashing through Jillian’s eyes, glad no more explanation was sought.

Jillian smiled and nodded toward the empty chair at the small table. “Do you mind if I join you?”

“Uh…no…sure.” Surprised at the enthusiastic woman who immediately sat down and nodded toward the barista, she tried to think of something to say. “Your shop is lovely. Really lovely.”

“Oh, thanks. My parents turned the old store into the coffee shop and after they gave it to me, I opened the art galleria upstairs.”

Madelyn’s eyes shot over her shoulder toward the wide, wooden stairs that cut through the middle of the shop. The carved spindles and railings were in the same wood as the paneling, adding to the dark, rich atmosphere.

“I’ll take you up later and give you the grand tour,” Jillian offered.

"Oh...you don't have to—"

"But I insist," Jillian interrupted. "I've got some friends arriving and I'd love for you to meet them. After all, since you're new in town, we need to make sure you have a proper Baytown introduction."

"I've been to Baytown before," she explained, fiddling with her napkin. "I'm just new now...or rather new again..."

"Well, it sounds like there's a story behind that statement," Jillian said, with a wink.

Before she had a chance to refute Jillian's assumption, the bell over the front door rang and, as she looked up, a group of women walked in. She sucked in her breath at a familiar face. *Katelyn MacFarlane...I'd know that thick, black hair even after all these years.* Her eyes shifted back to Jillian and she swallowed deeply as she watched her face light up. Unable to come up with a way to escape, she plastered a smile on her face as the women walked over to their table.

Jillian jumped up from her chair, greeting, "Girls, come on over. I'm just getting to know a new friend in town. She was just telling me that she's been here before but that's as far as we got."

Madelyn stood, politely nodding as Jillian introduced each one.

"This is my oldest friend in the world, Katelyn Harrison."

She quickly glanced at Katelyn's hand and saw the wedding band before looking into her face, which was more beautiful than she remembered.

"And this is Jade Greene, Belle Gunn, and Tori Evans."

*Evans...there was also Mitch Evans...I wonder...*startled out of her thoughts, she continued to smile as each woman greeted her, then realized they were all staring.

Jillian laughed and said, "I'm afraid I hadn't even gotten your name when my friends came in."

"I'm Madelyn...Madelyn Stevens."

She watched as both Katelyn and Jillian's eyes widened and she could see the wheels turning. Letting out a sigh, she held onto her smile as she said, "I actually grew up here...well, outside of town, but I remember you. I was a couple of years behind you two," nodding toward Katelyn and Jillian.

"Madelyn Stevens! I remember you," Jillian enthused, then halted as Katelyn elbowed her. Jillian twisted her head to look at Katelyn, her brow knit with surprise.

Katelyn stepped forward, reaching to take Madelyn's hands. "Oh, honey...I'm sorry. I just heard this morning about your dad."

Sucking in a shuddering breath, she blinked at the sudden rush of emotion. "Thank you," she managed to get out before Jillian tucked her arm with hers and began ushering her up the stairs. Calling for the barista to bring all their coffees to the galleria, she led the group upstairs.

Allowing herself to be ushered along, Madelyn's mind raced. *What have I gotten myself into?*

3

The public safety group was so large they were unable to meet in the police station workroom, so they moved to the municipal building's meeting room where large town meetings were held. Mildred and Mable, sisters and the police receptionists and dispatchers, hustled around to make sure the tables and chairs were in a large square so everyone could see everyone else.

Zac sat with Mitch Evans, Baytown's Police Chief and the other Baytown police officers, Grant Wilder, Ginny MacFarlane, Lance Greene, and Burt Tobber. He watched as others came into the room, all familiar considering the Eastern Shore of Virginia consisted of only two counties on the seventy-mile long peninsula.

Zac looked across the tables at Hannah Freeman, the Easton Police Chief, Wyatt Newman, the Manteague Police Chief, and Dylan Hunt, Seaside Police Chief. He knew that they, along with Colt, Liam, and Mitch, met monthly to coordinate any necessary law enforcement details. Other than the annual Emergency Management meeting, this was the first time he had been to a meeting with so many others in the area.

Within the two counties, there were about twenty small fire stations and several town police departments, as well as the two county sheriff departments. The arsonist had crossed county lines and, with numerous fires in the last six months, the emergency response teams were now meeting together.

He nodded at the Fire Chiefs from the other stations and watched as the other law enforcement officers sat down as well.

Colt Hudson, Sheriff of North Heron County, and Liam Sullivan, Sheriff of Accawmacke County, ran the meeting, reviewing the reports from each fire.

"We've been in contact with the State Police arsonist profiler and, I gotta tell you, there are a fuckin' lot of arsonist types," Colt said, shaking his head. "And within each of those types are lots of characteristics."

"So, we're looking for a needle in a haystack," Grant moaned.

Zac sighed, wishing the law enforcement personnel might have a way to stop the arsonist before it was too late and was left for the fire departments to have to deal with the aftermath of the destruction.

"So, far there's been little in common with the structures," Mitch said, looking down at the files in front of him, "other than they've all been empty. The fires have been set in sheds, empty garages, barns, abandoned houses."

"Thank God, so far they haven't struck homes with

people living in them or stores and businesses that would cause a financial hardship or loss of life," Liam commented.

Mitch looked over at Zac and said, "I know you've been a fire investigator. Any ideas?"

Running his hand over the back of his neck, he replied, "My fire investigation days were in the Navy and that was generally confined to the ships. I need to get the training here, but with each fire station only having a couple of paid employees and relying on volunteers for our staff and firefighters and rescue workers...well, it makes it hard to find the time." He watched the others nod in sympathy before he continued, "But what I know from the fires I worked on, it appears that the simple use of an incendiary device in a glass bottle—"

"A Molotov cocktail?" Ginny asked, leaning around to look over at him.

Nodding, he agreed, "Essentially. A gasoline soaked rag stuck in a bottle. The structures are old, wooden, some completely empty and some containing wood, papers, trash...things that will catch on fire easily."

The meeting continued for another hour as each fire station that had dealt with one of the fires gave their reports, as did the law enforcements involved. Zac grew frustrated at the lack of increased clarity with what they were dealing with. Lance leaned over and whispered, "Chill...these things aren't discovered quickly."

He nodded, but found it irritating nonetheless. "I

know...I've just got a really bad feeling that these will only escalate."

Lance nodded and, when his attention turned back to the reports from the others at the table, Zac found his mind wandering down a road he would just as soon purge from his memory. *The image of flames licking the walls, destroying everything in its path...everything I ever held dear.*

Madelyn stared in unabashed interest around the galleria as she was being led toward the tall windows overlooking Main Street. Jillian had hung local artist's work on the walls and used glass cases and pedestals to display pottery, sea glass art, wooden carvings, and bronze statuettes.

Before she had a chance to appreciate it all, Jillian was leading her to a round, glass-top table covered in lace doilies serving as the placemats. Sitting on the floral seat cushion, she admired the delicate, black iron chairs.

The others soon filled the chairs and accepted their coffees from the tray brought to them. The cup she had been drinking from made its way in front of her and she wrapped her hands around it again, sipping so that she would have something to do while she waited to see what the other women wanted to talk to her about. Self-conscious, her stomach clenched as she swallowed the flavorful brew.

"So, Madelyn," Jillian began, her voice soft, "I am so

sorry to hear about your loss. I'm embarrassed that I hadn't heard."

"Oh, it's fine," she assured, looking at the concerned faces around the table. "I just got in town early this morning and have only had the initial meeting at the funeral home. The obituary should appear in tomorrow's newspaper...I think that's what Mr. Melburn said." Feeling the heat of blush rise over her face, she rushed, "Not that I don't know...uh...there's just a lot..."

"Of course, there is," Tori nodded. "When a family member dies, there's so much to take care of and it can be overwhelming to keep everything straight."

She nodded, not knowing what else to say.

"I remember you," Belle admitted, a sweet smile on her face. "You were just a year behind me, I think."

"Yes, I remember you as well. You, Katelyn, and Jillian."

"When did you move away?" Tori asked.

Hesitating, she hated thinking of high school. Trying to think of how she could explain in simple terms what she never understood herself, she finally blurted, "When I was fourteen...I had just finished ninth grade." Seeing the lifted brows, she continued, "Uh...my parents split and my mom moved away, taking me with her."

"Did she come back here with you?" Jillian asked.

"No," she bit out, sharper than she meant to. Clearing her throat, she stared at her almost empty cup of coffee, before softening her voice, "She still lives in North Carolina and...well, they had not spoken to each other in almost fourteen years."

"So, this all falls on you," Belle said, her eyes filled with sympathy as her hand slipped across the table to clasp Madelyn's.

Looking over, Madelyn snorted, then immediately apologized. "I'm sorry. I'm just not used to talking about my family. It's...uh...awkward." Heat infused her face, but before she could blunder more, Jillian jumped in.

"We'd like to help. Truly, whatever you need."

"First, is the funeral," Belle said.

"Then there's the reception after the funeral," Katelyn began.

"And taking care of the property," Tori added.

Eyes wide, she sputtered. "No, that's not necessary. Really, I don't...I just..."

"Sweetie," Jillian said, placing her hand on her arm, "do you seriously want to handle this all by yourself?"

Chest heaving, she felt the sting of tears and blinked several times to gain control. Breathing deeply, she sat quietly, her thoughts churning. She knew it took strength to ask for help when needed. *Maybe they could help. The quicker it all gets done...the quicker I can leave.*

Jillian rose and moved to the top of the staircase, calling down an order. In a few minutes the server arrived with a pot of herbal tea, steam rising from the spout and a set of delicate china tea cups. Jillian smiled at him before she began pouring. "My grandmother always said that a pot of tea was needed in times of stress," she explained.

Accepting the cup, after pushing her now empty coffee cup away, she appreciated the calming beverage. She looked at the caring faces in front of her. Tucking her hair behind her ear, she tried to think of a succinct way to describe her situation.

Jillian's hand reached over the lace doily and gave her hand a squeeze. "Feel free to talk, Madelyn. Tell us anything you want us to know that will help."

Nodding, she offered a slight smile before beginning. "I suppose the simplest thing to say is just that my parents divorced fourteen years ago and when my mom left, she took me with her and Dad didn't...well, there was no communication." Shoulders lifting in a bare shrug, she pushed down the associated pain that stabbed her heart and said, "So, I had no idea what his life was like any more. I got a call from an attorney yesterday, informing me that my father had died that morning. It appears he had been sick recently and since the attorney was listed as the person to contact, the hospital had notified him."

Heaving another sigh, she continued, "Anyway, he said that I was listed as next of kin in his will and everything goes to me. So, after fourteen years, I'm back where I started, trying to figure out what the hell to do."

"And your mom?" Tori asked, her voice soft.

Scoffing, she said, "Mom never forgave Dad for his...failures. She's wrapped up with her second husband and they have their own life. So, when I called her last night to tell her I was coming to arrange the funeral and take care of settling his will, she just said 'good luck with that'." Snorting indelicately, she added, "Actually, Mom and I have a good relationship, but any mention of my dad and she turns into a shrew."

Katelyn, ever practical, stated, "What needs to be done first? Funeral arrangement? Reception?"

"Oh, no...no reception. I have no idea if Dad had friends, who they would be, and I don't know anyone. I think a small, graveside funeral. Mr. Melburn said he could talk to someone in the American Legion—"

"American Legion?" Jillian repeated, her eyes now bright. "Your dad was in the American Legion?"

"Well, according to Mr. Melburn he was." She tilted her head to the side, a crease lining her forehead. "But, I have no idea what that means."

"It's an organization for persons who served in the military," Tori explained. "And, it just so happens that my husband is the president."

"Our husbands are in it also and we are in the Auxiliary...that's for family members of veterans," Katelyn added, her eyes shining.

Licking her lips slowly, she pondered the pride in the other women's voices. "Okay...uh, I guess I'm still not getting the significance of Mr. Melburn's suggestion."

"Just think of it as an extended family," Jillian said. "The members would be more than happy to assist with the funeral and the Auxiliary will definitely assist with a reception."

"Assist how?" Rubbing her temple, she said, "I'm sorry to be so muddle-headed. All of this is so much more than I realized it would be. The funeral planning, I mean."

"I've been to a couple of funerals of other American

Legion members," Jillian said. "They can have a flag draped over the coffin—"

"He's being cremated."

"Okay, then they can have an honor guard carrying a flag, provide someone to do the eulogy, and the Auxiliary can provide refreshments for the reception."

Madelyn worried her napkin, her fingers needing something to fiddle with. "I...I'm not sure about a reception."

Belle leaned forward and said, "You know, honey, there may be friends of his in town that would like to get together to remember him."

Tears hit her eyes and her chin quivered. Swiping under her eyes with her fingers, she tried to quell the desire to curl into a ball. Sucking in a halting breath, she lifted her gaze to the concerned faces staring at her. "I didn't even know him..."

She lowered her eyes, not wanting to see the shared looks of pity she assumed would be passing amongst the others. Taking another sip of the now-cooled tea, she knew she needed to get back to the house to begin seeing what needed to be done.

Standing, she offered a heartfelt smile. "Ladies, it's been so nice of you to allow me to talk through this even though you don't know me."

"A stranger is just a friend you haven't met yet," Belle said, her smile genuine.

Jillian stood and offered her a hug. "We'll talk to our husbands and get back with you. We'll also take care of a simple reception. You don't have to worry about anything."

She nodded, unable to say anything in response. With goodbyes said after trading phone numbers, she walked down the stairs and back into the sunshine. Sliding her sunglasses onto her nose, her heart felt a little lighter than when she had entered. *Now to figure out what the hell to do with the house.*

4

The noise at the pub was growing as the crowds settled in. Zac sat with some of his friends, many of which had been at the emergency management meeting earlier in the day. A server brought over a pitcher of beer, winking at him as she walked away. He sighed. *Nope, not going there.* He did not want a short fling with someone he was going to be seeing around town all the time.

The door opened and a group of women walked in, heading straight for them. Mitch opened his arms for Tori while Grant did the same with Jillian. Jade slid onto Lance's lap and Belle sat down at the table. Katelyn moved to Gareth, her husband who ran a private investigation firm in town with her. Ginny looked over at Brogan, watching as he walked from behind the bar to where she was sitting, and wrapped her arms around his waist.

Before everyone had a chance to finish their greetings, Jillian spoke, "Everyone, we've got to talk."

Zac looked up in surprise at the seriousness of her tone and, considering Grant's lifted brow, he had no idea what his wife was going to say either.

"Do any of you know Lenny Stevens from the American Legion?"

Mitch nodded, "Yeah. He only came to a few meetings but he spoke at one of them. He was normally a quiet man, but seemed eager that night to talk about some of his experiences in the Navy."

Zac perked up, the memory coming back to him. "That's right. After that particular meeting, he and I talked for a while about the Navy. We never really had a chance after that to get together, but we said we'd share a beer sometime after another meeting." Looking up at Jillian, he said, "What's up with him?"

Tori replied, "He died two days ago at the hospital."

The group startled, almost in unison, and sounds of "oh, shit" and "fuckin' hell" filled the air. Nodding, Jillian said, "We met his daughter today. She's in town to arrange the funeral and happened to come into the coffee shop. At first, I just wanted to greet a new customer, but then we started talking and I found out who she was."

"She was a year behind me in high school," Belle interjected, "and she left after that year, so some of you probably wouldn't remember her."

"That would be when most of you were seniors or had just graduated and left for the military," Tori said, looking at Mitch, but Zac knew she was speaking to most of them.

"Sweetheart, I'll certainly let the other American Legion members know. I'm assuming the obituary isn't out yet?" Mitch asked, his hand squeezing Tori's waist.

"Madelyn said it would come out tomorrow, but she's struggling with everything now."

"And that's where we all come in," Katelyn announced, holding everyone's attention.

Zac's thoughts were tumbling back to the conversation he had with Mr. Stevens, a strange melancholy passing over him. Hearing Katelyn clear her throat, he jerked his eyes back to her face, seeing her cast her gaze around the gathering.

"Madelyn is overwhelmed with all that she needs to do and we volunteered to help."

"What do you need?" Brogan asked, staring at his sister, his normally hard face softened.

"Well, it seems that when her parents split, they *really split* and by that, I mean her mom took her away and her dad had no contact with Madelyn since then. So, here she is, having to plan a funeral and handle his estate. She was listed as his only heir."

"And before you think poorly of her," Jade added, "she appears to have been abandoned by her father and her mother was just as happy to have Madelyn stay away from him."

"God, families can be so fucked up," Lance said, shaking his head, Jade nodding her agreement.

"And, for those of us lucky enough to have the kind

of families that have never had those problems, we need to be ready to help," Katelyn pronounced.

Jillian looked toward her cousin, Mitch, and said, "Can the American Legion provide some kind of service...like an honor guard, or a flag, or...I don't know."

"She said he's being cremated," Belle interjected, "so there won't be a coffin to drape a flag over."

"We can still provide a flag for the service and then present it to her," Mitch said. "And we can certainly let the other members know."

"The service is going to be held at the funeral home, so it will be simple," Tori added.

"Did any of us know him well enough to speak or just say a few words?" Grant asked.

The group was silent for a few seconds, the Legion members seeming to struggle as they thought back to Lenny.

Looking around, observing none of the others appeared to remember much about the man who only came to a few meetings, Zac suddenly announced, "I will."

The others turned to him and he hastened to add, "I didn't know him well, but we talked a long time that night about the Navy. I could just mention a few words about that...you know, duty and service, and all that."

"Oh, Zac, thank you," Jillian gushed, her eyes warm. "I just felt so sorry for Madelyn today. She seemed incredibly lost."

"The Auxiliary is going to host the reception and we thought we could do it at the meeting hall. It could be set up before the service and then it's just a five-minute walk from the funeral home to the hall," Tori added. "I'll call the other Auxiliary members and we'll set it up nicely."

"Sounds like a plan," Brogan said and, with a wink at Ginny, he and Aiden headed back to the bar. The other couples settled into chairs, their conversations more subdued than before.

Zac looked around, his eyes landing on all his friends, most in couples, and he suddenly felt like the odd man out. After what happened to his dad, he was convinced love was not worth the pain it produced when gone. Looking down, he noticed his hand was absently rubbing over his chest, as though wondering why he felt so empty.

Hearing a roar of cheering from the front, he recognized a few of their single friends near the dartboard. Callan, still in the Coast Guard; Jason, a former Navy veteran, now owning the garage and a tattoo parlor in town; and pretty Belle, who had left the couples and wandered up front to cheer the game on.

Standing, he made his way there as well, joining in the rousing game.

Madelyn stood in the kitchen, wondering where to start. Unable to stomach the idea of cooking in the house, she had picked up a sub from the grocery store, where she also bought water, milk, cereal, cleaners, and garbage bags. With a sigh, she opened the refrigerator door and began taking every item out, placing it in one of the bags. Thankful there was not a lot to throw out, she soon had the refrigerator empty and was pleased to find it relatively clean on the inside. It only took a few scrubs with a soapy sponge to have it spotless.

Sucking in a deep breath through her nose, she let it out slowly before placing her carton of milk and water bottles inside.

She eyed the glassware, figurines, and other boxes on the counter and wondered who might want them. Giving her head a shake, she felt the snake of panic rising. *This is too much for me to handle. I only took a week off work...how will I ever get this done!*

Leaning her hip against the counter, she cast her eye around the furniture piled in the room. The pieces appeared old, but were in excellent condition. Carrying her water with her, she walked into the living room, her eyes now assessing the furniture piles in there as well. Running her fingers over the spindles of a chair she pulled out her phone and did a search for antique dealers in the area. Finding a few that looking promising, she moved into the kitchen again and found a piece of paper. Writing the names down, she determined to call them tomorrow. *I'll have someone appraise all this and sell it as a lot.* Pleased with her decision, she knew she just might be able to get back home in a week...leaving Baytown behind once more.

Climbing the stairs, she walked into her bedroom, flipping down the covers. Expecting dust, she was taken aback at the cleanliness of the sheets, almost as though he had been expecting her. Falling into bed, she lay there, her mind swirling, as sleep came uneasily and thoughts of her father invaded her dreams.

Sitting at his kitchen counter, pen and paper in hand, Zac stared into space, wondering what had possessed him to volunteer to offer the eulogy for a man he barely knew. *But, then, it sounds like no one really knew him well. Even his daughter.*

Curious, he walked to his bedroom closet where a stack of plastic storage tubs was stacked. There was little saved from his childhood, but he had managed to get a few things before it was too late.

Opening the one on the bottom, he dug through the items of his childhood and found the high school yearbooks. Pulling out the one from his senior year, he flipped through the pages, looking for the ninth graders. *Madelyn Stevens.*

A dark-haired girl stared back at him. Unsmiling. She did not look familiar but, then, as a senior, he paid little attention to the young girls in the school, preferring flirtations with the older ones. Still, as he stared at the picture, he saw the promise of beauty in her features.

Putting the yearbook away, he sat down at the counter, determined to not put off the eulogy any longer. Closing his eyes, he thought back to his few conversations with Lenny. The Navy. The early days of war in the Middle East and being on a ship. An aircraft carrier.

As the older man's war stories came back to him, Zac began writing them down. An hour later, he re-read what he had written.

Standing, he moved to his sofa, but did not turn on the TV. Instead, his mind was filled with Lenny Stevens...and Zac's own father. *Did they know each other?* Shaking his head, he wondered if they had been buddies many years ago. Closing his eyes in anguish, he forced thoughts of his dad from his mind until he was interrupted by a call out.

Jumping up, he rushed into the fire station, getting into his gear as the group of volunteers did the same. Heading out, he gratefully settled his mind on the danger ahead, leaving the past where it belonged.

5

Madelyn walked down the aisle to the front row of pews in the funeral home chapel. Like a dream, she felt as though she were floating near the ceiling, looking down on the gathering. The room was filled with more people than she could imagine her father knowing, all smiling politely at her.

Swallowing deeply, she wondered what they thought of her. *Do they think I abandoned him, when it was the other way around?* Forcing a neutral expression as she nodded toward the smiles sent her way, she sat in the front row, acutely aware that she would be there alone. All alone.

A shadow appeared next to her and she looked up in surprise as Jillian and a man slid into the seats next to her.

"No one should be alone at this time," Jillian whispered, her eyes warm.

As her gaze shifted from Jillian to the handsome

man accompanying her, she startled, recognizing Grant Wilder from high school. Every teenage girl had had a crush on the handsome football quarterback, but he only had had eyes for the pretty homecoming queen. *Looks like fairy tales can come true...for some.*

Feeling less conspicuous, she offered a grateful smile, then looked to the American Legion Chaplain in the front of the room, as he began his welcome. Scripture verse followed, along with the singing of *Amazing Grace*. He spoke for a few minutes about having met her father at the American Legion meetings.

"His fellow antique collector, David Wills, would like to say a few words."

She watched as a dapper, middle-aged man walked to the front, his smile wide as he began relating the many trips he would take with her dad as they looked for antiques to refinish or collect. Her heart felt a pang, remembering when she was a little girl and he would take her out to visit shops or auctions. Glad when Mr. Wills finished, she hoped the service was drawing to a close.

The chaplain spoked once more. "At this time, I invite Zachary Hamilton to come forward."

She heard shuffling from behind as a man, dressed in a dark suit, walked to the podium and turned to face the crowd. She sucked in her breath as recognition flooded her. *Zac...one of the Baytown Boys.* She remembered the dark-haired boy, all lean muscles and cute smile. She used to watch him at baseball practices, hating to go home too early. *What is he doing here? How did he know my father?* Palms sweating, she wiped them on her skirt, hoping no one noticed.

Zac looked out on the gathering, the attendees mostly from the American Legion, though there were a few other townspeople. His gaze roamed past his friends, landing on the front row at the beautiful, dark-haired woman sitting next to Jillian, her wide eyes pinned on him. Knowing he must be looking at Madelyn, he faltered at the realization that her early adolescent promise of beauty had been fulfilled. Her stare glued him to the spot and it took a second before he dragged his eyes away from her, remembering his eulogy. With a deep breath, he began.

"I had the privilege of meeting Leonard Stevens about six months ago at an American Legion meeting. He approached me after the meeting to say that he had served in the Navy, as had I, and he just wanted to shake my hand. Of course, it was an honor for me to be the one shaking his hand.

"He missed several meetings after that, but the next time he came, I invited him to the pub afterwards, but he declined. I got the feeling that he still wanted to chat but the pub might have been too noisy. Anyway, we ended up stacking the chairs by ourselves after the meeting and spent time talking. He asked about my time in the Navy, but I was most interested in his. He spent his tour of duty off the Saudi Arabian coast near the Iran-Iraq War exclusion boundary. He served as a radioman on the frigate, USS Stark, and he told me he was onboard during the Incident."

Zac grinned slightly, shaking his head. "I always

thought it was funny that the United States called it an *incident*. Guess that makes it sound better than attack. Anyway, an Iraqi jet aircraft fired missiles at the Stark."

Sobering, he continued, "He said thirty-seven crew members died that day and over twenty more were injured. I know a lot of people just assume that the Navy did little during the Gulf Wars, thinking of the land-locked countries, but between aircraft carriers, diving missions, escorting oil tankers and other craft, the Navy saw a lot of activity. But the attack on the Stark was different and I could tell it struck Lenny deeply."

He chanced a glance toward Madelyn, seeing her eyes still wide, his story obviously not familiar to her. He felt drawn in for a moment, staring into her eyes, seeing a strangely familiar, haunted specter in them. Clearing his throat, he said, "Lenny said that he was the radioman who was ordered to message the unidentified aircraft to identify themselves and when no such identity came back, he had to send the order again. Only one minute passed before the fighter fired their missiles. He remembered the whole ship rocked with the explosions and orderly chaos began. He stayed in the radio room, not knowing the extent of the damage, the ship listing to one side. He recalled how fear curdled in his stomach, wondering if he would ever get back home. It wasn't until later that he would know who had perished and the deaths stayed with him for years afterward."

Zac paused for a moment, casting his eyes over the group. "For those of us who served, in whatever branch or capacity, we go in knowing that death can be a reality, yet it is only when it occurs to those we know that we can truly appreciate the sacrifice of service. After we talked that night, he didn't come to the next few meetings. I saw him in town one day and he mentioned that he had been sick, but that he would be back soon. I wish I had had a chance to get to know Lenny more...I now feel guilty about that. But that night, he thanked me for allowing him to talk about his time in the service. He said it gave him some closure to talk about that day. So, to Lenny Stevens, I thank you for your service and you can rest easy knowing that we will assist your daughter in any way we can." Smiling toward Madelyn, he observed her shock at his words and the slight blush that rose over her cheeks.

Madelyn sat in stunned surprise during Zac's eulogy. She had never heard her father speak of being in the military, much less on a Navy ship during wartime. A flash of unfamiliar jealousy shot through her as she realized how much more of her father Zac knew than she did. *Well, that's not true*, she argued with herself. *He only knew the small bits Dad told him. I'm sure I am the only one with the knowledge that I wasn't worth fighting for.*

As the service came to a close, she pushed those negative thoughts to the back of her mind. *God, now I have to get through the reception.*

The inside of the American Legion meeting hall was utilitarian, but the Auxiliary had placed tables together, laden with food. Platters of chicken wings, vegetable and fruit trays, bowls of potato salad and pasta salad, and cakes, brownies, and pies galore. At one end, punch bowls and glass pitchers filled with iced tea sat near plastic cups.

Madelyn, escorted inside by a wave of well-wishers, smiled her thanks while battling light-headedness. Soon, the ladies had her seated at a table, a plate of food in front of her and an endless line of people expressing their condolences.

It seemed each one wanted to share a tale, experience, anecdote about her father, and with each reminder that she never really knew him she grew angrier. Refusing to let it show, she smiled, shook hands, nodded appropriately, and after what seemed like an eternity, the crowd finally started thinning and those left had gathered at other tables to talk amongst friends.

Mr. Wills stopped by, grasping her hands in his, and said, "My dear. You must be so overwhelmed. I know your father had a great many antiques in his house and I might be one of the few people in the county that know their worth. Please give me a call as you decide how you want to settle things." Before she had a chance to respond, he pressed his business card in her hand and walked off. Staring dumbly after him, she simply slipped the card into her pocket, before turning to the next person.

As Jillian, Katelyn, Belle, Tori, and Jade sat down at her table, she stood suddenly, desperate for a break. "I'll be right back," she said, a smile cemented on her face. "I just need to run to the ladies' room."

Turning, she quickly escaped, finding a hall nearby. A door to the outside was just beyond the restrooms and she gratefully pushed through, the sunlight hitting her face. Propping open the door with a rock to keep it from locking her out, she leaned against the warm brick building, closing her eyes as she breathed deeply, willing the day to be over.

Utter, bone-wearying exhaustion threatened to overtake her. *How do people get through these things?* She wondered if it would have been easier or harder if she were still a Baytown resident with a close relationship with her father. *Doesn't matter...I'm not and I didn't.*

Hearing a noise, she jumped, her hand landing on her throat. Blinking in the bright sunlight, she noticed Zac in the doorway, his eyes pinned on hers.

"I'm sorry," he said, staring at her. "I didn't mean to startle you, but I saw you leave and wanted to make sure you were all right. Then, I saw you standing there and realized...uh...well...I thought you might want to be alone. Which, I suppose, if you did, then I've just ruined that, haven't I?"

A snort of laughter erupted from her lips and she immediately covered her mouth with her hand, thinking both how refreshing it was to see him flustered and how inappropriate it was for her to laugh on the day of her father's funeral.

"Please don't stop smiling," he said, stepping closer. "It's the first real emotion I've seen from you today."

Like a cold shower, she sobered, adopting a composed persona. "I haven't thanked you yet for the kind words you shared at the funeral today. I'm sure my father would have been pleased."

Zac stared, silently observing as her robotic façade slid into place, and wondered what was going through her mind. Her pale complexion was flawless but it was her brown eyes that riveted him. Deep brown with gold flecks. Her dark hair was pulled back in a sleek pony tail at the base of her neck. Her dark dress was demure, yet classy. Wanting to know what she thought, he asked, "But were you pleased?"

Blinking, she startled, opening and closing her mouth a few times before blurting, "What?"

"I'm just wondering if you were pleased."

"Me? I don't see what I have to do with anything—"

"Because, Ms. Stevens, the funeral is for the living… those left behind. I just noticed that you seemed so uncomfortable inside."

Pinching her lips together, Madelyn wanted to rail at him, call him out for his impertinence. *He doesn't know me. How dare he judge me for my emotional state at my own father's funeral.* Swallowing deeply, she remained quiet, looking back out onto the quiet street.

"So," he continued, his voice as soft as silk, "I just wondered what you thought."

Whipping her head around to face him, causing the

loose strands of her hair to fly about her head, she glared. "What I think? What I think is that I am surrounded by people I don't know offering condolences for the loss of a man I hardly knew and hadn't seen in fourteen years! Who felt free to tell other people that he was in the Navy, saw things, lost things, but didn't even want to keep what he had!" Inwardly wincing at her harsh tone, she forced her grimace to stay firmly on her face, until she saw the hurt flash through his eyes.

"I'm sorry," he said, stepping backward. "I should not have intruded." With that, he turned and, after making sure the rock was still in the doorway, he reentered the building, leaving her standing alone.

Slumping back against the wall, she attempted to swallow the tears threatening to fall. Swiping her fingers under her eyes to clean any running mascara, she straightened, taking a deep breath before throwing open the door to make her way inside, once more plastering a polite smile on her face.

Entering the reception hall, she made her way back to the table, seeing the other women sitting there. Sitting, she apologized for her delay.

"Oh, sweetie, this day has been really hard, I know," Belle said. "You don't need to apologize for anything."

Glad that their conversations turned to other topics, she finally worked up the courage to ask about Zac. "The young man who gave my father's Navy eulogy, I believe he was one of the Baytown Boys?"

"Yes," Jillian acknowledged. "He, along with Mitch, Grant, Aiden, Brogan, Callan, and Philip. They all left for the military after high school...each finding their way back to Baytown."

Nodding, Madelyn recognized all of the names and had seen them all at the funeral, except for one.

Katelyn, watching her face, said, "Philip Bayles didn't make it back. He's buried in the town cemetery."

Suddenly remembering seeing Katelyn and Philip together in high school, she sucked in a quick breath, but before she could speak, Katelyn continued.

"I grieved for many years, but found love again."

A smile curved her lips, and she recognized it as only the second heartfelt smile of the day. The first one being outside with Zac. *Who I was completely rude to.* Before she had a chance to ask more about him, Jillian spoke.

"Zac had to attend the funerals of both his parents, so I always wonder how hard these are for him."

As the other women clucked in sympathy, her heart stopped. *Oh, my God, and I was such a bitch! Lashing out at a man who has suffered loss himself and was only trying to help.* Closing her eyes for a moment, she knew she needed to apologize. Glancing around the room to the few still in attendance and the Auxiliary women packing the food away, she observed he was no longer there.

As she stood, about to make her farewells, two attractive older women approached. Introducing themselves as Nancy and Claire Evans, Mitch and Jillian's moms, they hugged her before letting her know that they were packing the food for her to take with her.

Looking at the table, now loaded with Tupperware

containers, enough to feed an Army, she was about to protest, when two more women approached, Corrine MacFarlane and Marcia Wilder, Katelyn and Grant's mothers. Seeing her wide-eyed stare, they shared a look between themselves.

"I can see that this is overwhelming," Nancy said. "How about if we give you a little food to take back home and we can donate the rest to some of the needy families in the area?"

Madelyn's relief was obvious as her forced stance relaxed. "Oh, thank you. I would so much more appreciate that than to have it go to waste." As she stood there, surrounded by women, their men nearby, feeling more supported than she had in years, she let out a long sigh.

Another woman approached, her hand extended in greeting. "I know you're overwhelmed, but I wanted to say how sorry I was about your father. I'm Tonya Bayles. I believe you were in the same class as my daughter, Sophie."

Casting her mind back, she remembered Sophie Bayles, a little red-headed girl with pigtails. Smiling warmly, she nodded as she said, "Yes, I do remember her."

Tonya stepped back next to the others and Madelyn turned toward them, glad for what they had done and, yet, ready to flee.

"I want to thank you all," she said, reaching out to grasp Jillian's hand while her gaze landed on the entire group. "For the service and this reception. I don't think I could have done it alone."

"What are your plans?" Mitch asked, his hand resting on Tori's waist. "Is there anything we can assist with?"

She shook her head. "You've done more than enough. I'll call Mr. Wills and have the furniture assessed before I sell it. Then I'll contact a realtor to have the house go on the market before I leave."

"How long will you be here?" Tori asked.

Shrugging, she said, "I took one week off work so, hopefully, I'll get it all done by then. If not, then I should be able to handle things long distance."

As exhaustion crept over her body, she offered hugs of thanks and goodbyes before taking her few food items and walking back outside. Looking up, she noticed the sun had moved across the sky. A memory of her father taking her mother and her to the pier to watch the sun set filled her mind. Back before everything went to hell. *Maybe this evening...for old times' sake. Just one more sunset...this one for me.*

6

Zac stood at the end of the pier, watching the gulls dip into the water as the sun began its descent into the horizon. The blue sky was now lit with every shade of orange, pink, blue, and slowly morphed into adding shades of purple.

Leaning his forearms on the railing, he kept his eyes trained where the sky met the sea, the sight never getting old. He remembered his dad bringing him to the pier to fish on weekends when he was little. Before. Before life changed and there were no more fishing trips. At least not with his dad.

Rubbing his hand over his face, his mind moved to the funeral. Sighing heavily, he thought of Madelyn with her haunted eyes. After what she had said, he figured she wasn't just sad for the loss of her father. The funeral was just a reminder that she had already lost him. *I know all about that.*

The sky morphed into a darker purple and he stood

straight, saying goodbye to another day. Turning, he walked back down the town's long wooden pier, taking him toward the beach.

The day had stretched interminably, but he knew it must have felt longer to Madelyn. It was clear her relationship with her father had been strained...distant. And that could only serve to make her feel like a stranger at the funeral and reception.

He looked toward a bench near the edge of the pier and, as if conjured from his thoughts, there was Madelyn, her eyes trained on the bay. Her dark pumps were on the bench next to her and, while she was still in her dark dress, her hair was no longer pulled back. The breeze blew the tresses away from her face, giving her a much softer appearance than earlier at the funeral. He raised his hand, then hesitated, wondering if she would welcome him breaking the spell that the sunset cast.

Her gaze must have caught the movement because her head turned his way. He watched as recognition flitted through her eyes. Continuing to raise his hand in a small wave, the air rushed from his lungs as she smiled in his direction.

Walking over, she stood as he neared. "Hello, Zac."

"Madelyn," he greeted with a smile.

"Sunset watching?"

Laughing, he said, "It's practically a Baytown resident pastime. One of the perks of living on the bay."

Madelyn watched the crinkles at the corners of his eyes and a flashback from high school came to her, a time when she saw him running to home base during a Baytown baseball game, his smile just as wide. Blinking away the childish memory, she said, "Would you care to join me?"

Zac hesitated for only a second, wondering if her offer was sincere or if she were simply being polite. "I'd love to, but don't want to intrude on your thoughts."

Sighing softly, she said, "I'm sorry about earlier. I shouldn't have taken out my...frustration, on you. It was all just a bit much and I didn't handle it well. Honestly though, the last thing I want tonight is to be alone with my thoughts."

Nodding, he sat down on the wooden bench facing the water, now reflecting the evening colors. They sat in silence for a moment, but he found it peaceful. Many people try to fill silence with talk, but he appreciated the quiet. Glancing to the side, he observed her profile.

Her dark hair, long and loose, blew away from her face from the gentle bay breeze. Her nose, slightly upturned, gave her an impish appearance. Her complexion was pale as porcelain, but her cheeks were rosy. Her eyes were closed and he stayed quiet, wondering if she were in prayer.

Suddenly, they blinked open and she turned toward him. Her eyes were large. Brown, but in the final light of the day, he could see flecks of gold in them. As though a hidden treasure lay within. Mesmerized, he blinked when she spoke.

"I want to thank you for everything you did today... well, you and the others."

"It was our pleasure, I assure you."

Shaking her head slightly, she said, "To me, it was invaluable. If it had been left up to me, I would have had a private memorial with just myself, taken his ashes, and walked away. I had no idea what to do, who to notify...nothing. I am only going to be here for a week and felt overwhelmed. Though, I might have to call to have more time off."

He watched as her eyes darkened, the light dimming as though she had flipped a switch, and he wanted to turn it back on.

She continued, "The service was lovely and so were your words. I had no idea my dad had been in the Navy, much less had anything remotely adventurous happen to him." She looked down at her hands, clasped tightly in her lap. "It turns out there is very little I knew about him. But, at least, now I know he had friends." A rueful groan slipped out as she added, "Friends and a life."

"Madelyn, I don't know what happened with your family, but you aren't alone here. There are lots of people who will help and that didn't stop with just today. Whatever you need, you just have to let us know. I mean, hell, try to keep Jillian and Katelyn out of your business...it won't work."

A smile curved the corners of her lips and his breath caught in his throat at her beauty. "Thank you," she said, her words soft and carried off with the breeze. After another minute of peace, she said, "I'm glad that I got to see you tonight. I—"

His radio began to beep and he grabbed it off his belt. "10-38, 419 Easton Highway."

"This is Hamilton, Station 24, responding. ETA twenty minutes." His eyes, now alert, met hers. "Sorry, Madelyn. I've gotta go." He hesitated for just a few seconds, regret coursing through his veins, before he turned and jogged to his truck.

"That's fine. Be safe," Madelyn called out, watching him until he was out of sight. Sighing, she glanced over her shoulder as the night continued to claim the sky.

"Fucking hell," Zac cursed, his crew on the pumps, spraying water on the old, abandoned warehouse.

"Good thing the motorist happened by," Greg said, his words coming through the radio.

With a nod, Zac remained quiet, watching as the gathering fire responders battled the blaze. The warehouse was the largest building the arsonist had hit so far. *If it's him.* Trying to not make assumptions, he watched as the blaze licked the wood along the bottom and he knew a type of accelerant had been used for maximum destruction in as quick a time as possible.

Two more fire stations sent their trucks, adding to the three already there. The black smoke curled into the night sky, illuminated by the flames rising from the three-story building. Two more hours passed before the fire was completely out and some of the firefighters were able to go through the rubble, making sure there were no remaining pockets ready to flame again.

The State Police were sending a fire investigator but it would be early dawn before they arrived. Zac watched as the Easton police officers wrapped caution tape around, cordoning off the area. *Not that there are any trespassers here anyway.* He stood by the truck and looked around. The old warehouse was on a road between a few farms and the main highway, but not visible to the highway. *Someone knew it was here...abandoned...close enough for us to get to and yet far enough that the wooden structure was going to burn to the ground.*

Adam, the North Heron Fire Chief, and Roger, the Cherrytown Fire Chief, walked over to where he was standing. Adam, clapping him on the back, asked, "Any ideas?"

He shook his head, pulling off his jacket and tossing it to the ground next to the truck. Scrubbing his hand over his face, he sighed. "We gotta figure out a way to catch this guy. But it's like chasing a ghost."

"One of the reasons we love this area is because it is mostly rural, not much traffic once you get off the main road. Got low crime, although that's changing. But it makes it an arsonist's paradise. Too many fucking places, just off the beaten path, to start a fire."

Roger waved goodbye and walked away, leaving Zac staring at the destruction, watching the firefighters combing, careful not to disturb any possible evidence. "You know, I've been thinking of that." Seeing he had Adam's attention, he hesitated. "Nah, never mind. I'm just tired." With a smile that was more of a grimace, he walked back to his truck, calling for his volunteer team to begin the cleanup.

"It's beautiful, isn't it?"

"Sure, if you say so."

"What the fuck is wrong with you? You can't see the beauty in it?"

They looked out the van window, the line of trees hiding them in the dark. Brilliant yellow flames had risen from the building, and now the embers were all that was left. Firefighters wandered around like ants over a cookie crumb left on the sidewalk. "I guess it was pretty…when the flames were shooting up. Now, it's just a mess."

"You don't get it…it's fucking beautiful. The fire. The flames against the night sky. The red embers. The smoke going from boiling to curling in wisps. "Fucking beautiful," the whisper came, eyes still glued to the window.

A strange melancholy settled over Madelyn as she walked through the house. She had imagined this trip to be quick—a simple funeral where almost no one would show up, cleaning the house, calling a realtor. But Baytown held a different reality.

She remembered the girls of Baytown as a teenager, idolizing the beautiful young women seen through the filter of early adolescent eyes. The fact that they had so graciously invited her friendship and taken the time to arrange the reception still seemed unreal. *Not to mention the Baytown Boys.* A laugh escaped her lips as she thought of Mitch, Grant, Aiden, Brogan, Callan, and of course, Zac. As a ninth-grader they were as unattainable as climbing Mt. Everest, but now, they not only planned her father's funeral service, but Zac even delivered a eulogy.

When she left the memorial reception, she was sure that her plan was to call David Wills the next morning and have him come out and make an offer on the entire contents of the house. She would not have been upset to have him back a truck up to the front door and haul away all the furniture and other antiques her father had collected. Whatever was left, she would donate to Goodwill. Hire a cleaning crew to give the house a thorough scouring and then call a realtor. One week and she would be back home.

But, now, standing in the living room, her fingers drifting over one of the cabinets, she thought back to the words that were spoken today about her father. A good man. A man who preferred his own company but would come to the aid of others. Shaking her head, other thoughts battled to the forefront. *A man who drank so much, his wife left him, taking their daughter and he did nothing. A man who would talk about his war experiences with someone but never seemed to mention his daughter to anyone. A man who never tried to get to know his daughter. A man who'd rather spend time with antiques than his daughter. His daughter...me.*

Blinding anger choked her and she grabbed a vase nearby and, whirling her body around, threw it against the far wall. The crash resounded through the tomblike house as she watched it shatter into a million pieces. Slumping to the floor, she buried her head in her knees, waves of grief washing over her, her heart resembling the shattered glass.

7

The bedroom window faced the east and the early morning sunlight streamed in. Most people would have covered the glass with more than blinds, but Zac liked waking to sunshine. He would lay in bed for a few minutes as his mind ran through what needed to be completed during the day. And right now, his thoughts were a swirl. *Job challenges...arsonist...and a certain, beautiful woman with haunted eyes that was only in town for a week or so.*

Swinging his legs over the side of the bed, he stood, moving to the window to peek out of the blinds. The blue sky, dotted with fluffy clouds, greeted him as the sun was rising over the tops of his neighbor's house.

A shower later and on his first cup of coffee, he thought of meeting Madelyn last night on the pier. She said she had wanted to see him, but his call interrupted whatever she was going to say. Wondering if he should try to meet her again, he looked at the clock. Just enough time before he had to be at the station.

Within five minutes he was standing in Jillian's coffee shop ordering breakfast, smiling as she walked over to join him.

"You almost never come in for breakfast," she accused with a smile on her face. "In fact, I do believe that you and most of the boys hit the diner early in the morning."

"That's cause there, we can just say 'coffee'. Here, we gotta know words like latte, cappuccino, and ordering something skinny."

Throwing her head back in laugher, Jillian plopped down in the seat across from him. "You do not, silly. You can get a plain cup of coffee here and you know it."

He met her grin and dug into his eggs and bacon. After a moment, he caught her staring at him. "What?"

"Nothing," she grinned, "I just like watching someone enjoy the food they get here. And, I get the feeling that you'll talk to me when your stomach is full."

Wiping his mouth, his eyes twinkled. "Okay, okay. Yes, I have an ulterior motive for being here." Sobering, he wondered if this was a good idea—after all, the women had a gossip line that stretched for miles. Her hand reached across the table, landing on his arm and his eyes jumped to hers, seeing a seriousness replacing the usual mirth.

"Zac, you can talk to me. I promise, it won't go any further."

Nodding slowly, he tossed his napkin down and

held her gaze. "I was just wondering about Madelyn." Seeing the spark of interest in her eyes, he rushed, "Not like that...I mean, she's gorgeous and all, but she's leaving as soon as she gets her father's affairs settled. And I'm not enough of a cad to try to hit on a grieving woman."

"Zac, you're not a cad," she protested. "I know you're not exactly into relationships, but you seem to keep your...uh...affairs quiet. Not like Aiden," she added, rolling her eyes.

"I'm no monk, but yeah, I try to keep things simple. The few women I...well...see, know that it won't lead to anything. And I guess I must pick 'em right, 'cause they don't seem to want anything more than a night either. Honest to God, though, Jillian, it's probably a lot less than you think." Shrugging, he explained, "I just don't see romance in the same way that the rest of you do." Chancing a look into her eyes, he saw understanding and a flash of sympathy, the latter being something he hated. She said nothing, for which he was grateful.

"Anyway, I was wondering about Madelyn. I ran into her last night at the pier and we talked for just a moment before I got called out again. It just felt like there was something she wanted to say to me, but we didn't have time." Leaning back in his seat, he heaved a loud huff, shaking his head. "I thought about going by to see her...to see if she needed anything, but she was so closed off at the funeral and I didn't want to intrude. It's kind of like walking on a landmine around her."

Nodding, Jillian agreed. "I know what you mean. I get the feeling that there's a lot going on under the surface, but I have no idea why she was estranged from her dad."

He observed her eyes leaping to his, sympathy in them, so he hurried to ask, "So, you didn't really know her back in high school?"

"No, I didn't. They didn't live here in town and since she was a couple of years younger..." her voice trailed off, her eyes looking over his shoulder, but not focused. Sighing, she added, "It's embarrassing to admit, Zac, but in high school, while I like to think that I was a nice person, I was also more interested in watching Grant play ball, hanging with Katelyn, and picking out my homecoming dress." She dropped her head, shaking it slowly.

"Well, if it's any consolation, I was more interested in which girl's pants I could get into and know that Grant felt the same about you."

His grin met hers and they sat silent for a moment, their adolescent past slowly rolling by in their memories. "But, to get back to your original intent on seeing me today, I would say...take a chance and just go by to see her. She's probably lonely and would welcome the company. The girls and I were going to wait until tomorrow to go by."

Standing, he tossed down some cash and leaned over to kiss the top of her head. "Thanks, Jillian." Walking outside, he felt the sunshine beaming down as he made his way down the street.

Mildred nodded as Zac walked into the police station, her smile wide. "Chief Evans is expecting you."

Returning her smile, he said, "Ms. Score, you're as beautiful as ever. Hope Coach knows what a peach he's got."

She cackled, her hand sneaking up to pat her purple-grey curls. "He still remembers how to compliment his wife, just as much as he remembers coaching all you boys when you were younger."

"Well, tell him I said hello," he said with a nod, before moving down the hall to Mitch's office.

Mitch stood, welcoming him into the room. Looking about, it was the same type of ordered chaos as was in his office as well. They shook hands before settling down in the chairs. Mitch's was the old, creaky wooden one his father had used when he was chief, and probably the same one his grandfather had used when he held that position as well. Zac settled in the metal chair, noting the legs were not even and rocked slightly every time he shifted.

"You did good at the funeral yesterday," Mitch said, his gaze warm. "Not that I was surprised, but it was amazing the story Lenny told you and that you were able to share it."

"Thanks. It makes me wish I'd been around him longer. Maybe if I'd gone by when he missed some meetings, then...I don't know."

"Don't take that on," Mitch warned. "You can't save everyone."

His eyes jumped to Mitch's and his retort died on

his lips. Finally, after a moment of staring, he relaxed in his seat, mumbling, “Yeah...”

“So, what did you want to talk about?”

“Did you see the latest state budget?”

Mitch’s eyes narrowed and he said, “I always look it over but now you’re making me think I missed something. What’s up?”

Scrubbing his hand over his face, he said, “As you know, we’ve got five fire stations in North Heron County and fifteen in Accawmacke County, so that’s twenty in total. Each one’s got a paid Fire Chief, who is in charge of volunteers, training, and responding. For our county, only two have a separate Rescue Captain. So for the rest of us, we’re also the main EMT, in charge of those volunteers as well. I know each police and sheriff department has officers who have some medical training, but we’re spread thin. Okay, all of this you know, but the latest state budget is looking at giving the poorer counties an extra paid position. Accawmacke doesn’t qualify, but North Heron does.”

Cocking his head to the side, Mitch leaned forward. “Fuck, man, I can’t believe I missed seeing this.”

“Well, it was buried under a lot of other budget items, but the other chiefs started talking so I went back and read it over.”

“What exactly does it mean for us?”

“From what we can gather, Baytown would receive another paid position, one that would be more over the rescue, EMT side of the spectrum. I’m just wondering what’s the best thing to do.”

"You thinkin' of taking that job instead of Fire Chief?"

Nodding slowly, he said, "I'm thinking about it." Mitch said nothing, so he continued, "Been doing this a long time, Mitch. Hell, you know that. When I talked to the Navy recruiter in high school, I couldn't think of any other job but being a firefighter...and on a ship... fuck, I loved it." Leaning forward, he pinned Mitch with a stare. "I know y'all thought I did all that because of my dad, including taking over being the Fire Chief when I got back here. Hell, maybe I did. But if I could save one life from dying in a fire, it was worth it to me."

"And now?"

Dropping his head, he rubbed the back of his neck with his hand, massaging the headache that threatened. After a silent moment, he lifted his head and said, "It's not that I want to get out of firefighting completely, but this job is paperwork, reports, budget, and a fuck ton of training and scheduling. Shit, Mitch, I live in the back of the fire station. It's like I'm consumed...not by fire, but by the job."

"And the other position they're budgeting for?"

"I read their proposal. It would be heading up the EMT, which I already do, and continuing training for those volunteers, many of whom are also fire volunteers as well. Working closely with the Fire Chief, but only responsible for the EMT and not the firefighting."

Mitch rested his elbows on the desk, his chair squeaking at the movement, his eyes still on Zac. "It sounds like they're taking your job, which is too overwhelming for any one person, and splitting it into two manageable positions."

Grinning, Zac agreed, "Exactly! And instead of them hiring someone for the new positon, I'd like to take that one and then they can find a new Fire Chief for me."

Mitch met his grin with one of his own, and asked, "So, what are you having to think about? Sounds like you've already got it figured out."

Chuckling, he said, "Yeah, I guess I have. I swear, when I woke this morning, it was all muddled in my brain. But, talking it out loud to you, the answer is clear."

They stood then, friendly goodbyes said, and Zac headed back through the municipal building toward the fire station, his load feeling lifted. Glancing at his watch, he thought of stopping by Madelyn's house after lunch and that brought a wider smile to his face. Entering the station, his step was decidedly lighter.

After coffee and toast, Madelyn walked back upstairs, re-entering her room, armed with garbage bags, having made the decision to begin the reclamation process here. *If I tackle this room first, where my fondest memories are, the rest will be easy.*

Starting with the oak dresser, she opened the top drawer, finding it blessedly empty. She was hit with the memory of her mother taking things from the dresser and placing them in a large suitcase open on her bed as she cried. All her mother would say was, "I'm done. I'm so over it. You and I are leaving and starting over somewhere else."

She wondered if memories were going to assault her at every turn in the process of cleaning out her father's house. *It used to be my house too.*

She moved to the second drawer and found it empty as well. The third drawer was stuck and when she gave it a tug, it opened and she stared dumbly at the contents. Notebooks. She did not recognize them as old school items, so she pulled the top one out. Flipping it open, she stared at the pictures on each page. Pictures of her.

Her brow crinkled as she stepped backward, bumping against the bed as she tried to make sense of what she was seeing. Recognizing the photographs, printed on computer paper, she realized they had been from her Facebook page from years ago. When she was a teenager, she did not care about privacy settings and all of her photographs were easy for anyone to find. *But, why would he? I didn't even know he knew about Facebook.*

The notebook seemed to progress through her sophomore and junior year of high school. It had been hard to make friends so late in her high school career, but she had joined the band and ran on the cross country team. Pictures of marching band practice, races, and teammates filled one page after another. Then came the pictures of friends in school. No sleepovers...no homecoming dances. But at least she had made some friends.

The photographs were simplistic, but chronicled

her time after her parents divorced. Licking her dry lips, she moved back to the drawer and took out the next spiral notebook and discovered it was much the same, only now it was her high school senior year. A few more friends, a prom date, and graduation.

Lightheaded, she sunk to the floor next to the bed. There were five notebooks in all. She looked at the two from high school, three from college, and the last one was from the past couple of years. Fewer pictures were in that one and she realized she did not post as much as when she was younger.

By the time she finished flipping through the notebooks, she leaned back against the bed, her head tilted up toward the ceiling. Closing her eyes, she tried to make sense of it all, but her thoughts were scrambled. *If he didn't want to have anything to do with me, why did he search out my social media? Print out the pictures? Take the time to put them in notebooks?*

Blowing out a breath, she dropped her chin and stared at the closed books in her lap. *And, if he did want to have a connection with me, why didn't he just call?*

8

The knock on the door, while not unexpected, still managed to startle her. Sucking in her lips, Madelyn closed her eyes for a second, steeling herself. Inhaling deeply, she let it out slowly as she walked down the stairs and to the front door. Opening it, she smiled at the man on the other side, standing on the porch. His suit, impeccable. His hair, neatly combed. Blue-grey eyes, bright and eager.

"Mr. Wills, please come in."

"Ms. Stevens, I am so excited to be of service to you," he said, his words smooth and gracious. Stepping into the foyer, his eyes immediately swept the room. "Oh, my..."

If he had been a cartoon character, his eyes would have bugged out before turning into dollar signs. Forcing a smile, she said, "Let me be upfront with what I would like to do—"

He whirled around to her, his hand landing on her shoulder. "I understand completely, I really do. This is all too much for you to handle and I assure you that I'm perfectly capable of taking on the whole task."

"Well, to be honest—"

"What I'll do is assess all the furniture your dear father collected and give you an itemized list for the auction. I'm willing to get rid of anything that might not sell at auction."

"Mr. Wills, as I was saying, what I'd like is for you—"

He turned away from her mid-sentence, striding into the living room. "Of course, I'll pay a fair market value, minus my commission. I'm sure it will be more than acceptable to you and then you'll be able to move on with your life."

"Mr. Wills!" she shouted, her hands planted on her hips, finally drawing his attention. "I need you to listen to me and, please, do not make any assumptions about what I do or don't want."

His brow knit in a crease and he turned back to her. "Well, certainly."

Now that she had his attention nerves hit and she wiped her palms on her jeans. "I invited you over today to help estimate the value on what my father had collected. But, you need to know that I have decided to take some time. I'm not going to make a snap decision or a quick sale."

He nodded slowly, his expression softening. "I understand. I apologize if I was too eager."

Relaxing her shoulders, she smiled. "Not at all. I appreciate your enthusiasm. And while I will certainly sell most pieces to you, I don't want to be rushed. I will, of course, pay you for your time with the assessments." Looking into the room, she said, "Okay, where do you think we should start?"

Two hours later, many of the antiques piled in the living room had tags attached. David had introduced her to his system of identifying the period, approximate age, and condition of the piece before giving an initial estimate. He explained that the estimate of value was just a starting point and when he got back to his computer with the pictures he had taken and researched the pieces he would be able to provide her with a final value.

Another knock at the door sounded and, expecting David's assistant, she yelled for him to come in as she crawled over several items. Tripping over a low stool, she landed in a heap just as the door opened. Palms stinging, she looked up in embarrassment, seeing Zac standing in the doorway.

"Uh, hi..." she stammered, blushing as he bent forward to assist her to her feet. Even standing, she still had to lean her head way back to look into his face. When she had been near him at the funeral she was wearing heels but now, in her flat shoes, she realized how tall he was.

"Are you all right?" he asked, his hands still on her waist. "I came by to see if you would like to get lunch, but I didn't expect to have to use my EMT skills."

"Nothing hurt but my pride," she quipped, attempting to cover her embarrassment. The warmth of his fingers on her waist traveled through her body making her very aware of the effect he had on her libido. His dark hair looked as though he had just swept his hand though it and her fingers twitched at her side, itching to see if it was as soft as it appeared.

Hearing a noise, his gaze shot behind her, his eyebrows lifting. "Did I stop by at a bad time?"

"No," she rushed, stepping back. "David…Mr. Wills is here…helping me with—"

"Fuckin' hell," Zac said under his breath as he stepped inside and viewed the mess that he assumed was a living room. "What the hell happened in here?"

She opened her mouth to explain, but David popped his head around the corner, surprise on his face. His eyes dropped to Zac's hands still on her waist. "Oh," he said, "I didn't realize you had company. I thought we could go out to lunch and then I could take you to my office so we can start the appraisal process."

Deciding to keep his hands where they were, Zac noticed she stepped slightly closer to him. Inwardly fist-pumping, he smiled pleasantly at David.

"I don't think so, David, but thank you so much for what you've done today. I'll see you tomorrow and we can continue the downstairs. If you can, bring your computer tomorrow. That would probably save time, be more efficient."

David's eyes narrowed slightly at the dismissal, but his lips curled into a smile. "Of course. I'll see you bright and early tomorrow." With a curt nod toward Zac, he walked outside.

Zac shut the door behind David and swung his gaze back to hers. "I get the feeling he wasn't too happy with my arrival."

Blushing, she leaned forward and whispered, "I think I messed up his plans when I said I didn't want to rush the process."

He wondered about her change of heart, but then his gaze drifted over the furniture and the sheer volume of her father's collection would take some serious time.

Madelyn observed him staring at the mess and felt her blush deepening. "I...uh..." Sighing, she said, "I can't think of any way to explain this, other than to just say, welcome to my father's world."

Uncertain what to say, Zac nodded, his gaze moving away from the conglomeration of furniture to her face. "Hey, don't be embarrassed. I was just startled at the size of the antique collection your dad had. At least he collected something worthwhile. My old man just collected debts."

Madelyn opened her mouth, then closed it quickly. His words were so brutally honest and yet, said with a hint of humor.

He grinned, disarming her, and added, "Sorry if that was a bit too much. My dad's faults were well known in town, so I forget that not everyone knew him." Observing her gaze avoiding his, Zac said, "So, what's going on here?"

"My dad collected antiques and it seems that he filled the house." She sighed, adding, "I'm afraid the whole house looks like this. I had no idea, of course, until I got here the other day."

His gaze narrowed as he stepped further into the room. Madelyn watched as his eyes not only travelled over the furniture, but swept the ceiling as well. He walked through the room, calling over his shoulder, "The kitchen this way?"

"Uh...yeah...uh..." she said, hastening after him. Rounding the corner, she saw him looking up at the ceiling.

He grabbed a kitchen chair and stood, quickly removing the cover of the fire alarm. Her eyes were drawn to the skin now showing where his t-shirt rode up. *Good Lord.* His abs were tight and, from what she could see, well delineated. His tan skin was smooth with just a hint of hair leading to the top of his low-slung jeans. It took a few seconds of ogling before she lifted her eyes and saw his blazing at her in anger.

"There're no batteries in this," he growled. "Your dad had a house full of wooden furniture, like kindling ready to burn, and no fuckin' fire alarm?"

Snapped out of her lust, Madelyn opened her mouth a couple of times, shutting it when nothing came out. "I...I guess so."

"Are you staying here?"

Nodding, she said, "Yeah. I figured I might as well stay here so that I can work on the house easier. Not to mention, it's cheaper than a week or more staying at a hotel." She looked around at the mess in the kitchen and her shoulder sagged. "I have no idea how Dad lived like this but, then, I have no idea how he lived at all."

Zac heard the defeat in her voice and dropped his chin to his chest. Heaving a sigh, he looked up, his heart aching for the sadness in her voice. He knew a lot about regret and wondered if she felt the same.

"Look," he said, "I'm sorry. Really. It's just in my nature to look at things through a safety perspective. I'm sure David walked in and viewed a paradise of antiques which must have made you feel good, and then I come in and start barkin' and make you feel like crap." He easily hopped down from the chair and set it to the side, next to a pile of other chairs stacked on top of each other. He stepped over, placing his hands on her shoulders, her body feeling so much more fragile than he imagined it would. Now that he had seen the inside of Lenny's house, he realized what a massive undertaking she was forced to deal with.

"Hey, why don't I get you out of the house, take you to lunch, and we can pick up some batteries on the way back."

Madelyn stared for a moment, indecision filling her mind, before she nodded slowly and her lips curved slightly. "Okay...yeah, that'd be good."

Laughing, he threw his hand over his heart, claiming, "You're killing my ego, Maddie. I was afraid I was going to get shot down like David."

Narrowing her eyes, she poked him in the chest. "Somehow, I think, Zac, that your ego doesn't often get bruised. You strike me as the type who doesn't exactly have problems getting lunch dates...or any other kind of dates." As soon as the words passed her lips, she inwardly grimaced. *He probably thinks I've been thinking of him...and dates.* She hated the blush she felt climbing up her face and was grateful he appeared not to notice.

"Nah, I work too much to have many dates," he admitted. Sticking his elbow out, he said, "Come on, let's get out of the fire trap and have some good pub food."

"Finn's? I haven't been there," she smiled. "Well, not since I was a little girl."

"Then you're in for a treat," he promised.

Walking inside Finn's, the familiar scent caused Madelyn's eyes to grow large as a memory flashed through her mind. She remembered her father bringing her here occasionally for a burger when she was a child. The pub special was always bigger than she could eat and he would finish it for her. Of course, her father would have to order another beer, saying he needed something to wash it down with and that would make her mother angry. Sighing, she wondered if all her memories would be tainted with what had become of her family...arguments and abandonment.

A hand on the small of her back startled her back to the present and she twisted her head to look up at Zac as he guided her to the table. He called out greetings to a few people and she recognized the MacFarlane brothers behind the bar, both of their gazes landing on them before breaking into wide smiles.

The server settled them into a booth in the dark section that had been a bank vault in its original days. The dim lights cast a small glow over the occupants and, since the lunch crowd had already left, they found themselves alone.

"They've got lots of good food," Zac said, his eyes never leaving her bent head as she poured over the menu, noting the auburn highlights in her dark hair as it fell in a curtain, hiding her face.

Her head suddenly popped up and she exclaimed, "I think a pub burger sounds fabulous, and they've got one with crab and brie on it!"

"And fries?"

Her eyes lit and a smile split her face. "Of course."

Zac gave the order to the server and then sat back, staring at her. He had only been around her a few times and, yet, she appeared so multi-dimensional. He was never sure which Madelyn he was going to get...happy, sad, angry, or appreciative. *That pretty much sums up someone grieving.*

"What are you thinking?" she asked, her smile slipping from her face.

Blinking, he said, "Sorry. Nothing. Well, not nothing. I was actually thinking that you're a very interesting woman...with a lot going on."

Madelyn sucked in her lips, uncertain if that was a compliment or not.

Seeing her face fall, Zac inwardly cursed. He wanted to ask more about her—what she did, where she lived, the antiques in the house—but felt like every subject was a landmine. The server brought their beers and he took a long sip, grateful to have something to do.

At the bar, Aiden looked at his brother. "You checkin' out Zac and Madelyn?"

Brogan glared. "What the fuck? Are you a chick or what?"

"Jesus, Brogan, I'm just sayin' that it looks like he's crashing and burning."

Brogan shot a glance to the vault, seeing Zac staring down at the table and Madelyn's eyes looking everywhere but at him. "Maybe they're just...I don't know."

"Well, I'm gonna go talk to them," Aiden said, gaining an eye roll from Brogan.

"You sure you don't have an ulterior motive?"

Aiden, normally easy going, glared back. "Seriously, bro? Jesus, Zac's one of my oldest friends. I'm not cutting in on that action. I just want to help." With that he headed around the bar toward the vault, leaving Brogan watching from behind.

"Yeah, but she's only gonna be in town a week or two. That aint' what Zac needs," Brogan mumbled under his breath.

Katelyn came from the back with the takeout lunches for her and Gareth. Catching the last of their exchange, she said, "What was that about?"

Shaking his head, Brogan said, "Got no idea, other than it looks like Aiden might be growing up after all."

"Baytown's own Peter Pan?" she laughed, tossing him a wave on her way out the door.

"Maybe so," Brogan said to no one, his eyes still on the vault.

9

"Hey, y'all," Aiden called out, grabbing a chair and pulling it up to the end of the booth, startling Madelyn.

"Oh...hi," she greeted.

Zac sent a glare his way, wondering what his friend was up to.

"It's nice to see you out and about, Madelyn," Aiden said, his eyes fully on her. "I didn't get a chance to talk to you the other day, but I'm real sorry about your dad."

"Thanks," she said. Madelyn remembered the MacFarlane boys in high school and Aiden was the one who always had a girl, or two, on his arm. Seeing the grownup version, she could easily imagine him still having women lining up for a chance with the affable Irish charmer. Glancing at Zac, she noted a tick in his jaw as though he was grinding his teeth.

"How long are you here for?"

"Well, I took a week off work, but once I saw my

dad's house, I know I'll have to call and ask for another."

"Good, then you'll have a chance to get to know Baytown again. If you need someone to show you around, just give me a call."

"She's not here for a social visit," Zac bit out, kicking Aiden under the table. "She's taking care of her father's estate."

"Well, all the more reason for her to come out and enjoy herself while she's here," Aiden said with a wink.

"Uh..." she muttered, her gaze shifting between the two men, uncertain what silent messages were being passed.

"Don't worry about her not having someone to show her around," Zac retorted, his eyes pinned on Aiden. "I've got her."

Madelyn's heart skipped a beat, hearing Zac's proclamation, but instead of being annoyed, a warm feeling slid through her body. Her lips curved slightly as she relaxed in her seat.

"I think the lady should choose, don't you?" Aiden pushed, his grin now fully wide.

Furious with Aiden, first for interrupting and then for putting Madelyn on the spot, Zac was moving forward to get rid of him, when she gave her answer.

"Thank you for the offer, Aiden, and I'd love to spend time with everyone who was so kind in helping with the funeral, but," Madelyn's eyes shifted to Zac, seeing him staring at her, intensity in his gaze, "if I need someone to show me around, I think I'm covered."

A shit-eating grin spread across Aiden's face while

he pushed his chair back, standing. "Good choice, sweetheart. Glad you made the right one." Bending, he planted a kiss on the top of her head before walking back to the bar, where Brogan flicked the towel from his shoulder, hitting him in the chest. "What? Just thought they needed a little push, that's all," Aiden protested, rubbing the sting.

Madelyn looked across the table as a light blush rose over Zac's face.

Zac shook his head, still stunned at Aiden's tactics. "Sorry about him. Brogan swears their mom dropped him on his head when he was a baby." She laughed, a sound he wished he could hear more from her.

"You might be right. Anyway, I suppose it was a good way to get us back on track." Seeing his head tilt in question, she said, "It's okay to ask me questions, you know. I don't want you to feel like you can't."

He met her smile with one of his own. His forearms were resting on the table and he turned his palms up. "I'd like to know more about you," he admitted. "I can't imagine having to uproot your life for two weeks to deal with all you are facing here. What is your job?"

"I'm a counselor for a mental health group."

Eyes wide, he said, "We've got a good mental health center here in town. In fact, several of my friends have received or are currently in sessions. Mostly to do with PTSD, I suppose."

Nodding enthusiastically, she said, "That's what several of my friends specialize in. It seems there is a never-ending client list. Many came back from their times in the service having to work through issues."

"Do you have a specialty?"

"I work mostly with addictive behaviors."

"Really," he said, leaning forward. "Like drugs and alcohol?"

"Yes, but I work with young people, mostly adolescents or children, that have these types of behaviors."

"Damn," he said, his voice betraying his surprise. "It's hard to imagine young people with such problems."

"Oh, yeah. I've had teens already addicted to drugs or alcohol and elementary children already huffing. Even children that have a fascination with pyrotechnics...oh, wow, I just thought about this in terms of you being a fireman." She leaned forward, saying, "Have you ever had to deal with a child that continually set fires?"

Shaking his head, he replied, "No...not children. Well, actually, I've never had a case of someone with that kind of behavior." He grew quiet for a moment, his mind working over the arsonist case. Looking up he realized his silence seemed to have made her nervous, as her hands fluttered together. Without thinking, he reached across the table and grasped her hands in his much larger ones. "Sorry, I was just thinking about a case we're dealing with."

Her eyes sparked with interest. "Really? Can you tell me about it?"

"Not much to tell, really. We just keep getting called out for fires and they're all set intentionally. So, it looks like we've got a serial arsonist on our hands. Our departments are stretched to the limit and the State Police are now involved."

Madelyn observed the tension in his jaw and the frustration in his creased brow. "This is weighing on you, even as much as you like your job."

Zac blinked at her statement, realizing she was not asking a question but was, instead, seeing inside of him. Nodding, he sighed "Yeah." He wanted to say more, but found the words did not come, so he fiddled with his napkin. Looking up, he said, "What about you? I know you love your work, but do you love your job?"

"I'd like to pretend that I don't know the difference, but you've got it right," she confessed. "I do like working with people, but the large, city clinic where I work has gotten very..." she spread her hands out as she searched for the right word, "political." She chewed on her bottom lip before adding, "The director seems to have an agenda and that is less about being a good counselor and more about taking in more money. I sometimes wonder if he was ever a counselor or was always just an administrator."

"I feel that way sometimes about the politics of my job, as well," he said, leaning forward, his gaze locked with hers.

"It's so frustrating, isn't it—"

Interrupted by their food being served, they smiled as they dug in to their enormous pub burgers. Going for a french fry first, she moaned in pleasure at the perfectly crispy, seasoned potato. He could not keep the smile from his face as he watched her relish her food.

Relaxing, he enjoyed his lunch, not able to

remember the last time he had felt a connection with a woman. *And she's leaving in a little over a week.* Taking a risk, he swallowed his bite before asking, "I know you've got a lot to do, but would you like some help... and company, this week while you're here?"

In the middle of swallowing, she widened her eyes and nodded as she finished. Blushing, she laughed, "I'm sorry...I should take smaller bites."

"No way," he said, his smile wide. "I like to see someone enjoy food as much as I do."

Nodding, she said, "And, in answer to your question, I'd love to have your company this week. Please don't feel like you have to help me—"

"It'd be my pleasure," he hastened to add. "Really. It just seems like we have a good connection...I'd like to spend more time with you."

Wiping her mouth with her napkin, she smiled, "Okay, then. I'd love the help and to get to know you better."

An hour later, after sharing phone numbers, he was dropping her back off at the house. His fingers had lingered on the small of her back longer than necessary and now he found himself hating to say goodbye.

She stuck her hand out, "Thank you so much for lunch, Zac. I hadn't realized how much I needed some company."

He took her hand in his but, instead of shaking it, bent to kiss the back. Her smooth skin was warm to his lips and, for an instant, he wished it were her lips instead. Lifting his head, he held her eyes, saying, "It was my pleasure." Hesitating for a moment, he asked,

"There's a beach party coming up for the safety members. Would you like to go with me?"

Her smile melted his nervousness away as she beamed up at him. "I'd love to, thank you."

Bending once more, he kissed her cheek before heading back to his truck, a matching smile on his face.

Stepping inside, Madelyn looked around at the mess, no longer overwhelmed by the tasks in front of her. With her step a little lighter, she moved into the kitchen, tossed her purse down, and leaned her hip against the counter, wondering what room to start on next. Her purse vibrated and she pulled her phone out, checking the messages. *Zac?*

Had a great time. Can't wait to see you again. Z

Laughing out loud, she could not remember the last time she had smiled so much. Her fingers flying, she fired off a simple reply.

Me too! Maddie

Staring down at her phone, she wondered why she signed it *Maddie*. She had not gone by that nickname in more years than she cared to remember. *Dad used to call me that.* She had almost forgotten, having long since buried that underneath all the other memories she refused to think about.

Pushing off the counter, she walked into the living room to continue moving furniture about.

10

Zac parked outside the North Heron Sheriff's Department building, noting the number of cars already in the parking lot. Grant rode with him, the two discussing the case during the entire drive. Entering the building, they walked into the huge meeting room, the gathering even larger than the last time they met.

Zac nodded at the other Fire Chiefs, as well as the law enforcement personnel he recognized. Once settled, the State Police ran the meeting, but to Zac's surprise, they announced that they were on an as needed basis and not taking over the case. He knew the agency was budget constrained, as most government agencies were, but assumed they would be completing the actual investigations.

A guest FBI arsonist profiler spoke next and, at this, Zac leaned forward.

"There are a variety of arsonist types and they are delineated by their motives, which usually fall into one of the following categories. The For-Profit arsonist is attempting fraud and is the least emotionally or psychologically motivated of all arsonists. They are going for a high level of damage because they want to destroy the property for financial gain. This is not who you are looking for since, so far, the buildings have all been old and abandoned, with no financial gain to be had.

"The Thrill-Seeker arsonists tend to be adolescents, and are often groups rather than an individual. The motive could be relief from boredom or a gang initiation. The ignition method is uncomplicated and routinely accompanied by vandalism and theft. I also do not suspect this is what you are looking at, due to the settings in which the fires occur and the large area or range of fires.

"Juvenile fire-starters often start fires in their own homes. Again, I don't suspect this because your fires have been over a wide range of the counties, not something easily attainable by a child or teen."

Zac thought back to what Madelyn had told him of working with a child who was addicted to fire starting.

"Crime-Concealing arsonists are not concerned with the pyrotechnics of fire, but are wanting to use the fire to conceal another crime. So far, this also does not appear to be what you have either. Terrorists or social-protesters who start fires usually are quick to take responsibility for their group's agenda.

"So far, you've heard me talk about what you do not seem to be dealing with. But, the last type of arsonists, the Hero or Vanity Arsonists, are the most difficult. Because they blend in with you and me."

Zac glanced to the side at his fellow Fire Chiefs and lifted his brows, seeing their interest piqued as well. Still, fear gripped his heart as he knew what was coming.

"These types of arsonists are the hardest to deal with due to the number of firefighters that are in the area. I'm obviously talking about the immense number of volunteers your stations use and have used over the past several years. Now, that is not to say that it is always a former or current firefighter or law enforcement officer, but they make up a preponderance of this type. They are driven by boredom or vanity, wanting to be one of the guys, motivated by ego and crave the spotlight by arriving on the scene to help put out the fire. They are often young, inexperienced, or may even be a rejected applicant. They are driven by the desire to prove themselves. And," he cast his eyes around the room, still holding Zac's rapt attention, "they usually hit abandoned buildings. They are not trying to hurt anyone. But as you well know, people can die in any fire."

One of the older Fire Chiefs stood and asked, "So, how do we go about looking for this person? We've got twenty fire stations across the two-county area of the Eastern Shore, each of us utilizing a huge number of volunteers."

"Good question," the agent said. "You can start combing through your current and past records, looking for possibilities, but make sure you don't go on a witch hunt. Your job, and the job of the law enforcement personnel in this room, is to work on identifying the arsonist, hopefully before someone gets hurt. Not an easy task. You'll find yourself beginning to doubt those around you. You'll look at your personnel—that you've been trained to trust to have your back—and begin wondering if it might be them. But you need to work together, especially to see if you can find any location patterns with the fires."

"Fuckin' hell," Greg said under his breath to Zac.

Nodding, Zac agreed, but also wondered where they would find the time to comb through records. Scrubbing his hand over his face, he listened to the rest of the program.

As he walked out of the building after the meeting, he noticed the two women he hoped he would be able to meet with. "Janet. Ann," he called out, walking over to the two Rescue Captains.

"Zac," they greeted, smiles on their faces.

Janet was a tall woman, muscular, with a blonde bob, some already going grey, which she made no attempt to color. She gave off a self-assured air, confident and down to earth. Ann, several inches shorter and several years younger than Janet, had sharp eyes that made Zac feel as though very little escaped her notice.

"Do you have a few minutes? I'd like to talk to you about something." Grant had already secured a ride back to Baytown with Ginny, so Zac had time to talk.

"This got anything to do with the new Rescue Captain position coming up in Baytown?" Ann asked.

"You don't miss much, do you?" he grinned.

"Nope," she replied as Janet chuckled.

"I'd like to rely on your discretion at this point, since I'm not firm on a decision yet." Gaining assurances from both of them, he continued, "I'm thinking about going for that position. Right now, I'm running both operations, fire and rescue, and I'm stretched to the max."

"The last thing you need to do is burn out," Janet said, her warm eyes on him. "And the last thing this county needs is for you to burn out. You can't do your job properly if you do that."

"I think it comes down to what you love best," Ann declared. "I know you have a love of both firefighting and rescue, but if you had to choose one over the other... Of course, you'll still be answering calls for both no matter which job you have, but the decision will lie in the job you love the most."

"It appears the money will be about the same," he said. "I'd still be over the rescue volunteers, but a new Fire Chief will handle the scheduling of the fire volunteers."

"That's right. That's how it's handled at our station," Janet confirmed, nodding emphatically.

Ann, in a gesture of friendliness, said, "Take care of you, Zac, so that you can keep taking care of the county."

Thanking the two women, he climbed in his truck, his thoughts swirling for the entire trip back to Baytown...the jobs, the arsons, and the beautiful woman he wanted to see again, even if her stay was short. *After all...that's good for me.*

The hot bath felt wonderful on Madelyn's tired muscles. Having spent the afternoon moving furniture, she realized how out of shape she was. Sinking into the deep water, she grinned. *But the work was worth it.* Revitalized after her lunch with Zac, she had attacked the living and dining rooms with vigor. She took the lighter pieces of furniture that David had said were not valuable and hauled them to the back porch. Zac had told her he would help her move them to the shed later. That still did not cull the mess as much as she would have liked, but the welcome news was that there were a lot more valuable antiques than not, so that would be good when she was ready to sell.

She had looked at the tags David had put on the furniture, going through and making a list of what was in the room, it's type and date, taking pictures with her phone. She knew he was going to give her a report, but she felt better knowing she would have her own to use as a reference as well.

Sighing, she thought of how much work she had accomplished and they had only taken care of two rooms, albeit the two largest room. She also considered the conversation she was going to have to have with her boss and dreaded it. He was not going to like her asking for another week, but she knew there was no way she could be finished with everything in the next week.

Rising from the water, she stepped onto the bathmat and toweled off before climbing into her tank top and sleep shorts. Hearing her phone ring, she checked the screen and answered. "Hey Mom."

"Honey, how are you? Saul and I've been worried."

"No reason, Mom. The funeral was fine and I found some friends and acquaintances of Dad's to help."

"I'm surprised Lenny had any friends left. They weren't drunks were they?"

"Mom! Jesus, will you stop. They were all great. Dad belonged to the American Legion here and they did a lovely service." The phone line was quiet, and she sighed, suddenly exhausted to her bones.

"Well, please tell me you're almost finished with the house and will be back soon."

"To be honest, this is taking longer than I expected, so I'll be here another week."

"Another week? Did your supervisor approve that?"

"I've got vacation time saved up—"

"God, it's just like your dad to take up your vacation time."

"Uh, Mom. Dad's dead, so I hardly think he had anything to do with it."

"You know what I mean."

"Well, I have a lot to do. You and Saul could have come to help, you know."

"Honey, I didn't want Saul to be there. I'm sure you'll do a perfectly good job and then you can come back."

"Sure Mom. Listen, I've got to go, so I'll talk to you soon." Disconnecting, she wondered why she had not told her mother of the scrapbooks. Biting her lip, she acknowledged that, for now, she wanted something of her fathers that was just hers.

Moving into her bedroom, she looked at the notebooks now piled on top of the dresser, once more allowing her mind to wander down the path of attempting to understand what her father's reasons had been.

Turning on her heel, she walked across the short hallway to her father's room. Standing in the doorway, she allowed the memory of her parents living in this room...together...married...at one time, happy, to invade her thoughts. Inhaling deeply through her nose, she let the breath out slowly before stepping inside. The scent of her father's aftershave still hung in the air, sending her back in time.

"Daddy, you smell good."

"You think so, little Maddie? Your momma likes it," he said, nuzzling her neck and making her giggle before grabbing her mother around the waist and nuzzling her neck as well.

"Lenny," her mom laughed, "go on and wash up. Dinner's almost ready."

She set the table and waited, anxiously, for her dad to return, loving dinnertime as a family.

He sat down, bringing with him a beer, moving the glass of iced tea out of the way. She watched her mom give him a narrowed-eye look, but he just smiled and said, "Dorothy, a man's gotta have a drink at the end of the workday. It's kinda like a reward."

Madelyn looked at her mom and saw her grimace, but

since her dad always smiled and joked at dinner, she didn't think the drink must be a bad thing.

Startling at the memory, she pushed farther into the room, her pleasant memory being replaced with ones where he would drink from dinnertime right through to bedtime, eventually needing her mother's help in getting to bed. And then the arguments would ensue. *And I'd have to cover my head with all my blankets to get to sleep.*

Her lips pinched and as she moved past the dresser mirror she caught a glimpse of herself. For a flash, she saw her mother in the reflection.

Forcing the morose thoughts from her mind, she opened the top drawer, seeing his wallet, comb and brush, neatly folded handkerchiefs, and a few odds and ends. The second drawer held folded underwear and socks, and the two drawers below that contained some other articles of clothing, but nothing more.

Turning, she faced the room once more. *I've got to deal with his clothes and personal possessions.* Moving to the closet, she opened the door, seeing her father's clothes clean and hanging on hangers. Her assessing gaze moved over the collection of pants, shirts, and a dark suit with a few pairs of shoes and work boots lined up on the floor. Everything appeared so neat, so uncluttered. She remembered the day she and her mom had left, whiskey and beer bottles littering the house. Heaving a sigh, she muttered, "The last thing I need is more memories dragging me down." Realizing his clothes would easily be bagged for a trip to Goodwill, she felt relieved.

Her gaze moved to the shelf, seeing several boxes stacked in the corner. Standing on her toes, she managed to pull them down, sneezing as the dust rose from the movement. Curious, she set them on the bed and lifted the lid off of the top one.

More notebooks filled the box, each with a date written in permanent marker on the outside. Opening the first one, dated the year she turned sixteen, her heart jolted in her chest as she read the first words on the page...***Dear Maddie,***

Gasping, she stood, cold seeping into her heart, staring at the pages written in her father's longhand. *What the hell?* She unpacked four notebooks, her fingers clutching the one with the earliest date. Sitting on his bed, she opened the first page, suspecting that her world was about to change forever.

11

Dear Maddie,

Today was a good day. The sun was shining over the bay and I spent some time fishing off the pier. I work most weekends at Martin's farm, so I have a couple of days off during the week to help out at the hardware store. But sometimes, I have a day off and will go fishing, if I'm not searching for antiques. It reminds me of the times I would take you and we'd fish all day, catching flounder. We'd take them home and your momma would fry them up for dinner. Now, it's just me, but I still need to find things to do to fill my lonely days.

It's been a while since your momma took you away. I can't blame her. I gave into the temptation of drinking too much and too many times. She'd beg me to get some help but I just didn't see it. I never meant to become a drunk. There...I said it. I was a drunk. And your momma was right to take you away until I could get myself straight.

I'm just sorry that it took something so horrible to get

me to see the error of my ways. I've been in counseling recently. I know I needed to change and I've been working on it. Realized my dad, grandpa, uncle, and even a cousin drank too much. I just never saw it as a problem. They say you have to hit rock bottom and having you taken away from me was hitting rock bottom. I'd give anything to have you back home with me.

I messed up when I said I didn't want to see you. What I really meant was that I didn't want you to see me until I got myself sobered up. I talked to your momma and she said that she needs to make sure I won't go back to drinking and then she'll bring you back to me and we can be a family again. I'm working on it, sweet Maddie. I love you, Dad

Gasping as she finished the entry, she lay the notebook on her lap, unaware of her tears until one dripped off her chin and landed on the page, making an ink spot over the words *sweet Maddie.*

He talked to mom? She told him we would get back together? But, she always told me he was still a drunk who didn't want us in his life. Dizzy, she sucked in a deep breath, wondering what else he was going to say.

Memories flooded back, nights where her father had trouble walking up the stairs and her mother had to help him. The mornings when she would catch the school bus and her normally early-rising father would still be lying in bed. Her mother angry because he lost his job and she had to pick up extra hours at the pharmacy where she was a cashier.

She knew her father drank but she had no idea how much of a problem it had become until it was too late. *Was I that blind? Could I have done something?* She remembered lying in bed and hearing her parents argue but just figured that was normal.

Afraid to read more, she was also afraid not to. Turning to the next page, she continued to devour his words.

Maddie, I continue to ask your mother to let me write to you or talk to you on the phone, but she says it's not a good idea. She wants me to be completely better before I do that and I hope it's not too late when she determines that it's time. I'm trying, I really am.

I'm still in counseling and have joined a group called AA. It's been hard to face up to my past and to my problems. I always thought of myself as a good husband...I loved your mother from the first moment I laid eyes on her in high school. And when she gave birth to you, I could have sworn the heavens opened up and shone right down on me.

And then I celebrated with my buddies at the bar. Looking back, it seems like I did that a lot. Too much, in fact. I had no idea how much alcohol came to mean to me. It helped me get up and face the day when I wasn't too happy at my job. Then it made me feel better at the end of the day when I got off work. Alcohol with supper. After supper. And then, so much I don't remember.

But I'm getting help and my counselor says keeping this journal will be good for me. Just remember I love you, sweet Maddie, Dad

Blowing out a long breath of air from her lungs, she closed the notebook, unwilling to read anymore tonight. Her mother had told her when they left Baytown that her father was a "mean drunk" who did not care about them anymore. It stung, she had never seen that side of him, but she had been willing to go where her mother moved them because it was nice to not have to face the fighting anymore. And, if her father really did not want to be with them, then, in her adolescent mind, that was more reason to stay away. *I may have questioned it once, but after hearing it from his mouth that he didn't want to see me...I knew everything my mom said was true. But now...*

Her mother had also said that her father was someone who was toxic in her life. Her mom had remarried by the time she graduated from high school, so she never expected her father to be a presence in her life. Saul had been a decent stepfather and seemed to still be taken with her mother after all these years.

Placing the notebook back into the box, she carried it to her room, setting it on her dresser along with the scrapbooks he had made. Rubbing her hand over her forehead to quiet her tumultuous thoughts, she crawled into bed, willing her mind to ease. She knew sleep would be elusive, but if she was going to finish cleaning out the house so she could get back to her job in another week, she needed to focus on the task at hand. There would be time for reminiscing...and reading, later.

"Aren't you getting tired of this?"

"You gotta be kidding. This is what I live for."

"Fires? Come on. It was fun at first, but what if we get caught?"

"Caught? How the hell is anyone gonna catch us. Didn't you listen when I was reading the newspaper article about us? We're called the Ghost Arsonist. That's because we slip in and out like ghosts and no one can see us or figure out who we are."

"I guess so…I still think it's getting riskier."

"You trust me, don't you?"

A long sigh followed by silence flowed between the two. Finally, a tired, "Yeah," was heard.

"Good. 'Cause this is just the beginning. We're gonna be famous. You'll see." With that, they climbed into the van and pulled out of the driveway.

When the alarm sounded, Zac was jerked from a deep sleep. Blinking, his body moved before his brain had caught up. Scrubbing his hand over his face, he stood and hustled through the door and into the station.

Listening to the call, he yelled for the overnight volunteers to take the truck, since he had to drive the ambulance.

Jerking on his shirt, he fumbled with the buttons, desperately trying to shake the dream from his mind. *My old man…why the hell did I dream about my old man?* Pushing the image down to the recesses of his brain, he focused on the task at hand. Pulling out in front of the fire truck, he sped down the road.

Soon the fire scene came into view and he was glad to see Station 23, Cherrytown, had the situation well in hand. Another shed had burned to the ground and as his station responded, they relieved the firefighters that had arrived first. Seeing one of the volunteers, coat and helmet off, sitting by their truck, he parked the ambulance close by.

Alighting, he jogged over, the medical kit in his hand. "What's up, Roger?"

"One of my men, Buster, lives nearby and responded first. He tried to contain the fire until we could get here, but some sparks landed on his hand and arm."

Nodding, Zac moved in as the volunteer fireman's friends stepped back. "Hey, Buster. I'm Zac Hamilton, Chief of Station 24. Let's have a look."

It did not take long to treat the minor burns, but he explained what he was doing and the policy that would need to be followed. "You'll need to see a physician and your Chief will give you the paperwork necessary for the county to file. I know it might seem like a pain in the ass, but keep in mind, you agreed to this when you became a volunteer firefighter."

"Yeah, I know," Buster grumbled. "Seems like a whole lotta work for something so minor."

"We don't take chances," he replied, then laughed as Buster shot him an incredulous, wide-eyed look. "Okay, I'll amend that. We don't take chances with any injuries."

Bister grinned and headed over to his Chief as soon as he was finished. Observing the extinguished fire, he packed up his supplies before checking with Terry. "Same old, same old?"

Nodding, Terry said, "Looks like it. Investigator is on their way. Goddamn, Zac, this is getting ridiculous. This person has got to be stopped."

"Agreed. I keep thinking we're lucky no one's been hurt yet. But, my fear is that they're gonna slip up and something really bad is going to happen."

"I know what you mean…it's like I can feel it in my bones. It's only going to get worse."

A cold shiver ran through Zac, piercing him straight to his heart. Sucking in a deep breath, he called for his team to pack up and head back to Baytown. As soon as they were gone, he did the same.

Madelyn stood at the kitchen counter, mindlessly dipping her tea bag into the hot water. With barely a glance toward the mirror before coming downstairs, she knew what she looked like…messy hair pulled into a bun, no makeup to cover the dark circles from little sleep and red-rimmed eyes from last night's crying fest.

She knew David was coming over this morning and she still did not care about how she looked. Hearing a knock on the door, she moved slowly from the kitchen to let him in. Instead, she was faced with Zac standing on her front porch, his smile disarming.

"Mornin'," Zac greeted. It was hard to see her

clearly through the screen door and he hoped he was not intruding. "Uh…is this a bad time?" She unlatched the screen and opened it, her lips forced a smile but it did not reach her eyes.

"Hey," he said, stepping inside, placing his hand on her shoulder. "Are you okay?"

She wiped her hand over her face and shrugged. "Sorry, I had a bit of a rough night."

He was just about to ask her if he could help when another car pulled into the driveway, parking next to his truck. He watched as David alighted from his pristine vehicle before turning back to see her face as it fell. He hated the idea of her being alone with David Wills, whose ingratiating manner got on his nerves. "Mind if I stay?"

She jerked her gaze from the approaching David to his and nodded her head quickly. "Yes, I'd like you to stay, please."

Grinning, he nodded. "How about I make a cup of coffee while you get him sorted?"

Smiling the first smile since the previous night, Madelyn replied, "I've got some tea started but help yourself to the coffee."

He squeezed her shoulder and moved back to the kitchen while she greeted David and they decided to have him finish cataloging what was in the dining room first.

Watching David pulling out his laptop, papers, and tags, she turned and walked into the kitchen, halting at the sight of Zac standing in her space, his broad back to her as he poured a cup of coffee. Glancing over his shoulder, he said, "Your tea is ready, but do you put honey in it?"

Stepping into the room, she asked, "How about a lot of honey?"

"That bad, huh?"

"Yeah..."

"You want to talk about it?" Zac held her gaze, hoping she would trust him.

She pondered his offer before glancing back into the next room where David was working. Heaving a sigh, she shook her head, and replied, "Not now. But...sometime."

Stepping closer, he peered down at her, tucking a strand of hair behind her ear. "Anytime, Maddie. Just say the word. I'm here...really, I'm here for you."

Madelyn stared into his eyes, mesmerized by the intensity of his gaze and wondered how she could feel so lost and so found all at the same time.

"Madelyn, what do you want to do with these pieces of glass?"

The call from the dining room startled her and she shot him an apologetic glance. "Just a minute," she yelled back. Twisting her head back to Zac, she said, "I never asked you what you were doing here today."

"Well, I've got some time and thought I'd offer to help."

"Really?'

"Absolutely."

"I've got a few pieces of furniture that David said have little value and I'm going to put them in the shed for now. They were too large for me to move by myself, but I got them to the back porch." She took a sip of tea, leaning her hip against the counter and noticed he stepped closer as he reached around her to grab his cup. Instead of moving back, he stayed right next to her, his smile capturing her attention once more.

"You were saying," he prompted.

Startling, she stammered, "Yes…uh…yes. The furniture." Attempting to hide her blush behind the cup of tea, she sipped, keeping her eyes down. After a moment, she dared to look up and her heart skipped at beat seeing him still staring at her, a smile curving his lips.

Chuckling, he sipped as well before saying, "Just show me what to move and where to put it. And afterward, I'm hoping I can convince you to come to the American Legion Youth ball game tomorrow. Everyone'll be there and it's always lots of fun."

Meeting his smile with one of her own, she nodded her agreement. As Madelyn walked him out to the back porch, Zac's gaze dropped to her ass, perfectly showcased in tight jeans. She turned as she moved through the screen door and he barely lifted his gaze before being caught ogling. Glad to have the distraction of moving some furniture into the shed, he got to work.

As Zac lifted the broken table into his arms and carried it across the yard, Madelyn watched him walk away, his jeans cupping his ass and showing off his muscular thighs. His arm muscles bunched and flexed as he maneuvered the piece to set it down on the ground. As he turned around, she barely had time to shift her gaze so he would not see her interest.

"Is the shed unlocked?" he called out.

Jerking, she blinked. "Uh...sorry." She ran past him to unlock it, throwing the door open wide so he was able to enter.

"Where do you want it?"

It was on the tip of her tongue to quip, *"You, me, and anyway I can get it,"* but she covered quickly. "In the corner is fine. Thank you."

Walking back to the porch together, a genuine grin curved her lips, looking forward to the game tomorrow and spending more time with him.

12

"Run! Run!"

Madelyn jumped as Jillian, sitting next to her on the bleachers, screamed for the runner to advance to the next base. She had made it to the ball game as it was already in progress, her eyes scanning the field for Zac. Seeing him standing near home plate, talking to one of the little boys, she felt a tingle down to her toes.

Belle, sitting on her other side, said, "You have to forgive Jillian. She and Katelyn really get into these games."

Laughing, she nodded, "I can see that." Looking around, she asked, "Is this a school group? Zac said something about the American Legion."

Tori, sitting in front of her, twisted around and answered, "The American Legion runs the youth ball teams. They have three teams now, of varying ages. The Legion raises money for equipment and uniforms.

There's no charge to the parents, so they get a chance to have their children play sports regardless of their income."

"Wow, I had no idea the Legion did that but, then, to be honest, I know very little about them."

"If you were staying, then you could join the Auxiliary," Belle said, her expression wistful. "It's for family members of veterans and since your dad was in the AL, then you're eligible."

She opened her mouth to remind Belle that she was only in town for another week, but no words came out. Closing it again, she wondered why she did not say anything. Lost in thought, she startled when everyone around jumped up in the bleachers, screaming as a young girl crossed home plate. Leaping to her feet, she watched as Zac high-fived the beaming child.

"He's awfully nice," Belle said, shoulder bumping her.

Swinging her head around, she stared at Belle, a smile dancing on her face. "Uhhh..."

Laughing, Belle said, "You don't have to admit anything, but I have a feeling you've already noticed how nice he is."

Her lips twitched as she nodded.

"But," Belle added, her gaze observant, "you wonder about how soon you have to leave."

"Yeah...I, well I guess, it's not really good timing for noticing anyone."

"It's never a bad time to have a friend."

"That's sage advice," she noted, her gaze shifting to Zac.

A long sigh left Belle and Madelyn watched the smile slip, as she said, "Sometimes life teaches us things when we least expect it."

She wanted to ask what was going through her mind, but another shout from the crowd garnered their attention. With the game over, she found herself swept away with the women.

"We'll meet the gang at the pub," Belle explained, looping her arm through hers. "Ginny and Katelyn will help with the kids and then everyone will join us."

She looked over her shoulder, catching Zac staring at her. Smiling, she threw her hand up in a wave, catching his wink as she moved away.

Entering the pub, her heart felt lighter now as she recognized a number of the townspeople. Brogan and Aiden came from the game and settled behind the bar. Tori, Jade, Jillian, and Belle escorted her to a large booth near the back. Ordering pitchers of beer and lemonade, and plates of appetizers, they settled deeper into their seats, waiting for the others.

As the conversation flowed, she kept glancing toward the door every time it opened, a little sigh escaping each time she realized it was not Zac. A giggle caught her attention and she turned around to see the others grinning.

"Honey, if you keep jerking your head every time the door opens, you're gonna get a crick in your neck," Jillian proclaimed, much to the amusement of the others.

Blushing, she did not have time to deny that she was looking for someone, when the sound of a boisterous group came in. Ginny made a beeline for Brogan as the others made their way to the large booth and table. Grant and Mitch scooted in next to their wives, and Gareth walked over, hand in hand with Katelyn.

Zac followed behind, his gaze shooting over the gathering, landing on hers before a smile lit his face, spotting a space next to her on the booth bench. Walking over, he was waylaid by one of the servers placing her hand on his arm.

"Hey Zac, nice to see you here."

"Thanks, Sidney," he replied, his voice amicable but his eyes still on the table of friends.

"I thought maybe we could get together sometime. I'm free after work," she pushed, her eyes hopeful.

Jerking his head back to her, he was surprised at her offer, considering he was almost ten years older than she was. "Uh...I don't think so. I've got plans."

Pouting, she said, "Maybe some other time."

He glanced back to the table, seeing Madelyn's eyes now averted, a slight blush painting her cheeks. *Fuck!* Turning back to the young woman, he said, "Sidney, you just started working here, so I gotta warn you... Brogan's not too keen on his servers coming on to customers. Especially since you're so young."

Her eyes flashed anger as she flounced away, leaving him standing with his hands on his hips for a few seconds.

"Problem?" Brogan asked, coming up behind him.

"Nah...I got it covered." Plastering a smile back on his face, he turned around and walked to the back booth, noticing Madelyn had scooted toward the end of the bench seat, effectively taking away the place he planned on sitting.

Not to be deterred, he sat down, his hip bumping into hers as he gently pushed her over. "Hate to crowd you, but I've been waiting all morning to spend some time with you," he whispered.

"Of course," she replied, her smile too wide and her tone too bright.

Throwing his arm across the back of the booth, he leaned in and whispered, "You're the only one I wanted to see, Maddie."

Her eyes sought his before sliding back toward the bar at the young woman in a Finn's Pub t-shirt. Dropping her gaze, she sighed. "Zac, I'm only here for little while. I wasn't jealous when she wanted to be with you, but it did make me realize that I'm being selfish to want your company when I leave in a week...or more."

He caught her last words and asked, "Or more?"

"I'm not sure I can get all of Dad's affairs in order within another week. I thought I'd call my boss on Monday and tell him I need another week off." Blowing out a puff, she added, "I have no idea how he'll take that."

"Damn, how can he not understand what you're dealing with?"

"Well, he's an administrator now and I do have clients that have to be shuffled around to other counselors."

"Don't take on that guilt," he admonished. "You've

got a lot to deal with." A grin reappeared on his face as he latched on to the other part of what she said. "You want my company?"

Shoulder bumping him, she rolled her eyes. "Yes, I'd like to spend time with everyone."

"Hmmph," he groused. "I'm now thrown into the *everyone* category."

A giggle slipped out as she admitted, "Okay, okay. I want to spend time with just you as well."

"That's more like it." He liked that she was not coy. What she thought, she said. Dropping his hand casually to her shoulder, he gently rubbed the tension from her muscles.

Twisting her head to look up at him, she said, "I really liked the ballgame. I had no idea the American Legion did anything like that."

"It's just one of the many community service projects we have going," he explained. Before he had a chance to tell her more, the servers brought huge platters of wings and nachos for the group to share.

"You'd better jump in while you can," Belle laughed. "These guys know how to decimate whatever's put in front of them."

Seeing the hands moving quickly, she grabbed a few wings before Zac had a chance to get any.

"Hey," he complained.

"Don't worry," she said. "I figured I would get some for both of us." She continued to load her plate before sliding it between them.

Grinning, he squeezed her shoulder with his left

hand, diving into the food with his right. He noticed she did not have a glass. Pushing his beer over toward her, he asked, "Here, need something to wash it down with?"

"I'll just get some water," she said, looking at the server approaching, but he got there before she did.

"Two waters, please," he said, his voice low.

Smiling her appreciation, they continued to eat.

After a few minutes of no talking as the group munched, Tori looked over and asked, "How are things going with your father's house?"

Wiping the barbeque sauce from her lips, she said, "Slow. Really slow." Seeing the curious expressions from all around, she hastened to say, "As a child I remember my dad loving antiques, but it seems that in the years I was gone, it became an obsession. He filled the house with his finds. When I first entered, I thought I had entered something from the TV show about hoarders."

Gasping, Jillian said, "I had no idea you had to deal with that kind of situation."

"It's okay," she replied. "David Wills sought me out at the funeral and is going through everything. He's helping to decide what is actually an antique with value and what's not."

"He's got a good reputation," Tori said. "He inquired about some of my grandmother's antiques, but I wasn't selling them so I had to turn him down."

Mitch added, "If I remember, he wasn't too happy about that." Looking at Madelyn, he warned, "Don't let him strong-arm you. Only sell what you want and when you want. Tori's right...he's got a good reputation, but he can also be pushy."

Belle's eyes jumped between her and Zac and she smiled. "How long are you going to be here?"

"I don't know," she admitted. "I thought one week, then two. Now, I'm going to ask for another week off because I want to go through the house very carefully. I know David's methodical, but I find myself wanting to go over each piece myself. I don't want to make any rush decisions. It's also a chance for me to take some time off. I haven't taken a vacation in almost two years."

"Honey, you do need a break! How can we help with that?" Jillian asked. "Going through anything? Or, the guys would be glad to help move some of the furniture."

She saw the emphatic nods from around the tables, but she shook her head. "Thank you so much for the offer and I promise to take you up on it, if and when I need. Zac's already been helping with some of the heavy lifting."

She looked down at her plate, missing the knowing glances of their friends.

The others nodded as they continued to eat. No longer hungry, she fiddled with her napkin, suddenly overcome with melancholy.

Zac, seeing the change in her demeanor, leaned over and whispered, "You want to get out of here?"

Her jerky nod was his answer and he stood, offering his hand to assist her up. Seeing her chin quiver, he wanted to help her escape the prying eyes of their well-meaning friends. “Guys, we’re gonna take a walk and will see y’all later.”

Amid goodbyes, he casually placed his arm around her shoulders and led her out into the sunshine.

13

Zac itched to take her hand as they walked down the street toward the town pier but, instinctively understanding she needed peace, he simply guided her along with his hand on her lower back. Neither spoke as she allowed the sunshine and bay breeze to soothe her spirits. They walked onto the wooden pier and sat on one of the benches built into the sides. Slipping her shoes off, she leaned back, tilting her face to the warmth.

After a few minutes, she twisted her head, staring at his eyes, pinned on her. "Can I ask you something?" She caught his nod and she added, "And if you don't want to answer, you can just tell me, okay?"

He shifted so that he was facing her and reached up to tuck a windblown strand of hair behind her ear. "Go ahead, Maddie. You can ask me anything."

She sucked in her lips for a moment, gathering her courage before blurting, "Do you think we ever really know our parents?"

Not what he was expecting, Zac stared, his expression blank.

"It's just that what I always thought about my parents seems to not be what the reality was and I wondered if that was just me."

Heaving a sigh, he said, "I think we know what we remember and what others tell us. But I'm not sure we can ever really know what they were like. At least, not when all we have to go by are childhood memories."

She nodded slowly, before continuing, "I heard that your parents had died…and I just wondered…well, I know it's only been a week for me, but somehow, I thought…since my dad and I…I just thought…oh, hell, I'm not making any sense!"

"You want to know what it was like for me?"

Nodding, she said, "I know that is so personal. I'm a counselor and, yet, I feel so unprepared for what I'm feeling. I know everyone's grief is so different, but I feel lost."

She had twisted her body to face him and he took her hands in his. "I guess being raised in this town, I have no secrets. Everyone knows about Rod and Mary Hamilton. My parents were great. They loved each other and loved me. Then Mom got cancer when I was in elementary school and died when I was ten."

She gasped, her hands squeezing his. "Oh, my God, Zac. I must have been too young to know that or even understand that back then."

He nodded and added, "It was horrible but, honestly, one of the amazing things about living in a small town is I was immediately surrounded by other, good women who stepped in. Mitch and Jillian's moms, Nancy and Claire, Grant's mom, Marcia, the MacFarlanes' mom, Corrine, and Philip's mom, Tonya...they all made me feel loved. Made sure I had lunches packed, groceries in the refrigerator, made it to school and to practices. And not just for a few months, but for years. Hell, sometimes they still look out for me."

Madelyn stayed quiet, wanting to hear everything he felt like sharing, without interrupting him with questions.

"That was almost twenty years ago, but I still feel it. Still miss her. Still wish things had been different." Linking his fingers with hers, he said, "Your grief is so fresh...too real and too close. Don't try to make sense of it. Just let it flow. Cry if you want. Be alone when you want. Surround yourself with others when you want."

Emitting a small chuckle, she said, "Good advice. Are you sure you're not the counselor?"

"Don't be so hard on yourself," he chided gently, lifting her chin with his knuckle. "As a rescue worker, I'm always thinking of what I could have done better or differently, even though I may have saved a life. I guess it's the same for you. You can counsel others, but it's different when you have to go through it."

Nodding, she silently agreed. After another moment, she said, "The group here is so close...so supportive. They've taken me under their wing and, even though I'm only here for a short time, they make me feel part of something bigger than myself."

"This is a good place to live. I know I was itching to get away into the big, wide world, but four years with the Navy taught me that all I really wanted was to come back here and live. In fact, most of us Baytown Boys came back and we started inviting some of our military friends, who didn't have a supportive hometown when they got out of the service, to move here too. Jason and Lance are two who've done that." They were silent for a moment before he added, "I mentioned the Eastern Shore Mental Health Group and how some of my buddies see them for PTSD. You could probably get in to talk to someone about grief counseling. You know, counselors need counseling too."

"God, you're so right." Sighing, she said, "But I won't be here much longer." Wanting to move to a less emotional topic, she said, "Tell me about the American Legion. I had no idea what it was and, certainly, no idea my dad was even a veteran."

Laughing, he replied, "Oh, man, I could talk about the AL all day. It's the nation's largest wartime veterans service organization. It's committed to mentoring youth and to continued devotion to our fellow service members and veterans. I'm the finance officer and one of the founding members of our chapter here."

"Really? Now I'm embarrassed that I don't know more about it."

"Don't be. Most people aren't aware of what we are or what we do. Our baseball program is huge and, officially, it educates young people about the importance of sportsmanship, citizenship and fitness. But unofficially, it's great out here because it's the only sports many of these kids can do, since there's no fee for them to play. We only ask the parents to help out when they can and if that's just by coming to a game to cheer, then that's great."

"Zac, that's wonderful. What a service for the community. When I was at the game earlier, I was stunned at how many people came."

Nodding, his pride evident in his wide smile, he said, "We've got the whole town excited about the games."

"What else do you do?"

"There are a ton of programs, but one I really like is the Operation Comfort Warriors program. For us in Baytown, it kind of goes with our inviting others to come make their home here. But it supports recovering wounded warriors and their families, providing them with comfort items when they're in the hospital. Our Auxiliary works hard on this project."

"Belle mentioned the Auxiliary, but I had no idea what she was talking about."

"The American Legion Auxiliary is for family members of active duty military or veterans. So, wives, mothers, sisters, daughters, granddaughters can join. Hell, in fact, I think anyone can join who's willing to volunteer." He eyed her for a moment, appreciating the sunlight glistening off her dark hair before adding, "If you stayed, you could join as well. Of course, you could join when you go back home too, but I just thought it would be nice if you were here."

She smiled a wistful smile. Heaving a sigh, she said, "Baytown certainly has a pull to it. But, my home is in North Carolina. My job is there. My mom is there."

"And friends? Boyfriend?"

"No to the boyfriend. And as far as friends, I have a few. I mean, it's not like I don't have friends...just not a lot. Not like you do here. Oh, God, I'm rambling again."

Throwing his head back in laughter, he said, "I like it when you ramble. It's cute."

"Cute? Just what I want to be known as...*cute*." She rolled her eyes, but was unable to hide her smile. Silent for a moment, she allowed the bay breeze and warm sun to penetrate. Letting out a deep breath, she said, "Thanks, Zac."

Cocking his head to the side, he asked, "For what?"

"For just being here. For making me feel better. For being...a friend."

Leaning in, Zac watched as her upturned face moved closer to his. A whisper away, he murmured, "Good friends," before kissing her. The gentle brush of his lips on hers sparked a fire deep inside and he angled his head, taking the kiss deeper.

She sighed underneath his ministrations and he felt her body respond. Wrapping his arms around her, he pulled her closer until her heartbeat was next to his. The feel of her breasts against his chest, her legs sliding over his so that she was almost on his lap, and her lips pliant under his had his blood rushing to his dick and all thoughts of taking things slow flying out of his mind.

The sound of children's laughter from the beach brought Madelyn back to reality and she pulled away, regret in her sigh. "Oh, Zac," she moaned, "what are we doing?"

"If you don't know, then I must be doing something wrong."

She laughed, her eyes dancing for a moment before she sighed.

Cupping her face, he said, "Nothing says we can't enjoy each other while you're here. Not if we both know what the score is."

Her eyes, shadowed by the clouds overhead, held his. "What is the score...just so I'm clear?" she said, her words halting.

"We're two adults, both enjoying each other's company. There's no one to get hurt and when it's time for you to leave, we part as friends."

"Friends who were intimate?"

Nodding, he said, "Why not?" Seeing her hesitation, he hastened to add, "Maddie, this isn't an offer I've ever made before. I'm not the kind of man who goes around having indiscriminate sex. With my job, I hardly ever get to date and I'm not much of a one-night-stand kind of guy."

Watching her bite her lip while still sitting on his lap had him leaning in to give the swollen flesh a lick before kissing it once more. Leaning back, he watched a smile curve her lips. "And, this doesn't have to lead to sex. We can just enjoy each other's company. But, we'll know up front that, if it does, then we can both say goodbye when you leave and have no regrets."

"I'm not sure it works that way, Zac," she said. "Sex without feelings seems kind of...reckless with our hearts."

"Maddie, we'll have feelings. Feelings of friendship...just not the urge to declare everlasting love." A rueful chuckle rumbled from his chest. "I'm not sure that's an emotion I'm capable of anyway. To me, love equals pain."

Madelyn cocked her head, wanting to ask him more but then changed her mind. After all, having seen what her parents went through, she had to agree. Love certainly could equal pain.

Bringing her hands up to his face, she cupped his cheeks as she pulled him in for another kiss, this one owned by her. His lips were smooth and firm and as he opened his mouth she slid her tongue inside. Feeling the rumble from his chest once more, this time she swallowed the delicious sound.

"Okay," she whispered, thinking that, just for a little while, it would be nice to have sex with a gorgeous man, no strings attached. A chance to forget everything pressing down on her and just enjoy. "For as long as I'm here, we can be friends."

He lifted her hand and placed a kiss on her knuckles. "Here's to new and very good friends." Standing, he gently pulled her to her feet, wrapping his arm around her shoulder.

She looked up and smiled, saying, "I hope your place is good enough, because there's no way we're going back to my dad's house. I'm sleeping in a twin-sized bed in the room I had when I was a child."

Laughing, he said, "I think that can be arranged." As they walked down the street toward the fire station, his words took on a reluctant quality when he said, "I hope you aren't expecting too much. My apartment in back of the station is rather...uh...spartan."

"Does it have a bed?"

"Yeah," he grinned.

"Will it fit two people?"

"Yeah," his grin widened.

"Then we're good," she declared.

14

Madelyn expected to have to go through the fire station to get to Zac's apartment and was relieved when he walked her around the back of the building to a set of metal stairs attached to the brick. Leaning her head back, she realized how far up they would go, but her fear of heights was less than her fear of others seeing her blatantly walking into his apartment. Friends with benefits would be easier if no one else knew what was happening.

She linked fingers with his as they started up the stairs, the occasional creaking resulting in her heart skipping a beat and her hand clutching his.

Zac looked down at Madelyn, observing her lust-filled eyes had morphed into wide-eyed fright as her fingers squeezed his painfully. Just then the stairs groaned again and, hearing her gasp, he asked, "Are you afraid of heights?"

"Uh...not as long as my feet can stay on the ground," she tried to joke.

"Don't look down," he ordered, unpeeling her hand from his in order to wrap his arm tightly around her. "Just keep looking at me."

Swallowing, Madelyn obeyed, noting it was not difficult considering Zac's profile was gorgeous. Before she knew it, his hand was on the doorknob and within a few seconds, they were safely ensconced inside.

Whirling around, he led her deeper into the apartment, his eyes full of concern. "You okay, sweetheart?"

Now that her feet were firmly planted on the floor, she grinned as she stepped up to him, plastering her body against his front. Clasping her hands together behind his neck, she gave a little tug downward. "I'm perfect."

Grinning, he latched onto her lips, mumbling, "Yeah, you are." Not watching where he was going, Zac continued to kiss her as he backed toward the sofa. Flipping over the end, he landed on the soft, worn cushions, her body sprawled on top of his, their lips still attached. He grunted as her slight weight knocked the air from his lungs, but the feel of her breasts pressed against his chest again shot all thoughts of anything but getting her naked and underneath him from his mind.

As though she had the same thought, she placed her hands on his chest and pushed up, her thighs straddling his pelvis, his hard cock straining at the zipper of his jeans hot against her warm core.

Grinning, she pulled her shirt over her head, not

caring where it landed. He looked up, eyes wide at her breasts spilling over the top of her demi-bra. His hands followed his gaze, palming the plump mounds before jerking the cups down. Her breasts sprung free and he bent at the waist, latching his mouth over a taut nipple.

While he sucked, she unfastened the bra from the back, allowing it to be tossed to the side as well. Clutching his shoulders with her hands, she held him in place as she leaned her head back, pressing her breasts forward.

Feasting on a nipple, he felt her hands slide down to the bottom of his t-shirt and attempt to pull it upward. Letting go of the delectable bud for a few seconds, he reached behind his neck and grasped the offending material, pulling it over his head to land near her shirt on the floor.

Standing, his arms still wrapped around her, she clutched her legs about his waist, their naked chests plastered together. He stalked into the small bedroom, grateful for the double bed. It might not be huge, but it would fit the two of them. *Especially if she's under me.*

Twisting one more time, he laid her on her back, her bright eyes smiling back at him. She placed her feet on the bed to scooch higher, but his hands on her ankles stopped the movement.

"Oh, no, Maddie. Not until I've had a chance to taste you." Chuckling as her eyes widened, he unbuttoned her jeans before sliding them over her hips. She wiggled, assisting in the removal, her fingers grabbing her panties as he tossed her pants onto the floor. Standing over her, he dragged his eyes down, perusing her full breasts, her tapered waist, and full hips. Her legs, long and toned, no longer wrapped around his waist but lying open, her slick folds beckoning. His cock, already pressing into his jeans, strained, leaving him to wonder if his zipper was creating a permanent mark.

Leaning up, Madelyn propped her upper body on her elbows, observing as Zac divested himself of his clothes as quickly as he could. When he was down to his tented boxers, she lowered her gaze to travel slowly over his body. His dark brown hair was clipped neatly and his clean-shaven face gave off a boyish charm. Her eyes moved slowly, from his muscular chest to his defined abs, the V-muscles disappearing beneath his waistband. "You're beautiful. You know that, don't you?" she said, marveling at the muscles flexing with each movement.

"You've got that backward, Maddie," he countered, his gaze traveling down her luscious body. With a deft movement, he lowered his boxers, kicking them down his legs and onto the floor. No longer constrained, his cock stood at attention as he ran his fist up and down its length. He knelt on the floor tossing her feet over his shoulder before placing a kiss on the inside of each thigh. She shivered and he kissed the goosebumps away.

Unable to keep from jerking her legs, she could not contain the giggle that erupted. "I'm ticklish," she gasped, but then his mouth began to move higher and her mirth ended as her sex clenched in anticipation.

With the flat of his tongue Zac licked her slick folds,

memorizing the taste of her. *God, what would it be like to have this beautiful woman every night—wait, what? This is just sex. Sex between friends, true, but just sex. Just like I like it.* Pushing all other thoughts from his mind, he determined to make it memorable for her. *Nothing wrong with making her glad she agreed.* Plunging his tongue in, he grinned as she jumped, jerking her hips off the bed. "Mmmm," he mumbled against her clit, using his mouth in tandem with his fingers as he nipped, licked, sucked, and worked her into a frenzy.

She clutched the sheet in her fists before reaching down to grab his head with her hands. With one last suck, she screamed his name and he felt her hot core clench his finger as he continued to move his tongue around her clit, prolonging the orgasm.

The vibrations sent shock waves throughout Madelyn's body until she finally collapsed back onto the bed, her body boneless. "Oh, my God," she breathed, unable to think of anything else to say.

Zac chuckled as he lowered her legs gently off his shoulders. Kissing her mound, he began kissing upward over her tummy, nuzzling her sides as she squirmed.

"I told you, I'm ticklish!" she protested halfheartedly. Gasping for air, she moaned, "Zac, you're going to kill me."

"Well, I am a rescue worker. I can revive you."

"Mmm, and how would you do that?" she breathed as his mouth made its way up to her breasts, lavishing attention on each one.

"I think mouth-to-mouth is definitely necessary."

Proving his theory, he latched onto her lips, stealing her breath as his tongue tangled with hers. Angling his head, he delved and probed each crevice, memorizing the taste and feel of her.

As he lifted his head slightly, staring down at her warm eyes, she agreed, "I think mouth-to-mouth is absolutely necessary." Her hand slid down over his ass, moving between them to circle his shaft. "And then I think that you could...probe me with your cock...you know, just to make sure I'm alive."

Laughter bubbled up from his chest as he lifted his hips just enough for her to continue her ministration. "Oh, yeah, babe. I think probing is next on our list of things to make sure you stay alive." Shifting upward, he reached into his nightstand and snagged a condom, rolling it on with quick efficiency.

Lifting an eyebrow, she said, "Need those often?"

"Not nearly as often as you think. In fact, I should probably check to make sure the expiration date is still good."

Grinning, she said, "I know this is just between friends, but if you want to know the truth, it's been a while for me too. Last boyfriend was ages ago and I've never been one to troll the bars looking for a fast lay." Biting her lip, she added, "But in case it breaks, I'm on the pill."

"Good to know," he said, leaning down to kiss her sweet lips once more. "Nice to not be just another notch on your bedpost."

"My bedframe is metal," she retorted with a grin. Looking over, she realized his mattress was on a floor frame with no headboard. "Guess neither of us will be notching anything soon."

"God, you're amazing," he said, nestling his hips between her widely spread legs and lining his cock with her sex. *Beautiful, sexy, funny...I may have just found the perfect woman—oh, shut up and just enjoy it.*

"Fuck," he said, leaning down to capture her lips. Moving hotly over them, he felt the scorching heat of her body pressed close to his. Lifting his head, he held her gaze. Her nod was his permission, but he asked nonetheless.

"Tell me what you want," he ordered, teasing her core with the head of his cock. "I need to hear the words." Moving it slowly through her wet folds, he closed his eyes briefly, forcing himself to go slow. His cock strained to move inside, as though it had a will of its own. Sucking in a deep breath, he opened his eyes, carefully watching her flushed face as she held his gaze.

"I want you. Now," she answered, her breasts heaving with each pant as her hips bucked upward.

Dipping his lips to hers, he whispered, "You got it, babe," before plunging his dick into her hot, tight sex and his tongue into her warm mouth.

Moving in rhythm, he started slowly, his cock stretching her as it hit every nerve along the way. In and out, creating a friction that drove her to distraction. He nibbled along her neck, sucking on the tender area at the base where her pulse throbbed.

Madelyn slid her hands down Zac's back as her legs entwined around his waist, opening herself up more. Digging her heels into his ass, she heard him groan as she met him thrust for thrust. His back muscles bunched and stretched underneath her fingertips as she gripped him tightly.

"Harder," she moaned, squeezing her eyes shut as the world around her fell away, the only tangible sensation the rocking of her body as he powered into her. Shifting the angle of his hips, he continued to grind against her clit. Her world tilted as tremors began in her core and exploded outward. For a moment, she had no worries or cares...only sensations filling her mind.

Zac watched as Madelyn's teeth bit into her kiss-swollen bottom lip, her head thrown back against the mattress as he felt his balls tighten. Her breasts moved with each thrust and she panted each breath.

"Open your eyes. I need to see you when you come," he ordered. She obeyed, her gaze warm upon him. Her plump lips were smiling as he felt her inner muscles clenching around him.

Madelyn was mesmerized with how Zac's serious expression altered when his orgasm rocked through him. With his head thrown back, she observed the veins standing out on his neck as he powered through his orgasm.

Zac was stunned, feeling the immediate difference between Madelyn and any other woman he had ever been with. He wanted her again as soon as one orgasm passed. He wanted to make the next one better. Sex had always seemed perfunctory. Always an action. Not an emotion. *But, we agreed...no emotions. And I don't want to get too deep...do I?*

He dropped his head back to the mattress by hers as

he tried to catch his breath. Rolling to the side, he pulled her along with him. Their sweat-slicked bodies cooled slowly as their heartbeats continued to pound.

Pushing her dark, silky hair from her face, he watched her as her breathing slowed. After a few seconds, her eyes opened and focused on him, a smile curving her lips.

She reached up, wordlessly, and stroked his face. He noted a shiver running over her and pulled the covers over them, tucking her in close to his body.

Here, with her in his arms, there were no problems. No job decisions to be made. No furniture to be sorted. No thoughts as to when she might leave. It was as though the cares of the world could not touch them as they rested in their cocoon. He just hoped she felt the same.

Zac awoke with his arms empty and the bed catching the chill of the evening, considering the sun had almost set and dark shadows fell across the room. They had slept for hours, recuperating in each other's arms. Leaning up, he watched as Madelyn slid her shoes on, bending down to grab her purse.

"Hey," he called out, his hand rubbing over his chest.

She turned, her smile wide, noting the confused line creasing his brow. "You were sleeping so peacefully, I didn't want to disturb you. I get the feeling, with your job, you don't always get a lot of uninterrupted sleep."

He sat up, swinging his legs over the side before standing, unconcerned about his nudity. He watched as her eyes moved over his body and he was unable to contain the pride infusing his being. “See anything you like, Maddie?”

Barking out a laugh, she cocked her hip, and replied, “Oh, I think you know the answer to that, Zac Hamilton. I made good use of what I liked.”

Grinning, he stalked forward, his hands on her shoulders. “You’re kind of overdressed, aren’t you? Were you planning on sneaking out?”

“No sneaking to it,” she quipped. “But, yeah, I was going to head home.”

He tried to hide the disappointment from his face, offering a pretend pout instead. *This is what I wanted, friends with benefits for just as long as she was in town. A short tryst. Easy, fun, no emotions.* And yet he found himself blurting, “When will I see you again?”

She fiddled with her purse strap as she searched his eyes. “I don’t know. I’ve got to work on the house and get David to set up the auction to sell the antiques.”

Snagging his boxers and jeans off the floor, he jerked them on. “We’ve got a beach party coming up. Are you still coming?”

Her face brightening, she nodded. “Sounds good.”

Nodding, he walked her to the door, then hesitated. “I forgot you’re afraid of heights. Let me walk you through the station.”

“But, what if—”

“There’s only one volunteer on night duty tonight

and I promise he'll be in the break room watching TV if he's not already snoring. It'll be fine."

"Okay," she agreed, "but if I keep coming here, I'm going to have to traverse the scary stairs sooner or later."

"Or you can just come in through the station."

"I thought the idea was to keep this between us. No complications."

"And what's complicated about other people knowing? Or are you ashamed of being seen with me?"

Huffing, she said, "Not ashamed...just...uh well, it is Baytown."

"You're afraid of the Baytown gossips? Babe, the Mayor's secretary was sleeping with the Town Manager when he was engaged to someone else. And that's after the Mayor's wife had him sleeping on the couch because he hired her in the first place."

A giggle erupted from her but he was on a roll.

"Jillian had to put Grant into the friend-only category when he kept going out with women even though he obviously cared about her until he got his head out of his ass and realized himself that what he wanted all along was her. Don't even get me started on Brogan, who pined for Ginny for a year, even cutting his long hair to impress her, before finally making a move. Mitch had trouble making the moves on Tori because she was accused of murder."

"Oh, my God," she blurted. "Stop! I get it. You're saying that no one cares what we do."

He pulled her in for a hug, his arms tight around her body, noticing the way her chin fit perfectly underneath his. In fact, everything about her felt perfect. Kissing the top of her head, he said, "I don't want you to feel self-conscious. No one will judge you, and certainly not our friends. But, I'll respect whatever you want."

She leaned her head back, staring into his eyes and said, "I'm not ashamed of our friendship. I'll let you walk me out the front."

Grinning, he threw on a BFD t-shirt, and they left through the main station.

Halfway through the station she turned back to him suddenly, raising a hand and squinting her eyes in disbelief. "Wait, did you say Tori was accused of murder?"

Laughing, he put his hand on her back and finished walking her to her car down the street. "Baytown is just full of surprises." After opening her door, he bent to kiss her goodbye. "I'll talk to you tomorrow?"

"Count on it. I'll be at home, digging my way through Dad's things."

He stood on the street and watched as her tail lights grew smaller before heading back into the station, a strange sense of wistfulness filling his chest.

15

Madelyn climbed the stairs, reluctance in her steps. Reaching the top, she bypassed the bedrooms and headed straight to the small bathroom, turning on the water in the bathtub. As the water ran, she stripped off her clothes and stood in front of the mirror. Her breasts had pink burns from Zac's stubble where he had devoured her. Her neck sported small bite marks and she grinned at the evidence of his nibbles.

Lifting her gaze to her face, she wondered why she did not feel happier. *I'm only here a couple of weeks. It's just a bit of fun...no big deal.* But, she knew she was lying to herself. Sex with Zac Hamilton might have just been sex to him, but to her heart, it felt like more. *God, I don't need this complication!* As she settled into the tub, she realized there was no complication. Not to him and therefore not to her. *I can keep it light...keep it friendly. And then when I leave...well, I can take my sad heart back with me.*

The night was blessedly peaceful with no emergency calls, but as Zac lay in bed, his thoughts rolled over the day with Madelyn. She had asked about his parents and he had easily talked about his mother's death. While it had been on the tip of his tongue to talk about his father's as well, he hesitated. *What would she think if she knew he had been the town drunk?*

There were few secrets in Baytown, especially back in those days, and his father's drinking was well known. But she lived in the county and not in the town, so perhaps she had never heard of his dad. He had told her of the kindness of his friends' mothers when his mom died, but it had been a while since he allowed himself to think back on how his friends' dads stepped up as well.

His mind traveled down the path he rarely allowed, hating to think of the days when the other men in town were more of a dad than his own father was. He just accepted their offers to help him learn to play ball, how they celebrated when he made homeruns, and provided extra food when the Baytown Boys had sleep-overs. *Did I notice they treated me special? Or, in my teenage mind, did I just think it was normal?* He knew they would have stepped up for any of them, but looking back, none of the others seemed to need it.

Rolling over, he punched his pillow, his frustration over his dad growing. *How could he just leave me alone like that? And did he know what the other men in town did to fill his place?*

Sliding his mind back to Madelyn, he had observed the same specter of pain in her eyes when they talked out on the pier and wondered about the cause. He knew she and her dad were estranged, but had no idea why. Blowing out his breath, his proposal with the pretty counselor took over his thoughts. Sex without emotion. Friendship without declarations of love. *What a perfect arrangement...I thought. Who knew being with her was going to rock my world? And why does the idea of something more not scare me as much as it always has?*

Rubbing his chest, he felt an emptiness in his heart at the thought of her that didn't set well with him. *Since when do I need someone? Love equals loss, and that equals pain.* Closing his eyes, he knew he was not going to go back on his offer and, if he was being honest with himself, he secretly hoped she would stay longer than originally planned.

The American Legion meeting had adjourned, but Zac held back, putting the chairs away as most of the others headed to the pub. Steve and Ed Evans, Jillian's and Mitch's fathers, helped. Even in their late fifties, it was easy to see that the two men were brothers. Both sported short hair, grey interspersed with the light brown. Ed was slightly leaner, but after his heart attack, his wife had watched his diet like a hawk. Zac had noticed at the last AL picnic that Ed had stared with unabashed envy at his brother's plate until Claire snatched half the food off Steve's overladen dish.

As their task finished, Zac stuck his hands in his pockets and asked, "You guys got a minute?"

Steve looked at him, sharp eyes piercing his before casting a glance toward his brother. Both men turned and deftly took several chairs back down from the neat stack. Placing three facing each other, Steve said, "Let's have a seat, son."

Son. That was something he always noticed. Both Steve and Ed called him 'son'. But, then, so did most of the other men in town. *Was it a throwaway title, or did it mean something? And why the hell does it matter to me now?*

Shaking his head to rid himself of the tangled cobwebs that filled his mind, he sat leaning forward, his arms resting on his thighs. Staring at his clasped hands for a moment, he finally looked up and asked, "I want to know more about my dad...and why he drank himself to death instead of taking care of me. And why all of you had to step in to do his job."

Seeing the shock in their eyes, he continued, "I'm asking you two because I may have only been ten years old when Mom died, but it wasn't lost on me that you, and several other dads, took me under their wings when my own dad decided he didn't care about his own son anymore—"

Steve opened his mouth to protest, but was halted when Ed knee-bumped him, allowing him to continue speaking.

"For a long time, Dad was just sad and I got that. As young as I was, I got that, 'cause I was sad too. But when did you all know something was wrong?"

They sighed heavily at the same time before a look passed between them, indicating the secret-brother manner of deciding who would speak first.

Ed placed his hands on his knees, holding Zac's gaze steady and said, "We grew up with your dad. We'd bend an elbow when we were out fishing or at the end of a game. Like most young bucks, we'd get beer from one of the stores that never cared how old you were, and if memory serves, your grandfather had no problem with getting us a six-pack."

"Probably not much different than you boys in your teens," Steve added.

"We all went into the military and when we came back, we'd still have a drink or two when together, but family responsibilities took over." Ed shrugged, "Alcohol was not a big part of our gatherings."

Steve said, "Your dad drank, but none of us ever noticed a problem...not right away. Then we'd notice, long before your mother got sick, that he would be the last to leave the pub if we had a get-together. If we were out fishing, he'd go through a six-pack before the rest of us had two beers. And we'd stop while he kept going."

The two men shared another long look before turning back to Zac. "When your mom got sick, he stopped drinking. He was devoted to her. We'd all pitch in to make sure you were in school and taken care of when he was at the hospital or with her when she was sick from chemo." Shaking his head, Ed repeated, "Utterly devoted."

Swallowing hard, Zac remembered his dad admonishing him gently. *"Gotta stay quiet, son. Your mama's resting."*

"But then, when Mary died, he was devastated, like any man would be, and he took to drinking heavily. He wasn't a mean drunk...he was amiable, so it was easy to overlook because we all knew how much he loved your mom and her death pulled his foundation right out from under him." Sighing heavily, Ed added, "And that was a failing of ours...not recognizing that it was a problem until it was too late."

"It wasn't your job to keep Dad away from the drink," Zac fired back.

"No, but I think we all regret not trying harder."

"So, you took care of his son since he wasn't doing a bang-up job of it?"

Steve rubbed his chin, dark clouds moving through his eyes. "We took care of you because we loved you. We all did. You were, are, another one of our boys."

"A pity charge?"

Rearing back, Ed said, "We took care of all the kids, Zac. Not just you. I'm the one who took Grant to the doctor when he broke his arm in sixth grade, 'cause his parents were visiting Marcia's mom in Virginia Beach. Grant's dad sat with Jillian when she got sick at school and Steve and Claire were at a conference in Maryland all day. Philip's dad got to the hospital first when Mitch fell off the ladder until I could get there. That's what Baytown's all about...good friends who care about each other."

He sat quietly, letting more memories flow over him, his heart still aching from the knowledge his father did very little but drink as the years progressed.

"Your dad was not drunk all the time, but it did get worse. We just stepped in to make sure you had plenty of adults around to take up the slack where he was failing."

Steve eyed him with a steady stare. "Can I ask what's got you thinking about all this, son?"

Leaning back in the hard, metal chair, his breath left his lungs in a heavy sigh. Scrubbing his hand over his face, he shook his head in dejection. "I don't know. Maybe I've just always accepted how things played out but never really analyzed the actual reasons. I guess I always figured that dad just drank because he missed mom so much, and am only now realizing that maybe part of me also thought I wasn't enough to save him..."

"Oh, son, you couldn't have done anything. I'm sorry you've taken that on. It hurts to think that his inability to work through his grief impacted you so much," Ed finished.

Nodding, he agreed. "Yeah..."

"This trip down memory lane have anything to do with Madelyn being in town and her father's funeral?" Steve asked.

Heart suddenly racing, he looked up abruptly. "Why do you ask?"

"Well, I didn't know her dad well, but he drank a lot too."

Zac's brows lifted to his forehead at this tidbit and wondered if that had anything to do with her relationship turning sour with her dad.

"Seen you two together at the pub. She seems like a real nice girl."

He looked at Ed and Steve, but saw no mirth in either man's eyes. Just concern.

Ed said, "Of all the boys, you were the one who kept girls at arm's length. Oh, you'd go out and enjoy being with them as long as nothing serious ever happened. I figure there were a few hearts broken by you. Not like Aiden, who'd charm the pants off anyone and not have a second though. You were cautious with your heart."

"And now, your interest is snagged by someone and it seems like you're trying to get a grip on what that might mean," Steve finished.

Throwing his hands up in defense, he retorted, "Hey, she's only in town a couple of weeks."

"But...something's got you questioning the past."

"You guys are too insightful for your own good, you know that?" He looked at them pointedly and laughed as they tried to look unassuming. "I'm just finally at an age where I can look back and try to figure out my dad. And yeah, she's got me thinking about it. After what he went through, I've always equated love with potential loss and with that loss extreme pain. Wasn't worth the heartache."

They all sat quietly for a few minutes, the room silent as their thoughts churned. Ed looked at Zac before saying, "You know, growing up, you had a chance to see me and Nancy up close, being at our house a lot. Same here, with Steve and Claire. And I know Eric and Corrine MacFarlane included you in a lot of their family gatherings with their kids. You had the chance to see lots of solid relationships that weathered good times and bad. Your parents loved each other. You gotta know that love binds us together, son. Love does not have to equal pain.

"Obviously," Ed added, "long marriages will end with one partner losing the other and yes, that is loss and pain. But the love that was shared, the memories made will make the pain worth it."

Zac's hands twisted together as he tried to open his mind to what they were saying. Inhaling a deep breath, he let it out slowly, hearing the shuddering sound as it left his body.

"And, while your dad did not handle his grief the way he should have, he loved your mom and you very much."

"You can't hide away from love just because you're afraid of the pain. You do that, Zac, and you'll be a very lonely man."

Standing, they all embraced before replacing the chairs into the stacks and leaving the building. Saying their goodbyes on the street corner, he threw his hand up in a wave as he turned to walk the few blocks to the fire station, his mind swirling.

The night had been long and the day even longer. David was doing what she asked, but she found that having someone else in the house was getting on her nerves. It finally hit her in the late afternoon that she had swept into town, sure that once she got the funeral over with she wanted to get rid of the household contents immediately, and put the house on the market. Now, she wanted more. More time to look over the house's contents. More time to figure out what she might have meant to her dad. More time for her memories.

She finally thanked him and sent him on his way, letting him know that she needed a few days to grieve. He appeared to understand and made her promise to call him if he was needed.

Having found the writings from her father, she wanted to spend more time unraveling the mystery of who he was, who he had become, and why he had stayed away when it appeared that he wanted some kind of relationship with her.

She sat down on the crowded sofa, now slightly visible in the living room since some more of the less valuable pieces had been placed in the shed. Opening the notebook, she leaned back, her gaze traveling over the chicken-scratch penmanship of her father. Reading a few more entries, she found that she alternated between tears and anger with each one.

Dear Maddie, My counselor says that each day is a new beginning. I try to understand that and have come to realize that my battle with alcohol will always be present in my life. Something I must come to grips with and something that I will always have to be careful with. He talked about how we can become a new person though, not always identified by our drunken past even though we will always be an alcoholic.

It made me think of the sea glass we used to find on the

beach. Do you remember those days when I'd take you and your momma for a picnic? We would sit on a blanket, eat your momma's good cooking, and then hunt for sea glass. Those colorful shards of glass would fill up jars and you would set them on your windowsill. You always said you liked to see the sunlight come through the glass and watch the colors dance.

I talked to your momma yesterday and she still says that it's too soon for you to come back. I miss you something fierce and wish we were together again. But, this is a penance I have to pay. I'll stay sober so she'll bring you back and we can be a family again.

Your dad

Heaving a great sigh, she leaned her head back, the full realization that her mother had not been entirely truthful with her finally sinking in. Wondering what else there was to learn about both her parents settled heavy in her heart.

16

"This really is most inconvenient and, quite frankly, borders on inconsiderate. Not at all like you."

Silently counting to ten, Madelyn replied, "I've been a model employee, never taking a day off in over two years. I'm dealing with grief as well as trying to settle an estate. I do not think it is inconsiderate to ask for time off work to do that."

"Well, perhaps inconsiderate was not the right word, but surely you can understand how difficult it is to shift your clients around?"

"Probably no more difficult than when Susan had three months of maternity leave last year and I covered for her. Or when Stan had surgery and I covered for him for two months. Or when—"

"Yes, yes, I get it. You have certainly covered for some of the other counselors, but our policy is that bereavement leave is for three days only."

"Then show me someone who can travel, plan a funeral, and settle an estate in only three days!"

Silence greeted her, only serving to ratchet up her anger.

"How much longer do you think you'll need."

Closing her eyes in fatigue, she replied, "I need two more weeks to make sure everything is accomplished. I have that much time in saved leave, which I will take all at once."

"I don't like this, but I'll grant it. Just remember, when you come back, you'll be maxed out on all leave so don't come crying to me if you need a break."

"Julius, your compassion is overwhelming," she bit out, no longer hiding her sarcastic tone.

"I know," he replied seriously, "it's one of my best qualities."

Disconnecting as soon as she realized he did not even get her sarcasm, she tossed her phone to the counter.

Rubbing her forehead, she groaned as her phone vibrated an incoming call. **Mom.** *Nope...not even going there.* Refusing the call, she left it on the counter, deciding to get ready for the picnic with Zac. Hoping one good thing could be salvaged from the day, she headed up the stairs.

"You look gorgeous," Zac said, planting a kiss on her lips.

Grinning in response, she twirled in her sundress

on the front porch and, tossing her hands out to the sides, asked, "Is this okay for the picnic?"

"Hmmm," he pretended to ponder. "It might be too good. Perhaps we should skip the picnic and just hang out here, all alone." Growling, he swooped in, lifting her hair to nibble her neck.

"Oh, no," she protested. "I've been dying to get out of the house all day."

With a faked put-out sigh, undermined by the smile on his face, he assisted her into his truck, admiring her bare legs in the dress. Adjusting himself, he climbed into the driver's seat and started the engine. As they rumbled down the road, she asked, "Who's gonna be at the picnic? Anyone I know?"

Laughing, he said, "Babe, this is Baytown. Everyone knows everyone around here." Seeing her smooth her palms over her skirt, he recognized nerves. "I'm sorry," he assured, "there will be lots of people you know. It's the health and safety members and that includes the police, the fire, and the rescue. And, since it also includes the volunteers, you'll know a ton of people."

"I wondered why Jillian said she would see me there, but Grant is a policeman, isn't he?"

"Yep. So are Ginny, Lance, and Mitch. All of the MacFarlanes are volunteer firefighters, as well as the Evans. You'll also get to meet a lot of other townspeople there."

He noticed she remained quiet and he shot a glance over to her as she stared out the window. Reaching across the console he asked, "What is it, Maddie?"

"It's just that I enjoy meeting your friends and, well,

some are becoming friends of mine also. Then I almost forget that I'm going to be leaving soon."

The silence stretched between them, before he asked softly, "Do you know when you will leave?"

Shaking her head, she looked over at him. "No. I called my supervisor this morning."

"From your tone of voice, I take it that didn't go well."

"No. But I did get two more weeks off."

Her answer caused him to squeeze her fingers in support.

"But there're things that I'm finding out about my dad that make all this so difficult. Things that don't make any sense. I just..."

The truck turned down a lane heading toward the state park and she stopped talking at the sight of so many people.

"I didn't mean for you to stop talking," he said, cutting the engine off before turning to her.

She smiled but her lips barely curved. "Oh, it's fine. Let's go have fun."

He battled the desire to head back home and keep her in bed until she felt safe enough to talk to him, but he knew he was expected at the event. She had her hand on the door, but he held her back. "Wait for me, sweetheart."

He walked around, assisted her down and, slinging his hand over her shoulders, pulled her in with a kiss to the top of her head before they walked into the midst of the picnic.

Overwhelmed as Zac introduced her to first this

person then that, Madelyn's head swam with the people she met. Barely able to remember anyone's name, she was glad to finally sit at a table with some people she knew.

Ginny and Katelyn were across from her and she breathed an audible sigh of relief. Ginny asked, "Too many people?"

"I can't believe how Zac seems to know the whole town."

Laughing, Ginny replied, "It took me a while when I first started working as a police officer, but I soon found that it was nice to get to know names, or at least recognize faces."

A pretty brunette sat with them and glanced her way. "My husband, Greg, is the new Fire Chief at Easton. I'm Tabby."

Barely having a chance to greet her, another woman sat on the other side of Tabby and introduced herself as well. "Ellie," she said, in a clipped voice. "Husband's Terry. Chief in Mooretown."

"I'm Nola. My fiancé's the Chief in Cherrytown. 'Course it's not very big...sure as hell not as big as Baytown, but it's got that big-ass campground so he's always having to check on campfires."

Ginny left the table to join the other police officers and Madelyn spied another table with Tori, Jillian, and Jillian's mother, wishing she were with them. Smiling politely, she wondered how she could move without seeming obvious when another young woman plopped down next to her.

"Hi! I'm Sarah." Sarah smiled widely and said, "I

used to live in Baytown, but now live in the county. My boyfriend is over there. Tad Bunson. He's one of the volunteers for the fire department and works for Zac. He's hoping to get one of the paying jobs putting out fires sometime."

"Hmph," Ellie groused. "Not many of those to go around."

Sarah bobbed her head in agreement, but continued, "He follows all the news. Says the budget may allow for more jobs in Baytown." She shrugged as she looked around, "He's always looking to move up."

"Long hours...not much pay...hard work. Does he have a clue what he'd be getting into?" Ellie snapped back, tucking her slightly grey hair behind her ear.

"Maybe with all the news about the arsonist they'll get more money for firefighters," Nola offered.

Ellie grumbled again, her scowl firmly in place.

Madelyn watched the exchange between the women silently, finding the enthusiasm of the naïve young woman compared to the experience of the older one to be fascinating.

"I hear they're going to send some experts to try to find out who the Ghost Arsonist is," Sarah said, her eyes bright. "Isn't it exciting to think how our little area is becoming famous."

Tabby snapped, "That is not the kind of press we want to get. I want that maniac found and gotten rid of. I'm tired of Greg getting called out for the acts of a nutcase."

"Hmph," Ellie grunted, once more.

Katelyn kicked Madelyn under the table and jerked her head to the side. "Ready to get some food?"

She was grateful for the chance to escape the table of arguing women. Standing, she nodded her goodbye while accepting Katelyn's linked arm through hers.

"Sorry," Katelyn said. "I could tell the women were overwhelming you." She jerked her chin toward a group huddled to the side. "While Zac and the others need to just enjoy the picnic, I'm afraid the case has gotten the whole area in an uproar. And while the firefighters and volunteers are off discussing fun things, some of the significant others like to talk it to death!"

"It appears Ellie gets irritated with Sarah's enthusiasm," she said.

"Ellie's been around a long time so she knows the score. She's tired of the low budgets and gets frustrated. Some of the newer volunteers really get into the excitement. Hell, in Sarah's case, she's not a volunteer but she still gets stoked about what Tad's doing."

Steering her to another group, Katelyn and Madelyn greeted Tori, Jillian, and Nancy. Glad to be with familiar faces, their conversations stayed away from the arsonist.

"So, are you still working with David?" Jillian asked.

Biting her bottom lip, she hesitated. "Would you think I was crazy if I said I asked him to take a break?" Seeing the others' surprised expressions, she added, "It's just that when I came here, I wanted to get rid of it all immediately and go back home, totally unencumbered with my dad's possessions."

"And now?" Tori asked, smiling up at Mitch as he

walked over with a plate full of hotdogs, chips, and potato salad. "Thank goodness! This baby is kicking something fierce, he or she wants food!"

Mitch chuckled as he placed the plate on the table and put a hand to Tori's pregnant belly. Her heart warming at the sweet scene, Madelyn startled when Zac's arm came over her shoulder, presenting her with a similar plate. She twisted her head around to smile at him before turning back to answer Tori. "Now, I find that there might be more to my dad than I assumed and I'd like to take the time to go through his things more thoroughly."

Nancy nodded her agreement and said, "I think that's a wise decision, Madelyn. Life rarely fits into the neat boxes we like to put it in."

Wondering about her cryptic remark, her attention was diverted as Zac returned with his own platter, bumping her hip as he sat next to her at the end of the table. Soon the gathering included most of the people she knew and, still trying to remember everyone's names, she leaned against Zac's arm.

Zac finished his food and, tossing his plate to the side, threw his arm around Madelyn's shoulders, taking her weight as she ate slowly. Looking over, he caught Aiden's grin before noting similar smiles on his other friends' faces. The idea of their arrangement brought a new wave of wistfulness, finding he loved the way she fit next to him. Her beauty captured his attention, but what he felt was digging deeper than just a tryst with someone for a few weeks. Deciding to use the opportunity of having their friends around, and to take his mind off the woman in his arms, he announced, "Thought I'd let you all know that Baytown is getting state money for a Rescue Captain as well as a Fire Chief and I've decided to go for that position." Immediately shock and congratulations abounded.

"It's about time they divided the duties. If Mooretown can have both, I sure as hell never understood why Baytown didn't," Ginny said.

Nodding, he said, "I've been run ragged for the past couple of years and it just became official that we are getting the funding."

"But why the rescue over the firefighting?" Tori asked.

Madelyn laid her hand on his leg, offering silent support as he grappled with his answer.

"I love both, but find that of the two, I prefer the rescue aspect. Right now, I'm in charge of both, training and scheduling, and realize it's become my whole life."

Jerking his head toward Madelyn, Aiden said to Zac, "And you deserve a life."

Madelyn blushed and shifted away from Zac, but he was having none of it, his arm clamping her to his side once more. She lifted her eyes but found the others smiling at her. They seemed to have no problem with she and Zac together, but her heart clenched at the thought that their relationship was on a deadline. *We only have until I leave.* What had seemed like such a good idea, now sat like a stone in her stomach as she lay her unfinished plate to the side.

Tad walked over, his smile wide as his eyes sought out Zac. "I just heard you've put in the application for the Rescue Captain? Got any ideas for the Fire Chief position?"

Zac looked up at the wide-eyed, eager young man. "You interested?"

"Hell, yeah!"

"Come in tomorrow and we'll talk about the position. There's a lot you need to know before you decide to apply."

"Absolutely," Tad enthused. Grabbing Sarah's hand, he moved back to some of the others.

"Oh, the enthusiasm of youth," Katelyn quipped, bringing on laughter from the group.

17

Sex for clearing the mind was not a bad thing, Madelyn thought as she lay breathless underneath Zac's body, their sweat mingling and their heartbeats pounding in unison. They had barely made it back from the picnic before jumping each other, having left early so they had time before his shift started.

Now, warm and sated, she ran her fingers through his hair as his breath tickled her neck.

"Sorry," he mumbled, rolling to the side.

"Sorry?" she teased.

"Sorry for squishing you...not sorry for fucking you." As soon as the words fell from his mouth, Zac winced at their sound. What they had done was not fucking to him, but something more. Lifting his head, he observed the sadness in her eyes, but did not know what to say. *Is she sad about my callous word or is there something else going on?* Suddenly ashamed, he blurted,

"I didn't mean fucking...like just fucking. You know, like there was nothing else there."

She watched the blush rise over his cheeks and lifted her hand to cup his jaw. "It's okay, Zac. I don't want you to sugarcoat what we have."

Afraid to ask if her feelings ran deeper than friendship, he nodded, laying his head next to hers again, his hand drifting over her smooth skin. "Can I ask you something?"

"Of course."

"Can you tell me what's going on with your dad's things? I mean, I'm thrilled that you're taking your time, but I get the feeling that there's stuff you are discovering and I'd like to know what's on your mind."

He watched indecision wrinkle her brow and reached over to smooth the crease. "After all, we're friends, right?"

"I know...it's just that my mom always taught me to not talk about our family problems. You know the old saying, 'don't air your dirty laundry'?"

"But you're a counselor. You know the value of talking about problems."

"You're right. A good friend can be a great resource." Seeing him lift his eyebrow, she chuckled. "Okay, maybe this is a case of the counselor not following her own advice."

Zac shifted on the bed, leaning against the pillows piled on the headboard and pulled her up with him. Tucking the sheet around her body, both to keep her warm and to keep his mind from wandering over her perfect curves, he said, "Okay...let me have it."

Blowing out a deep breath, Madelyn twisted her body to face his and pronounced, "My dad was an alcoholic." She waited, her stomach in knots, to see his reaction.

His eyes softened. "I'm so sorry, Maddie. Really, so sorry."

She said nothing, unsure how to proceed. Hating the exposure, she forced herself to continue to meet his gaze. His hand met hers on top of the covers and he linked fingers, giving her strength.

"I suppose I should just start at the beginning," she said, grateful when he nodded his encouragement. "My memories of my childhood are of a happy family, a dad who would take me to flea markets, yard sales, and antique stores. We had picnics on the beach and watched the sunset. It was just the three of us, but I was happy...I assumed they were too."

Looking down at their clasped hands, she continued, "It wasn't until I was older that I noticed the constant beer bottles around the house...the way Mom would get angry and they would fight...the times he was stumbling and she'd have to help him upstairs to bed."

Sighing, heavily, she said, "And then it really got worse when he lost his job. I thought he was just let go because of the poor business but I heard them yelling at night and Mom said it was because he had gone to work...drunk."

Zac watched her struggle with the words and, while he wanted her to tell her story, he knew he needed to alleviate her fear. "Babe, I've got to tell you something before you go on. Something that I don't talk about a lot, mostly because everyone around knows." He saw the crease in her brow return and he leaned forward to kiss it away. With his lips still against her forehead, he whispered, "My dad was an alcoholic also."

Her head jerked away from his lips and her eyes locked on his. "Oh." Swallowing hard, her eyes filled as she repeated, "Oh."

"Maddie, from the first time I met you, I saw sadness in your eyes that went beyond your father's death...a kinship of sorts. But I had no idea about your dad."

Nodding, Madelyn realized how much he would understand her conflict. "Is this okay? Our talking about it?"

His lips curved slightly and, tucking hair behind her ear, he kissed her forehead again. "I think it's perfect."

She cuddled back into his embrace, her head resting on his chest, their fingers still locked together. "It was soon after Dad lost his job that Mom met me at the door one day during the summer after my ninth-grade year and she was packing our bags before loading them into the van. She said we were done and were leaving right then. I had no idea we were leaving for good, just figuring she wanted to visit her parents in North Carolina, calm down and then come home. Two weeks later, we were in an apartment and there had been no contact with Dad. When I asked her, she just said he had problems he needed to work on and had insisted that we leave."

"So, your dad wanted you two gone?"

"That's what Mom said." She hesitated before adding, "I had no reason to doubt what she said. It hurt that he didn't want us around, but why would my mom lie?"

Shaking his head, he replied, "I don't know."

"Anyway, she had me register for tenth grade in North Carolina and when I said I wanted to visit Dad, she agreed. I was so relieved to finally find out what was going on. My dad and I, we were really close, nothing about the situation was making sense. We drove back to the Eastern Shore and when I went to the house, Dad opened the door but said he didn't want me to come in." Twisting her body around so she could face Zac, she added, "I had no idea at the time what his reasons might have been. I was a pouty fourteen-year-old who wanted the life she had grown up with—both parents under the same roof, loving me, ignoring that my dad had a problem. I still remember what a slap in the face it was when he said I shouldn't have come to visit."

"What happened?"

"He shut the door and I burst into tears. I got into the car and Mom drove us back to North Carolina. She didn't say anything about Dad the whole way home and I just cried and then, when my tears were over, I got mad. Why would he do that to me? Why didn't he want me anymore, you know?"

"And your mom?"

"Later, she let me know that they were getting a divorce. She also said that he didn't want family around at all. I was angry, hurt...well, devastated. I thought he would change his mind. He always loved me. I couldn't understand where any of this was coming from. But, then, when no birthday or Christmas cards or presents came, I believed her." She huffed, her face screwing up in thought, "And as an adult? I just wrote him off, Zac. I didn't come back to find out why...or how he was...or anything." Her shoulders slumped, "I just wrote him off. God, what does that say about me?"

"Maddie, you were young...impressionable. You didn't just trust what was told to you, you gave him that chance because you loved him. But actions speak louder than words. And believe me, I understand the way an alcoholic can push away anyone and everyone who is important to them."

Nodding slowly, she sighed. "It's just that when I came here, I wanted nothing to do with my dad's things. I wanted to empty the house then put it on the market. Walk away and never think on it again."

"And now?"

"I found some things," she said.

"Things?"

"First, I found some notebooks that were like scrapbooks. He had gotten on my Facebook page and printed out a bunch of my pictures and pasted them into the notebook. It was like he was trying to keep up with my life from the moment I left. There were notebooks from high school and college. I haven't posted much in the last couple of years, but he had some as late as last year that I had taken at a counseling conference."

"Well..." he began, then hesitated, not sure what to say.

She sucked her lips in again, swallowing hard before she whispered, "That's not all." Seeing his rapt attention on her, she said, "I found other notebooks. He kept a journal and it's like letters he wrote to me over the years. I've only read some of the entries...the earlier ones...because it's so confusing and honestly, hurts so much, I can only read a few at a time."

"Letters? What do they say?"

"He talks about going to AA and being told to keep a journal. About how he needed to let me know how much better he was getting. And how when he talked to Mom, she said we could all be a family again."

"Shit, Maddie. What the fuck?"

"I know, right? I looked at the dates. Zac, Mom had already remarried when he wrote those."

Zac pulled her shivering body close, tugging more of the coverings over her still-naked body. Hoping his warmth would seep into her, he rubbed his hands up and down her arms.

"I don't know what to believe," she mumbled against his chest. "All I know is that I can't go back to North Carolina without some answers. I feel like I owe it to Dad to understand what happened all those years ago."

"Have you talked to your mom?"

She rolled her eyes. "No. I just don't know what to say to her right now. I know things were bad at home when we left, but what I don't understand is why she might have lied to me over the years."

They sat in silence for a few minutes before he said, "I don't know why people do the things they do. My dad lost his wife, but he still had a son. A son he couldn't take care of because he drank his grief away." He felt her arms flex, tightening on his waist, as he continued, "I never told you how my father died."

Madelyn shifted her body while keeping her arm around his middle, the tone of his voice foreboding.

"I was a senior in high school and had already signed to go into the Navy after graduation when it happened. By then, my dad was known as the loveable town drunk. I, honest to God, bounced between embarrassment and not giving a damn as I grew up."

"Oh, honey," she breathed, her heart aching for him.

"For eight years, other men and women in this town practically raised me. Doctor appointments, ball games, holidays. Hell, it was Ed Evans who gave me the talk about sex at the same time he talked to Mitch." Shaking his head, he said, "As tragic as that was, it was all I knew for a long time. No one ever talked about Dad...they just stepped in and made sure I was okay and Dad had some food in him besides just pickling his liver."

"I can't imagine," she said, her mind filled with the image of teenage Zac having to deal with his father.

"It's weird...I loved him, but he stopped being my father when Mom died. It was like I was living with a stranger. He wasn't a mean drunk...just a drunk. Negligent, I guess."

"How did he...uh..."

"Die?" A heavy sigh followed, and he said, "The week after I graduated, he fell asleep in his bed with a lit cigarette. It must have fallen onto the carpet."

Her body jolted and her arm squeezed spastically. A gasp escaped before she was able to hold it in.

He rubbed her shoulder and said, "The fire crew got there, but he died of smoke inhalation."

"Zac, I'm so sorry."

He sat quietly for a moment before saying, "I hated like hell that my dad died and had died that way, but Maddie...part of me was relieved his suffering was over. My friends and their families swooped in, taking care of everything and me as well. One month later, I left for the Navy. I directed Ed to have the house torn down and to sell the property. I'd taken what memories from what was left there that I wanted and, other than that, I wanted it all gone."

She opened her mouth then closed it quickly. She knew there was nothing she could say that would not sound like platitudes, so she gave him the gift of just knowing she was there.

"I know you're thinking that it must have messed with my head...that's why I went into firefighting...I'm constantly trying to save my father."

"I'm not thinking anything, sweetheart, other than to just be here for you."

His fingers ran through her hair, the softness soothing as he stroked it away from her face. "I had already chosen firefighting as my Navy career. I was a teen volunteer for the Baytown FD." He felt her jolt again and quickly said, "No, I wasn't on duty when my dad died. I was off with the other guys, celebrating before we all went our separate ways."

"Did you have time to grieve before you left?"

"In some ways, I had grieved the loss of my dad from the time I lost my mom. But, I was once again surrounded by such love and support, and I knew that dad was now with mom, and he wasn't suffering anymore. I think if anything, I never grieved the loss of what he could have been. It only hit me recently how angry I was, have been, with him all these years. I think, too, I took on some of the blame for him being the way he was, thinking I wasn't enough for him to live for. But Ed and Steve, Mitch and Jillian's dads, have helped a lot with that. I was a child and my dad fell into a deep pit of grief, that's all there is to it."

She leaned away from his chest to peer into his eyes. Seeing truth in them, she reached up to cup his jaw. "You are so strong, Zac. So much stronger than most of us."

"I think we all have that strength in us, Maddie. At least, those of us who were blessed to be around good people. I know my dad had an illness and that's why he couldn't take care of me. If I'm strong, it's because I had those good people to give me their strength when I needed it."

Once more, silence curled around between them, each to their own thoughts as she settled her head back on his chest. Finally, he lifted her chin with his knuckle and asked, "What are you going to do, babe?"

She squeezed her arm around his waist, drawing strength from his steady heartbeat. "I'm going to stay for a while. I want to finish reading the journals and going through his possessions. I want to try to understand the man he was and the man he became."

Secretly pleased she was staying in town longer, Zac nonetheless hated the reason she needed to be there.

She leaned up suddenly, a light blush crossing her cheeks, as her eyes sought his. "But don't worry, Zac. I know you only wanted a couple of weeks and that's fine...I won't—"

He shushed her with his fingers on her lips. "Shh, Maddie. I want you...I want this."

Staring into his eyes, she knew he meant only until she finally went back to North Carolina, but her heart ached realizing she wanted it to be a lot longer.

18

Two days. She had not seen Zac in two days and he crossed her mind continually. She missed his smile, the way he linked his fingers with hers, and the way held her tightly whether they had just had sex or were just talking. *If this is what it feels like to just be friends with benefits, what would real love feel like?*

Blowing out a puff of breath, Madelyn bent over her task. She realized she worked better without David's distraction. She had changed his system of categorizing, without undoing anything he had accomplished. The antiques with value were now divided into two more categories; those she would sell and those she wanted to keep.

The thought had surprised her, but after talking about her father to Zac, she knew she wanted to keep some memories. Allowing her mind to travel back in time, she recognized a few of the pieces as ones he had accumulated when she was still living at home and taking "antickkin' trips" with him.

The other furniture, pieces that had no real monetary value but were in good condition, she moved to a different part of the room. She lugged more of the household junk to the shed, deciding that she would have someone pick it up all at once to haul it to the dump or to the donation center.

Without David flitting about, she was able to think about her father. What had the past years been like for him? When the divorce was final, what did he think? And when Mom re-married someone else? She knew the answers to those questions might lie in the journal upstairs, but fear had kept the pages shut. She would read them, as her heart allowed. *And since I'm not leaving for a little while, then there's time.*

She stopped at a small table with Depression Glass on top. The green glass was exquisite. She picked the plate up and remembered her father showing it to her, *"Look at this Dancing Girl pattern, Maddie. Isn't it pretty?"* She remembered he explained it was actually the Hocking Glass Company's Cameo pattern, but was often known as Ballerina or Dancing Girl. A smile slipped over her face at the memory. Heaving a great sigh, she carefully placed the plate back onto the stack. David had explained that, while the pieces were not overly valuable, they were great collector items and he would be able to auction them easily, getting the most for the set.

Without hesitation, she picked up the plate again and placed it on the other side of the room where she was gathering pieces that she wanted to keep. The memory of her father buying the piece when she was with him was fond enough for her to want the keepsake.

Her gaze drifted over a spinning wheel sitting on top of a table, her smile still in place. David had been exceedingly excited for the eighteenth-century piece that had been painted blue in the nineteenth century. He had claimed it would easily bring over a thousand dollars in an auction. Shaking her head, she remembered when her father brought it home and her mother derided it. *"It's blue, Lenny. Why on earth would you want that piece of junk? You're wasting money and we've got precious little to waste!"*

Walking through the house, she was unable to stop the memories from flowing, both good and bad. As she wandered through the recesses of her mind, she realized the bad memories were outweighing the good.

Her phone rang, the ringtone indicating her mother. Hesitating, she knew she had put off the inevitable long enough. Moving to the kitchen counter, where her phone was charging, she answered. Before she had a chance to say her greeting, her mother pounced.

"Madelyn, honey, when are you coming home?"

Sighing, she replied, "Mom, I told you, things are taking longer than I thought."

"Not if you just have a junkman come to haul everything out and get a realtor to slap a For Sale sign in the yard."

"It's not that easy—"

"Honey, I don't understand. Two weeks ago, you wanted nothing more than to go to Baytown to bury your father and sell his estate. Now I wish I had gone with you. What's happening?"

Several seconds of silence passed before she answered, "I guess I'm looking for answers."

"Answers?"

She heard the surprise in her mother's voice and tried to explain, "I'm in the house where I spent the first fourteen years of my life. I have good memories here, as well as not so good ones. I'm trying to figure out what went wrong."

"Madelyn, you know what went wrong. I was always honest about that. Your dad drank and it got worse and worse. He spent money on the junk he kept collecting, sure he was going to find a great piece that was worth something. He went from being a loving husband and father to a drunk, plain and simple."

"Nothing in life is that plain or simple," she retorted, her guttural tone harsh and unfamiliar to her ears.

The silence stretched interminably before her mother reacted. "What is it, Madelyn? Please just tell me what's going on."

"I found myself staring at my room, Mom. Dad left it unchanged. It was as though I had just gone to school and he expected me back at the end of the day."

"Doesn't that prove that he wasn't thinking straight?"

"Not when I found scrapbooks that he kept where

he posted pictures of me from about the time I was sixteen until recently."

"Sc..scrapbooks?"

Now, she could hear the confusion in her mother's voice and decided to come clean. "Yes, Mom. And journals. When he started AA, he kept journals that detailed how much he missed me and you. How he talked to you and how you promised that we could be a family again. But you know what, Mom? You never told me he was in contact with you and those dates were after you had already married Saul. You want to explain that?"

"What did she say then?" Zac asked.

Madelyn lay on her bed, the lights out in the house, the dark night chasing away the last light of the sunset, talking on the phone with Zac. Her mind in turmoil after the conversation with her mother left her agitated and irritable.

Also, the time away from him had given her the fear of sharing too much. *How much do I share with a fuck buddy?* Not knowing the answer, as well as now hating the label, she had attempted small talk until he bluntly asked what was on her mind. So, she caved and had just told him about the phone conversation with her mother.

Zac had listened carefully to Madelyn as she explained her conversation with her mom, feeling her pain as well as hearing the frustration in her voice. He wished he could be with her in person, knowing she could use a hug. Instead, he was stuck at the station with a new volunteer, hoping they would not be called out tonight. He repeated, "What did she say, Maddie?"

"She just started crying and said I couldn't possibly understand the decisions she made back then and it was all to protect me." Sighing, she huffed, "I just don't know what to believe. It feels like one more blow to have to deal with."

"What can I do, babe?"

Irritation at their situation flew through Madelyn and she lashed out, "Nothing. There's nothing you can do." Immediately contrite, she sighed heavily again, the definition of their relationship weighing her down. "I'm sorry, Zac. You know, maybe this isn't such a good idea."

A sliver of fear sliced through Zac, wondering what *this* she was talking about. Before he had a chance to ask, she continued.

"I mean, my life is confusing enough right now without adding the extra stress of us."

"The stress of us? What the hell, Maddie? We're friends. We're close friends...getting closer...at least, that's what I thought we were."

"To what purpose, Zac? I'm a mess and my life just keeps getting messier. You've got a job that's overwhelming and a serial arsonist that's taking over your life. I don't even know what we are. Fuck buddies? Friends with benefits? A casual hookup to use sex to relieve our stress, when we know there's an ending when I leave?" Madelyn hated the words falling from her lips but seemed unable to stop them. The silence on the other end of the phone reverberated through her.

Finally, he spoke, his deep voice calm, but hard. "I thought you wanted this. I thought you wanted friendship and the closeness."

"I did! I thought I did. I thought I could have sex without the messy emotions of something other than friendship, since my time here is limited. But I miss you when you're not here and I want to be with you at night instead of my walls closing in around me. But that's more than we bargained for and now I'm not sure what we decided was a good thing."

She did not give him a chance to speak as her emotions continued to pour out. "Don't you see? Being with you makes me miss you when we're not together." Exposed, she squeezed her eyes shut, hearing the need in her words.

Madelyn's honesty moved through Zac, syrupy warm. The knowledge that her feelings for him were growing made him smile but, before he was able to reply, the alarm sounded. *Shit timing!* "Maddie, I've got to go, but this conversation isn't over. We need to talk." Seeing the volunteer running, he bit out, "Fuck, gotta go, babe. Jesus, I'm sorry. I'll call. I promise."

The airwaves were dead as Madelyn lay back, her phone screen now blank. Sighing, she shook her head knowing the decision to pull away from Zac was the right one. With her heart involved and his not, they had nowhere to go but down.

The emergency call had involved a domestic dispute ending in a husband with an injury to his forehead after his wife hit him with a frying pan. Ginny and Burt had taken the call as the police and were there as well. The wife was alternating between screaming obscenities at her husband for "cattin' about town" and then screaming at Zac for hurting her husband when he tried to patch him up.

Ginny was in the process of arresting the wife when the husband, still sitting with Zac working on his head, jumped up, knocking him over in the process, to protest his wife's arrest. Losing his cool, he bounded to his feet, fists clenched. "Mr. Washington, sit the fuck down or I'll refuse to treat you further!" Whirling to face the irate wife, he shouted, "And you, shut the fuck up or I'll press charges against you myself!"

The couple clamped their mouths shut, eyes wide at his outburst. Ginny, fighting a grin, continued to read the wife her rights as Burt placed the handcuffs on. Zac barely noticed Joe, the new rescue volunteer, standing to the side as though afraid to move. He finished placing butterfly bandages on Mr. Washington's forehead and had the volunteer take photographs, in case any visual evidence of the incident was needed in court. Sighing, he knew it would never make it that far. The husband would be in Easton, the county seat, the next morning, bailing out his wife and would not press charges. *Jesus, is this what love does? Maybe Maddie and I are better off as nothing.*

Driving back to the station, he reminded himself that he knew of so many marriages that were strong...

where the couple worked well together...where love endured. Scrubbing his hand over his face, he shook his head. *But how do you know going in which kind of marriage yours would be?*

He wrote the report before heading back to his apartment. Flipping on the light in the kitchen, he grabbed a bottle of water from the refrigerator, drinking most in one long gulp. Dropping his chin to his chest, he heaved another great sigh. It was too late to call Maddie and, right then, he did not have the energy. Guilt speared through him, knowing she was in the throes of grief and now having to deal with her mother. *Hopefully, she's asleep by now. And God knows, I'm no good for her at the moment.*

Still on call, he climbed into bed a few minutes later, glad for once that his apartment was at the station. Praying he had had the last call of the night, he fell into a fitful sleep.

19

"Are you sure no one's here?"

"I saw the obituary myself. Thought about the house but I didn't want to drive toward the front and possibly be seen. We can just come from the side and do the shed."

"It's got a lock on the door. You think something's inside? Like a mower with gasoline?"

Chuckling, they replied, "Then maybe we should just stand back a bit. Come on, let's get this thing burning."

Waking with the urge to pee, Madelyn stumbled into the bathroom, her way lit by the nightlight plugged next to the counter. Finishing, she washed her hands before making her way back into her room, yawning widely. Her eyes landed on the old digital clock by her bed, discovering it was a few minutes after two o'clock. Hoping she could go back to sleep, she crawled into bed, leaning down to grab the soft blanket lying at her feet. A strange light flickered against the blinds on the window and as she stared, her vision coming into focus, she tried to figure out what she was seeing. Climbing out of bed, she turned on the lamp on the nightstand before moving to the window and lifting one of the slats, peeking through.

Stunned, she observed flickering from the shed and, trying to see clearer, she grabbed the blind cord and gave it a tug, raising them all the way up so she had a full view of the yard. Flames were beginning to shoot upward from the shed and in the shadows, two figures stood nearby. One grabbed the other and pointed toward the house before they ran into the edge of the woods. By the time she grabbed her phone from the nightstand, she gasped in horror as the flames fully engulfed the shed. Narrow tail lights caught her eye, the left one flickering, shining red in the distance until they were out of sight. Dialing 9-1-1, she reported the fire as she ran down the stairs and out the door.

The shrill of the fire alarm sounded and Zac was up and out of bed in seconds. Having fallen asleep in his clothes, he moved to the station, calling out instructions to Joe as the fire volunteers on duty climbed into the fire truck.

Moving his head in circles, he stretched out his

tense muscles. A long night just got longer and he feared the arsonist had struck again. Climbing into the ambulance, he pulled out behind the fire truck, the address instantly plugged into their GPS. *North Heron County and not Baytown proper.* They were the closest station but he knew Adam would have his fire crew and Ann would have their rescue crew there as well. Glad for the backup, he followed his fire truck.

Suddenly, the familiarity of the street hit him and he glanced down at the address on their screen. *That's where Maddie's father's house is.* Another glance and the realization that she had called in the alarm had his heartbeat accelerating. Picking up the radio, he called Mitch. "Call out – fire in shed – it's Lenny's house and Maddie's staying there."

"Ginny and Burt are on their way. I'll head out now." Just before Mitch disconnected, he added, "Stay cool, Zac. Keep your head on straight."

Turning onto the street, he could see the flames licking the night sky. Maddie had alerted the dispatcher that the fire was in the shed, which he knew was away from the main house, but his heart still pounded as adrenaline poured through his body.

The fire truck pulled into position, the volunteers instantly moving to the equipment and water tank as he parked between the shed and the house. Other volunteers, arriving in their personal vehicles from home, drove up as well. Seeing Buster from the Cherry-town station and Tad parking just in front of him, he watched as they moved to the fire trucks. Jumping from the ambulance, he shouted to Joe, "Get over there! I'm going to check on the resident."

Running up the front steps, he tried the doorknob, finding it locked. Pounding on the door gave no response so he leaped off the low porch and ran to the back door, near the kitchen. Hearing the sounds of approaching sirens, he knew the North Heron stations were arriving. As he made his way around the corner he saw the backdoor open. Pushing through with such force the door slammed back, hitting the wall, he raced inside.

He began shouting her name once more. No response. "Fuck, Maddie...where are you?" He ran through the living room, hitting a spindly table with his boot, hearing the wood splinter as he hurried through. Cursing again, he was struck, not for the first time, with the flammability of the house she was staying in. While he had changed the batteries, and tested the smoke detectors, he knew her house could go up in flames instantly.

"Maddie!" No response. Running up the stairs, it only took a few seconds to see that she was not there. "Fuck!" The need to see her chased all other thoughts from his mind.

He ran back down the stairs and out the back door. Turning to the left, he noticed the hose connected to the outside spigot was stretched toward the fire, water spewing on the ground. *Oh, fucking hell, no!* Reaching down, he twisted the spigot off before running toward the shed, now completely engulfed. His feet followed the path of the hose, his mind warring between anger and fear at what he would find.

The hose sprayer lay in the grass, but no one was attending it. The firemen were doing their job, their faces lit from the flames, but he did not see her anywhere. Tad drove up and he shouted directions to him as he ran over to Roger. Just about to ask if he had seen the property owner, he glimpsed her standing to the side near Adam. His knees almost gave out from under him, the weight of his relief so intense, but he locked down the emotion and rushed over.

His fear for her, overwhelming and crushing, had him grabbing her arm and whirling her around, yelling, "What the hell, Maddie?" Before he had a chance to lash out again, her face stopped him cold. Tears streamed down her cheeks and her arms were crossed protectively around her waist as though to ward off the pain of her loss.

He pulled her into his arms, wrapping her close, cupping the back of her head against his chest. Her body bucked with another sob and he closed his eyes willing his strength to help hold her up. After a moment, he looked over her head toward Adam and mouthed *Did she tell you anything?* Adam shook his head before walking over to the firemen who had almost doused the flames.

He stared at the decimated, flattened, scorched earth that used to be the shed, the smoke hissing into the air as the water hit the dying embers. He knew the contents, having taken some furniture there himself, and easily saw it was all gone. Pressing her tighter to him, he recognized she had once more taken a life-hit, drowning in grief before she had a chance to come up for air. And he also knew, it didn't matter if love scared the shit out of him...he was already gone.

An hour later, the fire trucks had left and Zac sent the ambulance back to the station. They sat at her kitchen table, which had been cleared off enough for four people to gather around. Madelyn sat with a steaming cup of tea, placed in front of her by Ginny. Mitch and Colt sat opposite her, with Ginny and Lance leaning against the counter as Zac scooted his chair next to hers, their fingers linked on top of the table.

"I know this is hard," Mitch began, "but we need to get your statement."

Nodding, she cleared her throat, wincing at how sore it was. Taking a sip of the hot tea laced with honey, she said, "I saw a flicker of light when I came back from the bathroom and was curious. There's just an open field on the next property and I thought maybe I was looking at headlights. When I was a kid, sometimes teens would go there to party and my dad would have to chase them off." She whispered, "Funny, how that memory has stuck with me."

Zac watched, along with the others, as her face softened and her eyes drifted down to her cup. Giving her a moment, he finally squeezed her fingers slightly, holding her gaze when she lifted her eyes to his.

She blinked then jerked her eyes over to Mitch, blushing. "Sorry, I'm...well, sorry."

"No worries, Madelyn," he assured.

"Anyway, I saw flames at the shed, but they weren't big. I mean, the shed just had small flames on one side, but wasn't engulfed yet."

"And you called it in?"

"Yes," she nodded, then abruptly shook her head and said, "No." Seeing the confusion on Mitch and Colt's faces, she corrected, "I mean, I first raised the blinds to get a better look. It was as though my brain couldn't process what my eyes had seen."

Mitch nodded his understanding, implying she needed to continue.

"I saw the people and the fire, so I grabbed my phone off the nightstand and dialed 9-1-1."

She took a sip of tea, allowing the warm liquid to soothe her throat, missing the incredulous looks from the others.

Zac's eyes bugged as his fingers twitched against hers. "People? What *people*?"

Her head shot around and she blinked, her face blank. "What?"

"Maddie, who did you see?" he said, each word emphasized calmly, forcing his voice not to show surprise.

"Just two people...near the shed. They were just...I don't know...uh, just standing there."

Mitch and Colt leaned forward and, out of her peripheral vision, she noted Ginny and Lance's bodies had come alert.

"Men? Women? A couple?" Mitch asked.

"I...I don't know. I couldn't tell. They were mostly in the shadows before they ran."

"Ran?" Mitch reiterated. "Ran where?"

"To a car...or something. When I was calling 9-1-1, I saw red taillights as they drove away."

Turning her head toward Zac, he appeared to be barely hanging on, his jaw tense and his mouth in a tight grimace. Swallowing deeply, she said, "They saw me...I think. One of them looked my way and pointed before they ran."

"And you went outside with a hose, straight toward them?" Zac bit out, no longer attempting to hold on to his anger.

She turned to Zac, her eyes wide, both with fear and anger, saying, "I wouldn't have gone out if they were still there. But they left and I knew the fire trucks were coming."

"So, you ran outside to do what, Maddie? Put out a huge-ass fire with a hose?"

Nodding again, she glanced at the others before returning her gaze to his. "It was his things, Zac. My dad's things." Tears filled her eyes as she added, "It didn't matter that the things in the shed were things I wasn't going to keep. They were still things that he'd collected. I didn't reason it through...I just reacted."

Tears spilled from her eyes and rolled down her cheeks again and Zac's anger melted as he pulled her toward him, wrapping his arms around her body. His eyes searched Mitch's over the top of her head, and he nodded slightly, communicating his intent.

Mitch and Colt stood and she lifted her head, wiping her face. "Thank you," she whispered, attempting a smile.

"No thanks needed, Ms. Stevens," Colt replied easily, his dark eyes warm on her. "I'll be in touch and, just to let you know, since your property is in North Heron County, my office will be the official station for your investigation. Even though this is not their usual MO, since we have every reason to believe that this is possibly the work of our multi-jurisdiction arsonist, we will be working closely with Chief Evans and the State Police. You can expect to have a number of officials here over the next few days."

"Usual MO?" she asked, tilting her head to the side as she accepted the tissue handed to her by Ginny.

"If this is our arsonist, then this is the first time they have hit a structure that is close to an inhabited home and not abandoned."

"Maybe they didn't know I was here," she offered, then sucked in her lips. Blowing out her breath, she added, "Or they're escalating." Seeing the raised eyebrows of the officers, she explained, "I'm a counselor. I work with youth, but I specialize in addictive behaviors." Shrugging, she said, "Behaviors like an arsonist would probably escalate over time, just like the addictive behaviors in children and teens."

The others nodded their agreement. Mitch asked, "Do you have somewhere to go or someone to call to stay with?"

"Uh..."

"You can't stay here, Ms. Stevens," Colt advised. "Not if they think you saw them."

Her eyes widened and Mitch said, "Tori runs the Sea Glass Inn. I'll call her and—"

"I've got her."

Everyone in the room looked at Zac, including Madelyn. Before she had a chance to respond, he said, "No where she'd be safer tonight than with me in the station apartment. I'll make sure she's safe and I can sleep in the bunkroom."

"That acceptable to you?" Ginny asked, her assessing stare on Zac while speaking to Madelyn.

Unable to think of an alternate plan, she simply nodded. "Yes...I'm sure that'll be fine for tonight and then I can make other arrangements as I figure out what to do."

Zac nodded but knew, if it was up to him, her figuring out what to do would involve staying with him for a lot longer than one night.

20

Bright light was peeking through the blinds and Madelyn blinked, stretching awake, realizing it was much later than she normally slept. For a few seconds, she tried to figure out where she was before the events of the night came crashing back to her. She could smell the faint the scent of smoke in her hair.

Abruptly sitting up, she shot her gaze around the small room, finding herself alone. A glance at the pillow next to her showed it was still plumped, no head indentation to indicate Zac had slept with her.

The full ramifications of what had happened slammed into her, causing her breath to leave her lungs with a whoosh. The fire, the fear, the noise and sights, the interrogation, and then being brought back to the station by Zac.

She had protested feebly, but he was insistent. Trouncing her ideas of taking up Mitch's offer by telling her that the Inn was probably full this time of year or calling Belle, or, one of the other women, in the middle of the night would be unnecessary, she had agreed to come with him, unable to think of an alternative.

Glancing at her phone, she saw it was almost nine a.m., two hours past when she normally awoke. Hearing no sounds, she climbed out of bed, stooping to pull the covers up. Moving to the bathroom, she quickly finished before looking into the mirror. Hair awry, eyes red-rimmed from crying, and a swatch of soot across her face. Uncertain if Zac minded if she took a shower, she quickly decided she did not care what he thought, since she was desperate to rid the smoky smell from her body. A few minutes later, with the warm water sluicing over her, washing away the grime, soot, smoke, and soothing tense muscles, she groaned in relief.

Zac, stepping into his bedroom, seeing the made bed, heard Madelyn's moans of relief coming from the shower. His dick twitched, coming to attention, and he dropped his chin to his chest. Counting to twenty to get his erection under control, he knocked softly on the door. "Maddie?"

He heard the water turn off and tried not to imagine her naked just on the other side of the thin, wooden door.

"Zac?" her hesitant voice called out.

"Yeah, babe. Who did you think was out here?"

"I don't know who else has access to your place here," she replied.

"No one but me…and now you."

"Oh."

He grinned at her short, confused reply. "I've got some clothes out here for you."

"Clothes?"

Shaking his head, he said, "Stay with me, babe. What you came with last night was dirty and smoky. I've got them in the wash. Ginny packed you a bag last night before we left your place."

"Ginny?"

"You gonna keep asking questions or do you want the clothes?"

The door opened and she stuck her head out, her hair slicked back from her face and her body wrapped in a towel. Glaring, she said, "Can't you just leave the clothes and go away?"

"Another question," he chuckled.

"Zac," she groused. "What's going on?"

Sighing heavily, he stepped closer to her, watching her wary expression as he neared. "I made a decision last night. Well, I realized something last night and have decided I'm good with it. I want it, actually."

Instead of asking another question, she cocked her head to the side, waiting for him to continue.

"No more friends with benefits. No more casual anything." He watched as she stiffened her spine, lifting her chin in response, pain slashing across her face.

"Fine," she bit out. "As I said yesterday, I think we're better off separate."

"No," he retorted, "you said you didn't think that sex without messy emotions was something you could do. And, you said you missed me when we weren't together. And, you said that you wanted us to be together at night, instead of separate. And," he lifted his finger, pointing it right at her, "you said that it was more than we bargained for."

She blinked several times, stunned he remembered her words. Opening her mouth, she got nothing out before he jumped in.

"And I agree." He watched the confusion fill her eyes and grinned. "You're right, Maddie. It's more than we bargained for, so we're changing our bargain."

Her open mouth clamped shut as her eyes narrowed, waiting to see what he was going to say.

"Our new bargain is that we're going to be together," he pronounced.

"Together?" This time her voice was barely above a whisper.

"Yes."

"I...I don't understand."

"It's actually very simple. You and I are together. A couple. We have feelings and we watch them grow. We're close and we get closer. I kind of think that defines us being together."

He watched as she stepped fully into the room, her hands planted on her hips, and he struggled to keep his eyes on her face instead of the towel that was hanging precariously above her breasts. If he were honest, he hoped it just might slip down.

"You decided. You decided?" she said, her voice no longer a whisper.

"Babe."

She tried to ignore the way that one word slid over her, warm and smooth.

"You said you missed me. Were you lying?"

Pinching her lips together she shook her head. He stepped closer and she tilted her head back to keep her eyes on his.

He placed his hands on her shoulders, his thumbs caressing her neck. "Look, I know we both come from backgrounds where the shit our parents put us through made us think that relationships weren't worth it... weren't worth the trouble. But, the last few weeks have made me realize that when you meet someone special...someone who *gets* you, then it's worth it. I'm not going to lie. I was scared out of my mind when I started to feel more for you, and that was pretty much immediately. But, Maddie, I can't deny this thing between us. I don't want to. No matter what happens, you are worth it. I wouldn't give you up for anything. I want it all with you."

His arms slid down her back, pulling her gently into his embrace, his hands now rubbing her soft skin and his chin resting on her head, the scent of her floral shampoo filling his senses.

Madelyn's hands left her hips as she encircled Zac's waist, holding him tight as well. Her cheek, against his chest, felt his steady heartbeat. Closing her eyes, she allowed his steadiness to invade her tumultuous thoughts, calming her mind. Sighing heavily, she finally replied, "But, I don't live here, Zac. What about that?"

"I don't know, Maddie," he admitted. "I know that people have long-distance relationships all the time. North Carolina isn't all that far."

She tilted her head back to peer into his face. "And if we lasted? If the relationship continued to grow? What then?"

Shaking his head, he said, "I don't have all the answers. I figure North Carolina needs rescue workers too."

Blinking, her body jerked. "You'd leave Baytown? Your friends? Your life here?"

"Maddie, if we discover that we're the other half to each other's souls, then I'd do what I have to do to be with you."

Tears filled her eyes, but she did not reply. She simply tucked her head back underneath his chin and remained quiet, her mind swirling with thoughts that threatened to overtake her.

Madelyn stood in the driveway of her dad's house, staring at the black, charred earth that used to be the shed. She remembered when her father put the lawn mower inside, along with other gardening tools. He would place the tools and mower in one corner, allowing her to have the rest of the space for her imagination to take over. Princess castle, prairie house, cabin in the woods. Whatever struck her imagination, she had a place to live out her childhood dreams.

"Maddie, get out of the shed. You're getting dirty," her mom would yell from the back door.

"Leave her be," her dad would chide. "Little girls need to have a place to let their imagination run wild."

"Well, she gets that from you," her mom would retort.

She startled as the memory came back, realizing that after so many years of assuming her dad did not care about her she had hidden all the good times in her mind. Things like that he often encouraged her to play and explore. Fueled by her mother's comments about her father after they moved away, after he himself pushed her away, she had tucked those kinder memories away.

Rubbing her hand over her forehead, willing the pain to go away, she turned as she heard a vehicle coming down the road. David. Sighing, she wondered if she would have the strength for him today.

Plastering on a smile as he alighted, he hurried over, taking her hands in his.

"My dear Madelyn, I heard the news and am so sorry, but thank God, you're safe." He twisted around, seeing the blank place where the shed used to be. "Is it all gone and please tell me you didn't have the valuables in there?"

"Yes and no," she replied. "Yes, what was in the shed, as you can see, is gone, but I had only placed some more of the items to be gotten rid of in a yard sale or donated to a thrift store."

He nodded slowly, his attention back to her. "Oh, my dear, I see the dark circles underneath your eyes. What can I do to help?"

She looked toward the house and said, "If you can give me two more days, I'd like to have you come back and start hauling out the things for auction. That'll give me time to make some more decisions about the few pieces I'd like to keep. Then, once you've taken them to your shop, the house will be emptier and I can feel freer to decide my next move."

"I think that's a brilliant plan," he said, nodding profusely.

The sound of more vehicles coming down the road caught their attention, both turning at the same time. She smiled at the sight of Katelyn, Tori, Jillian, Jade, and Belle.

As they alighted from their vehicles and rushed over, David nodded and smiled, "I see you're well in hand. Give me a call and I'll have some men ready in a couple of days."

"Thank you…for everything," she said, her hand still in his. She felt the squeeze on her fingers before he said his goodbyes to the group and headed back to his car.

Immediately surrounded, she assured the women that she was fine, just shaken.

"I couldn't believe it when Mitch came home and told me," Tori exclaimed. "Then I was furious he did not call me right away so I could have come."

"You didn't need to be here in the middle of the night," she protested. "Especially pregnant, Tori. You shouldn't be around all that smoke. Believe me, my kitchen could barely hold the people here anyway."

"Who all was here?" Jade asked.

"Mitch, Ginny, Lance, and Colt—"

"Oh, that's right. This is the county and not the town," Jillian said. "Grant wasn't on duty, so he wasn't here. He called me this morning, but Tori had already called."

"And Jillian called me," Katelyn grinned, before turning to the others, adding, "and I called Jade and Belle, but Lance had already told Jade."

Belle looked at her and clucked, "Honey, you look exhausted. Where did you sleep last night?"

"Zac took me back to his place." Silence filled the air, only broken by the birds twittering. She looked at their faces, seeing expressions ranging from worried to wary to happy. "It's fine, honestly," she said, then sighed. "Actually, it's anything but fine."

Linking arms with her, Jillian marched toward her front door. "We're here to help and not just with the furniture. So, let's go in, take a load off, and you can tell us everything!"

21

Madelyn put the kettle on before setting out six cups for tea. The others carefully moved a few of the objects from the kitchen, placing them in the living room where she directed them, making more space in the kitchen for them to sit at the table. There were only four kitchen chairs, but she easily found two antiques that were sturdy and placed them in there as well.

Settling around the table, she bit her bottom lip, tucking a strand of hair behind her ear. "I'm not sure where to start."

"The beginning is always best," Belle said, her soft voice holding a touch of humor.

Nodding, she laughed as she agreed. "I remember Zac from high school. I used to have to wait for the second bus load and would hang out at the baseball field. They were all there...Grant, Mitch, Aiden, Brogan, Callan, Philip, and Zac. I was just a nerdy freshman, but I thought they were beautiful."

She grinned at the wistful sounds coming from Jillian, Katelyn, and Belle, and knew they remembered as well.

"Of all of them, I thought he was gorgeous and really sweet. I remember seeing Claudia Mooney hanging by the fence trying to get his attention and was secretly thrilled when he never gave her the time of day. One day, he was catching a ball near the fence where I was, and I was stunned when he bent over to grab it and looked right at me when he stood up. And then smiled." Sighing wistfully at the memory, she repeated, "He smiled, staring into my eyes." Then with a rueful snort, she added, "That spring, I heard he went to the prom with Claudia and I was so disappointed."

"Well, any of the boys would have gone with her," Katelyn said, "cause she put out for most of the team. I think she's the only girl my brothers both had...not at the same time, of course."

"Gross!" Belle cried, as the others shook their heads.

Laughing, Jillian said, "Well, she got married out of high school to a man five years her senior because she got knocked up. She strutted around town like her shit didn't stink, waving her engagement ring in our faces. Said he was some big banker."

"Wow," Madelyn said, wondering why Jillian was smiling.

"Seems he worked in a bank, but he did maintenance for them. Nothing wrong with that job, except it wasn't what she thought he did. It was a few years before she realized he wasn't rolling in money. It hit her hard, but with two kids, they stayed married. Then I heard she was getting a divorce and lost custody of her kids." Shrugging, she added, "Seems he came home and caught her doing it with the man installing their air conditioner. And the kids were home at the time. He got rid of her ass and got the kids."

"Wow!" she repeated, eyes wide.

"Who cares about Claudia?" Jade said, trying to pull them back to topic. "I want to hear the rest of Madelyn's story!"

Now the one laughing, she continued, "I left Baytown with my mom when I was fourteen, but I suppose Zac is just one of those heroes, like in a romance novel...the kind the heroine never really forgets."

"Now, it's my turn to say *wow*," Tori said, her lips curving.

"Anyway, I was surprised when he gave my father's eulogy. We started talking and it seemed he *got* me." Looking at the others, she added, "It went beyond our understanding of each other's grief experience. You know, both of us losing our fathers the way we did. You all know that his father was an alcoholic, but what I haven't told anyone else is that my father was too."

"Oh honey," Jillian said, reaching over to clasp her hand.

"Anyway, we seemed to have a connection and then...well, uh...we decided to be friends with benefits." Feeling the heat of blush rise on her cheeks, she laughed in embarrassment. "Maybe I just needed the sex as a stress reliever. I've never done that before, but with Zac it just seemed so right." Looking around the table, she breathed a sigh of relief at the smiles greeting her.

"So, how's that working out?" Katelyn asked, leaning forward, her eyes pinned on her.

"Good...at first...then not so good and now I think we're back to good."

"Huh? Sorry, but you're gonna have to break that down at little more for me," Jade said.

Taking a sip of tea, she said, "It was good. We're both mature, consenting adults who decided that we liked each other and there was no reason not to enjoy each other's company, in every sense of the word, while I was in town."

"Sounds easy," Tori said, "but..."

"But, I realized it was all wrong. To be honest, I've never been someone's fuck buddy before. I'm hardly a blushing virgin, but my sex partners were always men I was in a relationship with." Lifting her shoulders, she sighed, "It seemed simple, but then I found myself quickly missing him when we weren't together. I really wanted to spend more time getting to know him...be with him."

"Emotions got in the way of just good ol' sex," Katelyn quipped.

Nodding, she agreed. "Yeah. It's not like on TV or in books where they make it seem so easy to be in a 'friendship with benefits' relationship. Sex without messy emotions. Even if it's short term and exclusive. I felt empty on the inside. I told him that I just didn't think the way we were would work anymore."

Belle leaned forward, her eyes full of sympathy. "And he just wanted things to stay the same?"

"No, not at all."

At this proclamation, the other women all blinked in unison, their mouths open. Seeing their look-alike expressions, she laughed. "As it turns out, he wanted more too." Her voice softened with the memory. "He even said that he'd be willing to date me long-distance or, even, go back to North Carolina with me."

"What?" Jillian and Katelyn shouted.

"I was just as surprised as you are. I mean this is his home...his friends are all here. And from what he's told me, even though he doesn't have blood-relatives here, your families became his."

"That's so romantic," Belle breathed, her eyes wide with wonder and her smile filling her face.

"What are you going to do?" Tori asked.

"I'm not sure," she replied honestly, her eyes searching theirs. "My life is rather topsy-turvy at the moment, which makes it not the best time to make life decisions. But, I can tell you this...I'm in no rush to go back to North Carolina right now. My boss is unsympathetic and things with my mom are...uh...unsettled. I've still got to come to grips with my father's death and there are some things I'm finding out about him that change things...I want to keep exploring that." Shrugging again, she said, "So, at least for now, I'm here and I guess Zac and I are officially dating."

"Oh, I hope you stay," Belle gushed, gaining a nod from Jade.

"Baytown may seem like everyone's all up in your

business," Jillian said, "but believe me, when you're down, these are the people who'll run to your aid."

"I used to spend my summers here with my grandmother, but grew up in Virginia Beach," Tori explained. "She left the Sea Glass Inn to me and, I have to tell you, I rushed back here first chance I got and would never live anywhere else."

"I've only been in town for about two years," Jade threw out, "but I love this place. Lance is a transplant here also and we have no plans to leave."

Finishing their tea, they moved into the living room, taking stock of what needed to be sent with David for the auction. As the others admired the antiques her father had collected, their comments about Baytown rolled around in Madelyn's head, wondering if her father knew Baytown would be hard to leave when he left his estate to her.

Katelyn looked at a few photographs lying on one of the tables. Bending down, she exclaimed, "Is that your mom with Tonya?"

Walking over, she said, "Yeah, that's Mom. But who is she with?"

"Tonya Bayles. You know, Philip's mom."

"That's right...she told me that her daughter and I used to play, but we weren't close by the time I was in high school."

Katelyn walked away to check on some other furniture, leaving her to stare at the two women in the photograph. *I wonder...*

Zac sat in the office of the fire station, combing through the applications from the past five years of volunteers. He started by dividing the lists by age and sex of the applicant, considering the profiler had told them that most vanity arsonists are young and male.

The Baytown stations, both fire and rescue, had a huge number of volunteers, but he knew the North Heron County had almost three times as many. He did not envy Adam and Ann their jobs. Greg at Easton, Roger at Cherrytown, and Terry at Mooretown were smaller stations and probably did not have as many to review.

An hour later, his eyes were crossing. There was nothing that jumped out and he felt as though he was getting nowhere. No single volunteer was at all the fires. No one was on site first each time.

Standing, he moved to the door that overlooked the large bay holding the two fire trucks and a smaller bay with the ambulance. Volunteers milled around, checking and cleaning the equipment as well as the trucks.

Tad looked up from talking to one of the newer volunteers and waved. "Hey, Chief," he called out.

He jerked his chin up in greeting, his eyes continuing to rove over the group. Old, young. Male, female. Multiple ethnicities. He had ridden out with each of them at one time or another, trusted them behind the wheel of a multi-ton truck, having his back during a fire, resting easy in the knowledge that any one of them would give all they had to save a life.

"Hey, honey," he heard Tad call out and watched as

Sarah walked into the station. She had a bag in her hand and a huge grin on her face as she approached Tad.

He observed the young man puff out his chest as his girlfriend approached, before walking her around the bay, showing off the equipment. She *oohed* at the appropriate moments and Zac shook his head as he looked down at them before turning to walk back into the office. Glancing at his watch, he had just enough time to review a few more applications before he had to make his meeting.

Greg asked Zac about Madelyn's property and the others shook their heads in frustration that the arsonist had stepped up his attacks by setting a fire so close to where someone lived.

"Do you think they thought the house was empty since her father had died?" Adam asked.

Terry leaned in, his forearms resting on the table, a worried look on his face, and said, "Surely the arsonist isn't going to start fires in occupied buildings." He turned to Zac and asked, "Is she alright?"

Nodding, he said, "Yeah...luckily the shed only held some furniture that she was going to get rid of anyway, but that close to her house was scary."

"Can you believe that with the economy the way it is, the state is considering cutting our funding for equipment and training?" Terry asked.

The other's cut their eyes to him, faces revealing

tight grimaces. Zac watched as Terry continued, "And now we've got a serial arsonist, worst case the state has ever seen. They have to bring in the State Police and FBI, and they still want to cut our budgets for buying new trucks."

Ann looked over at Zac and asked, "Did you make up your mind?"

He nodded, then shifted his gaze around the table. "Since the state has cut the equipment budget, they have approved Baytown for a Rescue Captain as well as a Fire Chief, and I've applied for the rescue position."

Congratulations abounded and Greg, sitting next to him clapped him on the back. "With the size of station you run, it's about time the positions were split into two."

Terry nodded his agreement and said, "Baytown's larger than Mooretown, so I've always been surprised you didn't have both."

"I've handled both, just like Greg and Roger here, but it's been hard."

Roger added, "I've heard that because of the arsonist and the attention it is giving our area, we might get more money added into our budgets. At least, that's what the state representative said in his press conference."

"Jesus, we need the money, but I can't believe we have to deal with the arsonist to get the attention," Greg retorted. "Fuckin' politicians. At least with this being an election year, they might just help us out after all."

Changing the subject, he asked, "When are we

having another joint Health & Safety meeting with the entire Eastern Shore group?"

"We just got an email as you all were on your way here," Adam said. "It'll be in a few days and the State Police will be there as well. I've got a feeling that they'll be taking over the investigation."

As their meeting broke up, Terry approached Zac. "I'm glad Baytown's splitting your job up. Maybe that'll make the higher ups realize how much we're needed, especially with the arsonist out of control."

Waving goodbye, he headed out to his truck. Driving back to Baytown his mind was whirling. They had also discussed their findings, as each had already devoured their volunteer's applications, looking for any indication that someone might be a vanity arsonist. There were a lot of possibilities, but he hated to become suspicious of someone he worked with.

Pulling into town, he took a detour before going back to the station. Parking in front of Harrison Private Investigations, he climbed out and headed inside. Grinning at Katelyn, who was standing in the reception area, he smiled his greeting.

"I know it's impromptu, but any chance you and Gareth are available?"

Eyeing him carefully, she replied, "Good timing. Come on back."

He followed her down a short hall, waiting as she poked her head into an office on the left and said, "Honey, Zac's here and wants to talk to us." She looked over her shoulder and asked, "Official?" Gaining his nod, she turned back to Gareth and said, "It's official."

The three settled in the workroom, a small room opposite of Gareth's office, and he wasted no time getting to the point. "I've got a little money in the BFD budget for investigations and it hasn't been used this year because everything's been internal. Also, the State Police are handling most of the arson investigations, but they haven't been looking into our personnel...yet. I've been trying, but I'm too close to these people. I work with them, have to trust them, and can't imagine anyone being a vanity arsonist."

"You want us to take a look to see if anything sticks out...and maybe do some checking into them?"

"Yes. I also have the notes from the Easton and Cherrytown departments. They both said they'd like to have you look at theirs as well. Terry at Mooretown said he was afraid of using any of his budget for this and is still looking his over."

"You got it," Gareth announced.

'That was easy," Zac said, smiling at his friends, eyeing the way Katelyn, professional as always, leaned in slightly toward her husband.

As they stood to leave, she walked him to the front and said, "Can I butt in and say something?"

Cocking his eyebrow, he said, "Katelyn, when did you ever keep your opinion to yourself?"

She laughed, playfully hitting his arm. "Okay, okay. I probably deserved that." Her mirth sliding away, she said, "I just wanted to say that I think you and Madelyn really work. I'm glad for you."

He smiled, but added, "I'm glad for me too."

As he turned to leave, she said, "Just so you know,

us girls are working to show her how great Baytown can be as a place to live...permanently."

His gaze shot to hers as his smile widened. Lifting his hand as thanks and goodbye, he headed back outside, the warm sun hitting his face as he felt some of his stress lift away.

22

Nancy, wearing her Auxiliary President Pin, announced to the group, "The meeting is now called to order. Please rise for the presentation of colors."

The members stood in unison as Katelyn walked forward, carrying the American flag and placing it in the holder at the front of the podium. The Methodist minister said a prayer and then the group said the Pledge of Allegiance before singing the National Anthem.

Madelyn participated as a guest, her eyes shooting around, taking in the American Legion Auxiliary meeting. The members were varied in age and ethnicity, but all with the same expression of reverence on their faces.

Jillian, as Vice President, approached the podium and said, "I will now read the Preamble to the Constitution of the American Legion Auxiliary.

"For God and Country, we associate ourselves together for the following purposes: To uphold and defend the Constitution of the United States of America; to maintain law and order; to foster and perpetuate a one hundred percent Americanism; to preserve the memories and incidents of our associations during the Great Wars; to inculcate a sense of individual obligation to the community, state and nation; to combat the autocracy of both the classes and the masses; to make right the master of might; to promote peace and goodwill on earth; to safeguard and transmit to posterity, the principles of justice, freedom and democracy; to participate in and contribute to the accomplishment of the aims and purposes of The American Legion; to consecrate and sanctify our association by our devotion to mutual helpfulness."

She took her seat and Nancy continued the meeting, including a roll call, reading of minutes by the secretary, and financial report by the treasury. During this time, Madelyn's gaze moved over the card held in her hand with the preamble printed on it.

She lifted her eyes, listening as the different committee chairpersons gave reports on the many activities for the community the Auxiliary was committed to. Looking around, she felt a warmth sliding over her, the bond of the women in the room palpable. The girls had been right. Baytown was small, but mighty in the ways its inhabitants opened their arms to gather someone in.

Her mind traveled back to the eulogy that Zac had given for her father. Whatever had caused her father to drink so much, be it habit or something else, she was grateful that he had taken the time to talk to Zac. Without that, she would never know about his service or experiences in the military.

While the meeting continued, she realized coming back to Baytown had given her the gift of her father again, even after his death. Battling back tears, she listened as the meeting drew to a close.

As the women prepared to leave, she approached Tonya. "Mrs. Bayles?"

"Oh, Madelyn, please call me Tonya."

Smiling, she asked, "I was wondering if you had a chance to talk to me sometimes in the next few days. I found a picture of you and my mom and...I...uh..." Suddenly unsure what to say, she floundered.

Tonya's smile turned sad as she reached out to place her hand on Madelyn's arm. "And you hoped I could talk to you about your parents?"

Nodding, she replied, "Yes. If it's an imposition, I understand—"

"Oh, my dear, it's not an imposition at all." She lifted her hands slightly to her sides and added, "But, I will tell you that your mother and I did not part ways as the best of friends, therefore you might be uncomfortable with what I have to say."

"No, no," she assured. "I've discovered some things that don't make sense and would love to talk to someone who was there back in those times."

"How about tomorrow afternoon? I'd love to have you come to my house."

"That's perfect. Thank you so much."

Tonya reached out to pat her shoulder. "Please don't thank me yet. I promise to be honest, but warn you to only ask the questions you really want answered."

After sharing contact information, she walked away, leaving her more certain that there was more to her parents' relationship than she knew.

The sounds of laughter all around had Madelyn smiling as she and a large group of women walked to the pub. The meeting had concluded but she found the night usually ended the way the American Legion meetings did—with the friends heading to Finn's.

Entering through the old, red painted door, her gaze shot around, seeing Brogan and Aiden behind the bar with their dad, Eric, helping out as well. Ginny and Corrine moved in to offer hugs and help. Mitch, Ed, and Steve Evans, as well as Gareth and Grant, were standing near the bar, waiting for their wives to come in and as they did, the men quickly moved to claim them.

Lance, off to the side, had eyes only for Jade, a smile sliding into place once she snuggled into his embrace. Belle, Callan and Jason rounded out the group.

Not seeing Zac, she wondered if he had been sent on a call. Trying to keep her smile firmly planted on her face, she nonetheless felt the sting of disappointment. Arms circled from behind, one across her chest and the other about her stomach, pulling her back into a muscular wall. Words, whispered at her ear, said, "You have fun, babe?"

As Zac's warm breath tickled her ear, she grinned wider, no pretense now needed. Twisting her head around, she nodded. "Yeah, it was nice. I felt strangely closer to Dad being at the meeting." She turned around, her front now pressed to his, and added, "I'm glad that he had you to talk to."

Regret moved through his eyes as he replied, "Oh, Maddie. I barely knew him and we only talked a couple of times."

"Yes, but he had never talked to us, at least not to me, about his time in the military. To know that, even for a short while, he had the opportunity to connect with you over the Navy, makes me feel better."

Bending to take her mouth in a short kiss, he gave her body a squeeze before saying, "Want to join the others?"

Nodding, her lips curved in a sly smile. "Yeah, but then I'd like to go home. Just you and me."

Lifting an eyebrow, he complained, "Oh, don't do that to me, sweetheart. Now I've gotta go make nice with our friends when all I want to do is get you naked!"

Laughing, she pulled him over to the back of Finn's and entered the fray of their friends. Katelyn brought pitchers of sweet tea as well as beer over to the tables and she shot her a look of gratitude.

Garreth quickly took the tray from her, whispering, "Call me to get the heavy trays."

Brogan laughed, "Hell, sis has been carrying trays for as long as she could pick one up."

"Yeah, well, she wasn't pregnant then," Garreth growled.

The room grew quiet for a few seconds before erupting in congratulations. "Way to tell everyone, sweetheart," Katelyn laughed, before answering the multitude of questions coming her way. "I'm about two months behind Tori and no, we don't know what it is yet. We just told our parents the other day and hadn't figured out when to tell all of you yet."

Brogan stalked over, giving her an evil eye, before pulling her into a huge hug. "Love you, sis."

Aiden shoved his way in, wrapping both his siblings in his arms.

As the group continued their chatter, Nancy asked Madelyn, "How's the work going with your father's house?" Nancy asked. "You have to know we were all so upset over the shed burning."

"Thank you. It was devastating, but more because of my memories of playing there. As far as its contents, I had placed old, broken, or invaluable pieces there to be given away to the thrift store. David Wills has identified the valuable furniture pieces and I'm going through everything, the good as well as just what's sentimental, and he'll come tomorrow to take the pieces going to auction."

"That's a lot of work," Tori said. "I remember when my father died how I had to help my mom."

"Yes, but it's brought a sense of my father being

back in my life, and I'm realizing that perhaps things were not always as I thought."

"They often aren't," Corrine stated wisely.

Steve eyed Zac's arm around her shoulder and asked, "How long you plannin' on staying in town?"

She noted the stares of the entire group and felt Zac's body stiffen next to hers. "I've decided that I'd like to stay for a bit. I'm not anxious to return to North Carolina right now, although my job status is tenuous."

"You should check out the Eastern Shore Mental Health Group," Jade said. "I heard from our school psychologist that they're looking for more counselors. I think it's hard to find qualified counselors that want to live and work here."

Smiles had greeted her answer about staying and Zac leaned over to whisper, "Sorry, babe. My friends can be protective."

Twisting around to stare into his eyes, she aimed her smile at him. "And that's one of the reasons I'm interested in staying."

Kissing her again, he leaned back, enjoying the company, but mostly, enjoying the feel of the woman in his arms pressed next to him. The laugher and stories abounded, but soon the group appeared ready to disperse.

"You ready to say goodnight?" he whispered, grinning at the flare of lust in her eyes. "I'll take that look as a 'yes'." Standing, he took her hand and pulling her to her feet, they said their goodnights before heading out into the starry night.

They made it to the station, but with a fairly large group of volunteers present, Madelyn begged Zac to take the outside stairs.

"But—"

"I know the stairs' height freaks me out, but I don't want to walk into your apartment in front of so many people."

They stood at the back of the fire station and he nodded, but hated the feeling of sneaking around. The idea of finding a place in town for him to call home had taken root, but they were too new for him to mention it. "Okay, babe, but walk next to the wall and I'll keep my arm around you."

Nodding, she focused on the brick wall, refusing to look over the side of the stairs as they made it to the third-floor entrance. She rushed through the door, breathed a sigh of relief and that was the last breath she got before her lips were in a battle with his as he pressed her against the wall.

He wrapped his arms around her, crushing her breasts against his chest, thrusting his tongue in her welcoming, warm mouth. Her arms clutched his hair, pulling him down to hold him in place. The kiss was demanding and unyielding as his tongue invaded her mouth, searching every crevice, tangling with her tongue, dueling for dominance, before he pulled back slightly.

"You okay," he asked.

"Mmmm," she replied, her hands attempting to tug him back to her.

"Just wanted to take your mind off the stairs."

Grinning against his lips, she said, "You succeeded, but now I want you to take my mind off of everything but your body."

Grabbing her hands in one of his, he brought them over her head, causing her breasts to push out as her back bowed. Using his free hand to explore, he glided down her shoulder, over her breast, stopping to rub his thumb over her nipple, before making his way down to slide into her pants, cupping her mound.

Her groans were captured in his mouth, sending a direct signal to his cock, which was already at attention. He leaned his hard body in, touching every inch of the front of hers, chest to knees and, with his hips jutted forward, his cock pressed into her stomach.

Sliding his hand under her sweater, he continued his upward path, coming to rest on her breast. Teasing, alternating between feather soft touches and then pinching her nipples, he soon had her squirming against his body, begging not so silently.

"Please, I want to touch you too," she rasped through kiss-swollen lips.

He let go of her hands and she immediately grabbed his face, holding him as she assaulted his lips again. Using his other hand under her ass, he lifted her easily, allowing her to wrap her legs around his waist. His swollen cock was now painfully pressing against her warm sex and he was desperate to rid them of the clothing that still separated their bodies.

Lifting his leg slightly so that she was seated on him, he jerked her sweater up and over her head. Raising her arms only long enough to have the sweater pass, she immediately reached back to him, clutching his shoulders as she pulled his head back to her chest.

He pulled the tops of her bra cups down with his teeth, freeing her breasts. With them at face level, he continued his assault with his mouth. Sucking first one nipple in and then moving to the other, he was aware of the movement of her crotch against his leg, trying to create the friction that she needed.

Lowering his leg, he set her feet back down on the floor, offering her support until her legs were steady before he reached behind him to grab his shirt. Pulling it over his head, he leaned forward, pressing her against the door once more, recapturing her mouth with his. This time, flesh against flesh, breasts against chest.

Their hands moved to each other's pants at the same time, fingers tangling. He grunted and she took this to mean that he wanted her to stop so she slid her hands back to his shoulders as he deftly undid her jeans zipper and jerked them down her legs. As he did the same with his, she slid her pants down, snagging her panties as she went. Kicking off her boots as she divested herself of her bra, she was naked by the time he had a condom rolled on his cock.

Both stared unabashed at the beauty in front of them. He suddenly could not remember the features of any other woman he had been with before Maddie. Not their features, their faces, their shapes. All he could see in his mind was the perfection that was standing in front of him, staring at him with her warm, dark eyes. Eyes that were not just shining with lust, but something else...something intangible. Something he wanted to explore.

She stared at his cock, jutting out toward her. Watching it twitch, she grinned. "Seems like you've got something on your mind, cowboy."

"Oh, yeah. I know exactly what I want."

Picking her up, she wrapped her legs around his waist, this time her sex directly on his dick. Wanting to make sure she was ready, he slid his finger into her wet folds, moving it deeper and deeper, looking for just the right spot to make her scream. "Perfect. So fuckin' perfect."

Madelyn felt the pressure building, the coils tightening, and knew she was close. *Hell, I could have come just dry humping his leg*. About to crack a joke about her impatience, the feel of his fingers deep inside of her sex, tweaking just the right spot, jolted the words from her mind as sensations crashed over her.

Opening her mouth to beg for more, he bent his head and sucked her nipple into his mouth, biting down just enough to give a sharp pain then soothing it with his tongue. She felt her inner muscles clamping down on his fingers as the orgasm washed over her.

Zac looked at the beauty in his arms, her head thrown back against the door in ecstasy, eyes tightly shut, mouth open, the only sound emitted a sexy moan. That sound almost had him coming just with his cock pressed against her stomach.

Placing his aching cock at her entrance he rasped,

"Ready, babe?" A nod was all the answer he received, but he wanted her eyes. "I want to see you," he rasped, barely hanging on as she dipped her chin and graced him with her smile.

"I'm here," Madelyn whispered, "and I want you... now." She almost added the word 'always' but stopped herself. It was just as well, for within a second, her sex was impaled on his cock. Balls deep, he began thrusting, tossing all thoughts from her mind.

One hand under Madelyn's ass for support, the other pressed against the door next to her head, Zac thrust, sliding in and out of her warm sex, the friction nearly taking him over the edge quickly. Forcing his mind to hold back, he wanted her to come again before he lost himself in her body.

Demanding, "Mouth," he sealed his lips over hers when she brought her mouth back to his. Deep. Controlling. His tongue mimicking the movements of his cock.

Madelyn knew the pressure was building, soon to bring the most incredible euphoria. Feeling Zac's hand move between them and tweak her clit sent her over the edge again, waves of pleasure shattering her into a million pieces. Shouting out his name, she thrust her head back against the door as her inner walls grabbed at his cock.

The feeling of his cock being milked by Madelyn's muscles was all it took for Zac to lose control. His head reared back as he powered through his orgasm, continuing to thrust. Neck muscles straining, face red and tight, he emptied himself into her waiting body with such force, he hoped the condom held.

Lowering her body to the floor, he held her until her legs steadied underneath her. Keeping his large hands on her waist, he leaned over, looking into her eyes as they stared up at him. Grinning at the same time, he nuzzled her nose before sliding his mouth to her ear, whispering, "Ready for round two?"

Giggling, she darted around him, grabbing his hand in the process, running to his bed. He left her just long enough to head into the bathroom, with the explanation, "Gotta deal with this."

As he stalked out of the bathroom, he observed her on her back, smiling up at him. Climbing into bed, he lay on his side next to her, exploring every delicious curve.

Thinking it would be hard to orgasm again so soon after what they had just done, Madelyn was surprised to feel the electric shock from her nipples to her womb and down to her sex.

Zac rolled another condom on before moving his finger through her slick folds, then lifted her on top, placing his engorged cock at her entrance.

He gently entered her, slowly, wanting to feel each delicious inch. She moaned at the fullness and the pressure that immediately began to build. With a final push, he was in all the way, pumping slowly.

"The last one was because all I could think about at the pub was getting in you, but now, this is more for you to have control."

"I'm good," she assured in a whisper and he began

to begin move faster. The friction was soon sending her over the edge again as the shock waves pulsated from her inner core outwards.

She grinned and, as her orgasm flooded her senses, she raised up and down, her hands on his chest, riding his cock. Her inner walls grabbed his dick and natural juices made the movement easier. Her breasts bounced in rhythm to her rocking and he palmed the full flesh, tweaking her nipples.

She lowered her face, whispering, "I want to be with you," and he hesitated for a second, staring into her eyes before taking over, thrusting upward.

Lost in the emotion and the words, Zac felt his balls tighten and knew that he was close. Throwing his head back, he powered through his orgasm, pulsating deep inside as her channel tightened around him again.

She crashed on top of his sweaty body, both still shaking with the intensity of the moment. Neither spoke for several minutes, the emotions of what they were feeling overwhelming.

As they slowly recovered, the cool of the night finally penetrating the heat they had generated, he tucked her in tightly to his body, jerking the cover over them.

Madelyn lay with her head on Zac's chest listening to his heartbeat, her fingers absently moving over his muscles. Gathering her courage, she said, "I didn't see the best in my parents' marriage. I didn't think it was holding me back, but maybe it was. No matter what, though, I want you, I want the emotions...even the messy ones...with you."

He lifted her chin with his knuckle, staring into her eyes. "Me too, Maddie. Everything...good, not good, messy, clean...you name it, I want it."

She sucked in her lips but, no longer hesitating, told him what was on her mind. "I need to let you know that I've made a decision." Seeing his rapt attention, she said, "I'm staying. I'm staying in Baytown."

23

Madelyn stared out her living room window watching the moving truck David had arranged to come drive off with the antiques she had decided to auction. As the dust settled from its trek down the lane, she turned and cast her gaze around the almost empty room. Sucking in a deep breath, she moved easily about the room, her fingers trailing along the few pieces that she wanted to keep. Pieces that she remembered collecting with her dad when she was younger.

Alone, she walked into the kitchen and fixed a cup of tea. As the kettle heated, she viewed the empty counters and floor space, now void of the pieces that he had piled in here as well. Zac had wanted to be with her today but had training. The girls had all offered to come as well, but she politely turned away their offers of help, explaining she wanted to do it herself and then be alone with her memories for a while. They understood, but made her promise to meet them at Jillian's coffee shop the next day.

So, now, she had plenty of time to breathe a little easier with the clutter gone from the rooms. To make more space for his antiques, he had gotten rid of some of the basic furniture, so it was now time to contact the thrift shop to come get what she was donating.

Once her tea had steeped, she carried the cup up to her bedroom, glad the stairs were now clear, the falling-hazard now diminished. Setting the cup on her night stand, she picked up the journal she had been reading, knowing she had a little time before she was expected at Tonya's. She had read the entries that carried her through her high school year before spending the last few nights with Zac.

Flipping the pages, she settled on the bed, steeling herself to read more of her father's thoughts.

Dear Maddie,

I write this with a heavy heart. I'm devastated that we will not be a family again. I've been sober for two years and believed your momma when she said we could be a family again. I did not fight the divorce at the time because I knew I had messed up. I drank, spent money I didn't have, and was not a good husband, father, or provider. But, I always thought we would be together when I proved I was clean.

Today, she let me know that she got remarried. I wonder what is going through your mind. What your momma has told you about me.

I lost the chance with your momma, but it breaks my heart even more to think that I've lost the chance to be your

father. Will he walk you down the aisle? Will he hold your babies? These are the thoughts that make me want to turn back to the bottle.

But I won't. I call my AA sponsor and we talk. I attend the meetings and gain their support. I refuse to go back to what I was.

Your momma told me that you are very fragile and I should not contact you. She says that you have decided that her new husband is your father and I no longer have a place in your life. It breaks my heart to think that my past behavior has hurt you so much, but I'll support her decision. One day, maybe when you are stronger, we can have that conversation, where I can tell you I'm sorry. But until then, I'll keep my journal, writing as though you are here with me.

Love, Dad

Stunned, she stayed on the bed, her breath ragged as she stared at the words on the page. Rubbing the back of her neck, attempting to ease the tension, she wished she knew the truth...was this just her dad's ramblings or had her mother really orchestrated the divide between her dad and her for all these years?

Arriving at Tonya Bayles' front door, Madelyn reached for the doorbell, hesitating for a second, her nerves threatening to overtake her. Before she could change her mind, she pushed the button, hearing soft chimes ringing inside.

Tonya opened the door almost immediately, her smile warm and inviting. "Come in, come in."

Entering, she noted the comfortable living room to the right and the dining room to the left in the traditional Colonial home. Tonya led the way to the living room, indicating she take a seat on the sofa. A teapot and two cups were sitting on the coffee table and she waited while Tonya poured the tea.

Her eyes drifted around the room to the many family photographs. Seeing Philip in his Baytown Boys baseball uniform, big smile on his face, she recognized Zac, Grant, Mitch, Aiden, Brogan, and Callan standing with him. Next to that picture was one of him in his military uniform with his arm around his sister. The mantle held the folded flag and her heart felt heavy as she thought of the loss of his life. "I'm so sorry, Mrs. Bayles, for your loss."

Tonya's gaze followed Madelyn's and she said, "Thank you, my dear. Time makes the tears come less often, but as a counselor, I'm sure you know that grief never leaves us. But please, call me Tonya."

Smiling, she nodded. "I also recognize Sophia. How is she?"

A flash of pain shot through Tonya's eyes, before she replied, "She's fine. She lives in Tennessee since graduating from college."

Licking her lips, she sipped her tea, feeling as though the subject of Sophia was difficult for Tonya. "I want to thank you for agreeing to meet with me today."

Tonya settled back in her chair and smiled. "I have to confess when I got home and told my husband you wanted to meet, David warned me to be careful. He said that there were things that only your parents know...or knew, to give you the answers you were looking for."

"But you will talk to me? At least, talk to me about them?"

Tonya nodded, setting her tea cup onto the table. "Yes." Tilting her head to the side, she said, "Do you have specific questions for me?"

Shaking her head slowly, she replied, "Well, of course, I'd like to hear what your thoughts were about my mom and dad." Her hand fluttered in the air and she shrugged, "Anything really."

Tonya leaned back in her chair. "Well, I suppose I should start at the beginning. I met your mom when you and Sophia were in the same pre-school. Let's see, that would make you about three years old." Smiling at the memory, she said, "Sophia was painfully shy and you were also. The other kids were running around like crazy and the two of you stood to the side. I wanted to rush over but the teacher told us to just let you two have a chance to get used to everyone. Your mother and I ended up going to get coffee together. We did not know anything about each other, but we bonded over our fear that our daughters were going to hate us for leaving them at the pre-school. I even think a few tears were shed that morning...by us!"

Her smile wide, she continued, "When we got back three hours later, we found all the kids still running around and the two of you were off together playing in a corner. You hugged each other when it was time to leave and Gwen and I never worried after that. You two were inseparable and your mom and I began a friendship that meant a lot to me."

She smiled in return and eagerly looked at the picture that Tonya handed to her, seeing two little pigtailed girls with their arms around each other.

"After that, of course, came school years. Sometimes you and Sophia were in the same class and others, you weren't. But you stayed friends all through elementary school. I think it was middle school that the two of you began to drift apart slightly, which is normal."

"That's right," she nodded. "I was in the band and started running track in seventh grade. I think I remember Sophia being in the horticulture club and even FFA." Eyes wide, she exclaimed, "She had baby goats!"

Laughing, Tonya said, "Yes, yes. My parents had a small farm outside of town and they let her raise the baby goats."

They sipped more tea, memories floating through the air like dust motes, bright in the sunlight before settling.

She looked up, seeing Tonya's face pinch as though a memory came to her that was not so pleasant. Tonya's eyes met hers and she sighed.

"And now for the not-so-good memories," Tonya said, her voice laced with regret. "Gwen confided to me that your father was drinking more and more. I hurt for her and tried to offer a listening ear, but as the years rolled by, it became worse."

"I remember the way things got worse," she replied. "We didn't take family trips anymore. We didn't even go to the pier to watch the sunsets. I'd hear my parents arguing at night after Mom helped Dad up the stairs. And I remember hearing her crying about him losing his job. I know she took extra shifts at the pharmacy to make more money."

Nodding, Tonya said, "My heart hurt for Gwen, but other than suggesting she try to get him to AA, I had no idea what to do other than just be a listening ear. Your parents weren't involved in any of the activities that we were and I hardly saw them together."

"I'm sure you were helpful."

"I don't know," Tonya said, as more regret passed through her eyes. "The times I saw your dad, and I only saw him when he was sober, he was such a pleasant man. And I know that no one on the outside can know exactly what was happening. I don't know how much you knew, but it seems as though you were very aware of the problems."

"I knew things weren't right, but Dad was so loveable, it was hard for me to understand why Mom was so upset with him all the time. I was too young to completely understand their problems." Looking at Tonya, she said, "But I get the feeling there's more."

Sighing, Tonya said, "Madelyn, my husband is right. The only two people who can tell you exactly what was happening are your mom and dad and, of course, he can't tell you anymore—"

"But, he is," she interrupted. "After we left, Dad joined AA and his counselor encouraged him to keep a journal...letters to me, actually. I've been reading them."

Tonya's eyes went wide at that proclamation.

"It's just that what Mom always told me isn't aligning with what Dad wrote. He says that he was talking to Mom and that she promised we would be a family again. But, she always told me that he didn't want any relationship with us."

Tonya took another sip of tea before saying, "I'm sure it was difficult for your mom to know what to tell you, but I wish she had been honest with your dad. Once she met Saul, I think she was ready to leave Baytown and just start over with him."

Her brow creased, she said, "Saul? But she didn't meet him until we moved to North Carolina." She watched Tonya's eyebrows rise in surprise, her mouth opening, but nothing coming out.

24

Madelyn focused on Tonya's wide-eyes and her heart squeezed as a new reality pressed on her chest. "She knew Saul when she was here...married to my dad."

Tonya pinched her lips together and shook her head. "Oh, my dear, I'm beginning to think this is a bad idea. You should really talk to your mother—"

"No. I mean, I will later." Swallowing hard, she said, "I'm not asking you for all the details...I just want to know what you know. I realize that you can't tell me what was going on with Mom from her perspective, but you can tell me what you know. Please...I'm so tired of the subterfuge. I'm twenty-eight years old and feel like so much of what I know is wrong."

Leaning forward, taking her hands in her own, Tonya's face filled with concern. "I wish I could tell you that I was a perfect friend to your mother, but I'm afraid that wasn't the case." Sitting back, she said, "You mother kept Saul a secret for a while, but one day, she called me and asked if I would come over. Once there, she told me that she had met a man who made her feel safe…secure. She never meant for it to happen, but they fell in love. She wanted to know what I thought she should do. I told her that she needed to stop the affair… if she wanted to divorce Lenny, then do that first and then have a new relationship as a free woman." Sighing, she said, "I know I sounded judgmental, but it was just how I felt. I know Lenny's alcoholism was hard to live with, and it wasn't difficult to see how she would yearn for a better relationship. But, it seemed so wrong for her to be sneaking behind his back. To be honest, I hoped that if she talked to your father and told him that she was going to ask for a divorce, it would shock him into going to AA and then they could stay together. Or, he would continue to drink and she would be vindicated in going through with the divorce."

"But she didn't," Madelyn said, sadness in her words.

"I don't know for sure, but she indicated to me that she wouldn't. In fact, she was very angry that I wasn't completely on board with her plans. We had some words…not very kind words, and she said that if I couldn't be a supportive friend, then I had no place in her life."

"Oh, wow." Shaking her head, she had no other response.

"That was about fifteen years ago and I was younger, less touched by life. I walked out of your parents' house and never went back. I regret that, more than you can know. Within the year, I heard that you and your mom had moved away. I didn't know where, but I confess to calling the office where Saul used to work and was told he left his job and moved away also. I figured then that she and he had gone together and taken you with them."

"And my dad?"

"I went by once...I'm not even sure why, but Lenny met me at the door and had been drinking. He wasn't mean, but he was angry. Said that Gwen wasn't there and he had no idea where she was. That was the last time I saw him. By then, my Philip had been killed in service and I never really thought about Lenny after that."

Blowing out her breath in a long, slow stream, she set her tea cup on the table and fell back against the cushions of the sofa. The silence in the room gave her thoughts a chance to swirl before settling into place.

"Things make more sense now...and yet, it just brings up more questions," she said. "I remember thinking at the time, that Mom choose North Carolina to be closer to her folks, but we didn't see them that often. I remember her not waiting long before she introduced her new friend, Saul, to me. I never saw them as anything but friends for a long time...they were careful to not show any romantic inclinations but then, after we had been there almost two years, she announced that she was getting married. I knew she filed for divorce the year before, but since Dad didn't want anything to do with me, I was filled with teenage anger, and was just glad Mom had someone nice to be with."

She looked over at Tonya, seeing sympathy in her eyes, and said, "But why would she lie? Why would she not tell Dad she wanted a divorce? Why would she tell him that they could be together when she was with someone else?"

"Oh, sweetie, I have no idea about that. Maybe she felt desperate? That can drive people to do irrational things. But, I know that she is the only person that can give you that information."

Confusion morphed into anger as the realization struck her that her mother's lies caused her to miss out on the last fourteen years of her father's life. His presence in her life. Sucking in a shuddering breath, she stood quickly. "Thank you for talking to me, Tonya. You've helped me tremendously."

Standing, Tonya grasped her hands. "I hope I haven't made things worse."

"No, no. Not at all. While there's still a lot to learn, I feel better knowing that it does seem that Dad didn't reject me."

"Madelyn, you were loved by both your parents. Each of them had their flaws, as do we all, but remember they both loved you."

Nodding, she forced a tremulous smile on her lips before stepping out into the cloudy day. The grey skies matched her mood.

Zac sat in the counselor's office, noting how much neater it appeared than his. He wondered if Charles hid his mess behind his desk. Dragging his attention back to the current topic, he sighed heavily. He had already talked about his mother's cancer, death, subsequent swooping in of his friends' parents, his dad's drinking, and now had come to the final part of his tale. Before he spoke again, Charles interjected.

"You've given me a great deal of background, Zac, and I'm impressed with how you have handled it all."

Shrugging, Zac said, "I missed my mom…I still miss my mom. I would have given anything to not have lost her at such an early age, but I was surrounded by such loving, supportive people that managed to help take care of me and raise me. But it was more. Talking to you has brought up memories that I hadn't really thought of. Like how Nancy Evans always found time to talk to me, just one on one, and she made me feel like I could say anything to her. Sometimes I would talk about Mom…sometimes cry…sometimes, we'd just share cookies and I felt better. Corrine MacFarlane always had me over for lunch after church on Sundays, and I was just part of their big, loud family, not feeling like I was the odd one out."

"Counselors call those people 'resources'. I always try to get my clients to identify their resources and use them as they are needed."

Nodding, Zac smiled. "My girlfriend and I were just talking about that. She said I had used my resources to fill in the gaps my mom left behind. And while it's not a complete substitute, it was healthy."

"Your girlfriend sounds like she knows what she's talking about."

"She should. She's a counselor." Seeing Charles' eyes widen, he explained how Madelyn was now staying in town and had been a counselor in North Carolina.

"Tell her to come in, if she's looking for a job. We are desperate for another counselor." Shaking his head, he said, "But I digress. You were going to tell me more about your dad."

"Yeah," he nodded. "About a month before I graduated from high school, Dad fell asleep with a cigarette in his hand. It fell onto the carpet and smoldered. The carpet caught on fire, but not with huge flames. Instead it smoked like crazy and Dad died of smoke inhalation quickly. By the time the neighbor saw smoke coming from an open window and the fire department got there, the flames were just starting but my dad was already dead."

Shaking his head, Charles said, "And you continued with your plans to join the Navy?"

"No reason not to."

Silence filled the office, before Zac said, "I was angry with my dad for a long time. Not just when he died, but when he mourned mom so much that he forgot he had a son. When he grieved by looking through the end of a beer bottle and forgot to look at the son left behind. Honestly, when he died, I felt a sense of relief." Sighing, he asked, "What does that say about me?"

"It says you're normal." At Zac's head jerk, Charles continued, "Your father had an illness but he also let that illness interfere with his ability to raise his son.

You were fortunate to have such a supportive extended family in all the others in town who stepped in to assist. But, it is true...your father let you down."

Nodding slowly, he silently agreed, feeling the guilt ease off his heart. "I loved Dad. By the time I had served six years, I had seen a lot more of the world that existed outside of Baytown. I realized that there are many flawed people, many reprehensible and, while my dad was drunk most of the time, his heart was in the right place."

"You mentioned that you wanted to take the position of Rescue Captain instead of Fire Chief. Is this somehow tied into your feelings about your dad?"

Rubbing his hand over the back of his neck, he grimaced while shaking his head slowly. "I've always been interested in firefighting. I was a teen volunteer with the Baytown Fire Department. When I talked to the Navy recruiter, I wanted to join them as a firefighter. My dad's death came after that, so it's not like I went into firefighting as a result of his death. And when I moved back to Baytown, I jumped at the chance to be the Fire Chief and also head of their rescue service. To give back to the town that helped raise me has been what I've always wanted to do."

"It sounds like lifesaving is in your blood," Charles noted.

Nodding, he agreed. "I think that perhaps I never properly mourned my dad's death because the truth of the matter is that I lost him a long time before that." Leaning back in his seat, he looked at Charles and said, "I just never thought of it that way."

Shaking Charles' hand, he set his next appointment with the receptionist before leaving. Running to his truck in the rain, he decided to find Madelyn, desiring to let her know that the clinic definitely wanted to talk to her about a possible job. *Things are looking up*, he thought with a grin on his face.

"Things are so messed up," Madelyn cried, tears flowing freely as Zac entered her house. He enveloped her in his arms, pressing her face to his chest, feeling her tears wet his shirt almost immediately.

"Babe, what's wrong?" Remembering she was going to meet with Tonya Bayles, he ushered her to the sofa, pulling her down onto his lap, cuddling her close. Holding her for a few minutes, he tried to offer comfort, allowing her to cry. When her sobs turned into hiccups, he wiped her tears with the pads of his fingers. "Please, sweetheart, you're scaring me. Can you tell me what happened?"

Leaning back, Madelyn felt foolish and grabbed a tissue from the box on the end table, wiping her eyes and nose. Blowing out a cleansing breath, she began to tell Zac what Tonya knew about her parents.

As she came to the end of her tale, she sucked in a shuddering breath and whispered, "For fourteen years, I thought my mom left my dad because of his drinking. But instead, she met Saul and they kept it quiet for years until she could divorce dad and they could get married. All these years, they lied to me."

She jumped up from his lap and stood in the middle of the room, her hands spread out to the side. "And this...all this mess I just cleaned up, didn't have to be this way. Dad's loneliness for the past half of my life didn't have to be that way. My relationship with my dad for all these years...which was non-existent, didn't have to be that way." Clenching her hands into fists, her face twisted in anger, she said, "Her lies changed the lives of all of us."

Unsure what to say, Zac stood and placed his hands on her shoulders, drawing her close again, feeling her body tremble as she encircled his waist with her arms. "I have no idea what to say, Maddie. I'm so sorry you're going through this. It seems as though you can't get over one hit before taking another. Are you going to talk to your mom about all this? Find out her side of the story?"

She nodded, but whispered, "I don't know when. Right now, all I want to do is stay here and be with you."

They stood in silence in the middle of the room, he offering comfort and she accepting all he had to give.

25

Madelyn stared at her phone for several minutes, her thumb hovering over the call button. Finally, steeling her spine, she hit dial. Zac had encouraged her to wait until she was calm before calling her mom and she had agreed. That was why it was now, later in the evening, that she had decided to take the plunge.

Her mother picked up on the second ring. "Madelyn, honey, I'm glad you called. Have you decided when you're coming home?"

Letting out a slow breath, she replied, "I'm not coming back, Mom. There's a lot I want to do here."

"Like what?"

She could hear the irritation in her mother's voice and grimaced. "I want to see if I can find out more about the area I grew up in. I've met so many wonderful people here...people here who have been very kind to me during this difficult time. One in particular...you might remember her. Her daughter and I played when we were little."

"Oh...uh...who is that?"

"Tonya. Tonya Bayles." Silence met her ears, so she plunged on. "It seems she remembers you. Remembers you very well. All about you."

"Oh, Madelyn," her mother said, her voice now soft.

"Mom, she told me that you met Saul there. On top of the journals Dad kept where he said he talked to you and thought we were going to be a family, it appears that you've done a lot of lying to me for most of my life—"

"No...not lies. Not everything. Honey, you need to let me explain—"

"No, Mom, I don't. I don't need to let you do anything. Maybe someday. Maybe later. But right now, I'm planning on staying here. I've met someone special and I've made friends, and now I'm going to interview for a job here as well."

For once her mom did not try to talk her out of anything. Instead, she said, "Madelyn, I'm so sorry you're finding things out this way. But there is so much you don't know. At least give me a chance to explain. I love you so much." Her mother's voice broke with a sob.

"I love you too, Mom," she whispered, her heart aching. "I just need some time right now." Disconnecting, she dropped her phone into her lap.

Staring around the living room of her dad's house, the emptiness appeared stark. David had taken all of the antiques and other items to be auctioned back to his warehouse. She had gotten rid of all of the trash, leaving only the barest of furnishings. She had kept the sofa and one end table with a lamp in the room. The dining room was empty and the kitchen only held a small table with two chairs. Upstairs, she had him take the furniture from her dad's room, leaving only the furniture in her bedroom. The pieces that she planned on keeping were in a storage facility in town.

She was showing the house to a realtor the next day and hoped it sold quickly. *But then where will I live? I surely can't live with Zac in the firehouse!*

"Where are we going?"

"I thought you needed a night out. Away from your dad's house, away from the firehouse, and away from anything negative."

Madelyn looked out the window as they pulled up to the Sunset View Restaurant near the marina. "Oh, I've never been here." She glanced at his khakis and navy shirt with the sleeves rolled up on his forearms and looked down at her dark jeans and asked, "Am I dressed properly?"

Laughing, Zac said, "Babe, this is Baytown... anything goes."

Glad she had chosen a light green, jersey wrapped shirt to dress up her jeans, she alighted from his truck once he opened the door for her. Entering, she was pleased to see that the dress code was casual. They followed the hostess to a table by the window overlooking the bay and the timing was perfect for watching the sun set. "Oh, the name for this restaurant is perfect," she gushed.

As she sipped wine and they waited for their appetizers, she caught him staring at her. Dabbing her mouth with a napkin, she whispered, "Do I have something on my face?"

"Just beauty," he replied, his eyes warm on her.

Rolling her eyes, she laughed. "That was kind of corny, but I really liked the compliment," she admitted. As her mirth settled, she added, "Thank you. I haven't had much to laugh about lately."

"No, you haven't, but I'm hoping that things are going to start looking up for you."

She met his smile as she took another sip. Turning to watch the sun as it lowered, she shook her head. "Crazy, isn't it?"

"What is, Maddie?"

"Everything that has happened in the past month. From finding out about my father's death, having so many people help me get through it all, to meeting you. Not to mention, the casual hookup we began with, which was so out of character for me." Seeing him lift his eyebrows in a pretend leer, she laughed again. "And then, as we got closer, to discovering that I'd like to explore staying in Baytown longer."

"Do you feel like you're moving too fast? Or that *we're* moving too fast?" Zac asked, attempting to keep a light tone to his voice, but fearful of her response.

Shaking her head slowly, her brow creased as she

pondered the questions. "No...I really don't." Taking another sip, she continued, "Sometimes life happens fast. We can go for a long time and have no major changes in our lives, but that's not necessarily a good thing. Neither is it always a bad thing to have things change quickly. I think it's about balance. I think it's about what we do with the changes. I think it also makes a difference if the changes lead to something good."

"And us...we're something good?"

Her smile widened as she replied, "To me, I think we're something amazing." Hearing his sigh of relief, she asked, "Were you worried?"

Chuckling, he nodded. "Kind of. I don't want to rush you. I know we're new...I know some people would say that you shouldn't make major decisions when life is crazy. But, I know what I feel for you. You get me. You understand me. Our backgrounds are somewhat tragic, but they allow us to understand where each other are coming from. It's like you're my other half."

Her intake of breath was audible, her already wide smile brightening. "Oh, my God, Zac. That is the sweetest thing anyone has ever said to me." She leaned, meeting him halfway, their kiss sweet but filled with meaning.

Interrupted by the server delivering their Thai shrimp appetizer, she grinned as they settled in to eat.

"When will you know about the Captain position?"

"Soon. The town council will let me know next

week. At the same time, they'll talk about the new Fire Chief, if they've decided on a candidate."

"Who would you like to see get it?"

"I don't know if there are any outside applicants from another area. You'd have to live here to be the Chief, so it's not like some big city. I've really only had Tad talk to me about it and I know he's got enthusiasm. He's only twenty-three, but, then, I was around that age when I took the position too."

"Anyone from another local station interested?"

Shrugging, he said, "None of the other Chiefs have said anything specific. Roger, Chief at Cherrytown, and Terry, Chief at Mooretown, both mentioned having someone who had some questions about the position, but I've heard nothing. I'm probably closest to Greg, the Chief at Easton, and he's said nothing."

"Well, I've only been around Tad a few times, but he does seem enthusiastic about the job." Grinning, she added, "And I think his girlfriend would be thrilled."

Barking out a laugh, he agreed. After a moment, he eyed her nervously. "I hate to add one more thing to your ever-growing list of changes, but I've been thinking about a change I need to make," Zac said.

Lifting her eyebrows, she licked the sauce from her lips before asking, "More than the job change?"

Keeping his eyes on her, he said, "It seems like ever since I got back into town from the Navy, I've been rather staid. I was pretty young when I took the Fire Chief job, but my experience sold the town council to take a chance on me. And, I had no one but myself to care about, so when they offered the cheap apartment in the back of the station, it was perfect. Rather bare and basic, but worked. With my job heading the fire station and EMT program keeping me busy all the time, a place right there has been convenient.

"I've been watching my friends buy houses, or fix up a place, or become involved with someone and get a place together, but I still just stayed complacent with where I was." Fiddling with his napkin, he said, "I guess one more thing that you and I have in common is that we're both facing some changes all at once...and I agree, that's not a bad thing."

Pushing her now empty appetizer plate away, she gave him all of her attention, reaching over to place her hand on his arm.

"I'll still be busy as the Rescue Captain, going out on most calls, but I'll have a little more down time since I won't be overseeing the entire program. I have no idea who will become the Fire Chief, and I doubt they would want to live in the apartment, but I need a change. So, I've contacted a realtor to look at some places in town to rent...a small house, perhaps."

Eyes wide, she said, "That's wonderful, Zac. I mean, if that's what you really want to do."

"It is."

"Can I ask if you're doing this because you want to or because of...um..."

"Because of you?" he finished for her. Seeing her nod, a blush crossing her cheeks, he answered, "I'm not pressuring you into anything, Maddie. I'm doing this because it's the right time. I won't lie...I'd love to have a place where we can spend the night and not be afraid of alarms going off or someone knocking on the door. And, if we keep going, then I'd love to think of us finding something together, but I know that's down the road."

"I just don't want you to feel like you have to change anything about yourself for me."

"I'm not." Holding her gaze, he linked fingers with her on the tabletop and amended, "Well, not entirely for you. Sure, I'd like a place of my own to bring you to and maybe to share with you sometime, but I needed to do this for me anyway."

Their meal arrived and they kept the conversation lighter as they enjoyed the food, watching the sun sink into the horizon.

Zac stood on the sidewalk, staring at the small, two level, pale blue house. Like so many of the homes in Baytown, the pastel houses created a colorful beach town feel. The house was small, an older home that had been remodeled. And the rent fit his budget, not being much more than what he was currently paying. With the raise he just received for his years being the Fire Chief, and all the money he had saved over the years, he knew that he would be able to buy a home. But for now, renting was perfect.

His eyes roved over the roof angles, the dark blue shutters, and as the realtor walked toward him, he wondered if Maddie would like it as well. *God, has it only been a month that I've known her? And I'm already thinking of living with her.*

"Mr. Hamilton, nice to see you."

Shaking her hand, he followed her up the short walk and into the house. The front door led into the large, open living room, the dark wooden floor gleaming. A brick fireplace centered on one wall and the rest of the room was painted a pale bluish-grey. His mind had already hung his flat-screen TV over the mantle.

As she droned on and on about the upgrades and remodeling, his eyes swept toward the smaller dining room. With a crinkled brow, he realized he would need to buy a table with chairs. A hall divided the house and he followed it to the large kitchen, complete with a breakfast bar dividing the area. *Yep, my stools would fit there perfectly.* The cabinets were painted white and the walls were in a pale yellow.

The addition of a laundry room had been added to the original home and, stepping through, he discovered it led to a back patio in a small, fenced yard. *Not much to have to tend, but a great place for a barbeque or just sitting under a tree.*

A half-bathroom was tucked next to the kitchen and, moving past, he grinned as he walked up the stairs, his gaze landing on the large bedroom, complete with a huge master bathroom.

"Of course, this house usually rents to a single or couple due to the single bedroom, so for your purposes, it would be great. That's why the rent is so reasonable."

"Yeah it would," he said, his thoughts running to finally getting out of the fire station and into his own place. Turning abruptly, he stuck out his hand. "Where do I sign?"

As soon as the paperwork was completed and he paid the first month's rent, he headed back to the station. Eager to get a move arranged, his plans were halted by a call out.

26

"I'm sure you're wondering about my objectives in interviewing for a counselor position," Madelyn said to Charles as they sat in his office. He had already reviewed her resume, called her references, and they had discussed her specialties.

"I would like to hear about your decision at this time in your life. You see, it isn't easy to get qualified counselors in this area. We have one itinerant counselor who travels three days a week across the seventeen-mile bridge tunnel from Virginia Beach. I live in Baytown and have for almost ten years. But," he smiled, "it takes a special person to want to live and work in this area."

"I understand," she agreed. "I was forthcoming about my leaving this area when my parents separated, then divorced, and why I had not been back." Seeing him nod, she continued, "But, I'm sure you wonder if this is a hasty decision and one that I might go back on quickly. While none of us has a crystal ball, I can say that I will not be returning to my job in North Carolina and for the foreseeable future, I want to stay in Baytown. I feel the need to connect with the place I called home for the first fourteen years of my life, as well as continuing the newfound friendships."

"Do you think this is simply a path in your grief journey?"

Holding his gaze, she replied, "I would be a fool not to consider that part of my desire to stay in Baytown is to connect with the father I lost, not only in death, but many years ago. So, yes, part of this is due to my grief, but that's not necessarily a bad thing, Charles. If my father hadn't died, leaving everything to me, then I would have never come back here. I certainly wouldn't be searching for answers because I didn't even know I had questions."

He smiled at her reply and nodded for her to continue.

"But I do want to explore, not only the area, but my memories, emotions, and feel that this is the perfect time for a life change." She stared out of his second-floor window for a moment, a sliver of the bay visible, and added reverently, "It's as though this place is calling to me. And it's a call I want to answer."

Grinning, Charles nodded. "Yes, I quite agree and couldn't have said it better. I will say that we're desperate for a children and adolescent counselor. I'll need to speak to the mental health board, which is run by the board of directors at the hospital. I can get back with you in a couple of days with their decision."

Standing, she shook his hand enthusiastically. "Thank you so much," she smiled before turning to leave the building. Walking out into the sunshine, she sucked in a deep breath, before walking down the street toward Jillian's shop.

"Things are heating up. I think we need to stop...or at least slow down."

They chuckled. "Heating up. What a choice of words."

"Stop laughing. You know what I mean. This is getting scary after we did that place where someone was living close by."

"You know that was a mistake. That man had died and I didn't think any one was there anymore."

"What if that woman from the window saw us? She's with the Fire Chief now. Maybe we should lay low for a while."

"No! We just have to be more careful, but I'm not stopping. And don't worry about her. If she saw anything, we woulda known about it. But just to be sure, I've got a plan to make sure she stays quiet." Moving closer, their shoes almost touching, they said, "And you're right along with me. No backing out now."

Turning, they walked away leaving the other person's chest quaking, wondering what they had gotten themselves into.

Driving into town, Madelyn was stunned at the crowds already gathered for the Eastern Shore Annual Fire & Rescue Volunteer town fundraising party. Zac, and the others, had warned her it would be huge since it encompassed all the two counties represented and this year it was held in Baytown. As she managed to find a parking spot along a residential street and walked toward the cordoned off Main Street, she realized it was not only a great fundraiser, but good for local businesses as well. Jillian's shop had a booth set up on the sidewalk and her employees were selling coffee to patrons in a long line waiting for the tasty brew.

Waving to her, she continued along to the block where the fire station stood, seeing the fire trucks and ambulances out, firemen in uniforms giving tours and letting kids climb into the driver's seat while their doting parents clicked pictures. Zac appeared busy, but as soon as he saw her, he motioned for her to come over.

Bending to kiss her chastely, he grinned, seeing wide-eyed awe.

"This is freaking amazing," she gushed, tossing her hand out, indicating the activities all around. "Is all this for the Fire and Rescue?"

"Yep. Baytown does their own separate block party just for us, but this is for raising money for both North Heron and Accawmacke counties. That's why there're so many people here today. It'll go all day and then into the tonight with several bands playing. It'll raise about ten thousand dollars...at least that's what we did last year and I'm hoping to top it this year."

"Well, I'm super impressed."

"There's a large chicken farm in Accawmacke and they've agreed to match our donations this year, so we could top twenty thousand dollars."

Grinning, she lifted on her toes to place a quick kiss on his lips. "Do you want me to hang out here?"

"Nah, I'm gonna be tied up here for a little while longer before the next shift of workers comes in. I think Roger's department comes in about an hour. You want to walk about the town and check out the activities and then swing back here? We can walk to the harbor together to see the booths over there. I think they're doing an oyster roast." Zac watched as Madelyn wrinkled her nose. "Don't like oysters?" Seeing her shake her head, he pulled her in close. "No worries. They have lots of different food." Nuzzling her neck, he let her go, watching as she walked down the street.

"Looks like you've got it bad, Chief," Tad called out, slapping him on the back. "Guess I'll soon be calling you Captain, huh?"

"Hopefully," he replied. Looking at the eager, young man in front of him, he asked, "Did you fill out all the paperwork for the Chief position? I sent in your recommendation."

Smiling widely, Tad nodded. "Yes, sir, I did. And thank you...if I get the position, I won't let you down."

Several more families came by with their small children, all excited to climb into the fire truck, so Tad ambled off, good-naturedly, giving them the guided tour.

Madelyn wandered down Main Street, smiling at the many people she now recognized and visiting in several of the shops. Continually looking down at her watch for when Zac would be able to catch up with her, she bumped into someone. Looking up suddenly, she smiled. "Charles. I'm so sorry. I wasn't looking where I was going."

"No worries," he assured, before introducing her to his wife and children. His smile genuine, he said, "I was going to call you tomorrow. I know this isn't a very professional way to do this, but the hospital board approved your employment."

Eyes wide, she gave a little jump as she grabbed his hand, pumping it up and down. "Oh, thank you. Thank you."

"Why don't you come in on Monday and we'll finish the paperwork and get you acclimated."

"Sounds perfect," she beamed. Watching his family move away through the crowd, she could not keep the grin from her face.

"Hey gorgeous," Zac whispered in Madelyn's ear as his arms wrapped around her from the back. Seeing Charles walking away and the huge smile on her face, his heart leaped at the news he hoped she heard. "Anything I should know, based on your expression?"

Clapping in glee, she twisted in his arms to place her hands on his shoulders. "I got the position. I'll find out the particulars on Monday, but for now...looks like I have a new job in Baytown."

With a whoop, he lifted her by the waist, giving her a twirl. Catching the attention of a few townspeople, he winked as he set her down. "Come on, let's grab some food before heading over to the music by the harbor."

Walking hand in hand, Madelyn's cheeks began to hurt from the perpetual smile on her face. Glancing to the side, viewing Zac's profile, she realized she could not remember the last time she felt so happy.

He caught her staring and shoulder bumped her. "What?"

Giving a little shake, she replied, "Nothing really. I'm just happy."

He stopped, lifting her hand to his lips and kissed her knuckles sweetly. "I'm glad, babe. Me too."

By the time they got their food from one of the many booths and found a group of friends ready to share their blanket, the mayor was up on the podium.

Corwin Banks took the microphone, waving to the crowd as though it were election year. After his words of greeting, he made the announcement that the preliminary figures from the benefit that day appeared to be exceeding what they had been in years past. As the crowd cheered, he grinned as though he personally had donated all the money instead of the community having come together for the fundraiser.

Corwin continued to hold on to the microphone for a few more minutes, touting the benefits of Baytown, particularly the improvements that had occurred while he held office. Finally, as the crowd's interest was waning, he said, "And, just to let you know, we are proud to announce that the city council has decided that our own Zachariah Hamilton will be the newly appointed Rescue Captain—"

The gathering erupted in more cheers as Zac sat, stunned at the mayor's way of announcing the decision. Smiling, he stood and waved as more well-wishers clapped him on the back.

Jumping up, Madelyn hugged him tightly before he dipped his head and planted a kiss on her lips, bringing more cheers from their friends.

"I'm so happy for you," she said, her eyes shining. "What a day for both of us!"

"Leave it to Corwin to make your announcement part of his speech, stealing your thunder," Brogan grumbled as others rolled their eyes.

"Whatever," Zac replied with a laugh. "I'm just glad I got the position."

"What will they do about the Fire Chief?" Tori asked.

"They'll now be able to officially advertise for the position and review applications."

"So, you'll still do both jobs until they decide?" Jillian asked, her brow crinkled with concern.

"Pretty much the same as what I'm doing now, but I've told Corwin and the town manager, Silas, that they need to make a decision by the time the grant money comes in for my position, which is in about three weeks. After that, they'll be without a Fire Chief."

After another hour, he turned reluctantly toward Madelyn and said, "I hate to do this, but I've got to go finish the cleanup of the station. You want to hang here?"

She thought for a moment before saying, "You know, I think I'll head home. This is great and I love hanging out with everyone, but now that I know I have a new job, I'd like to get some work done this evening before I meet the realtor tomorrow."

Thinking about a realtor, he said with a grin, "Can I come over later? I've got a surprise to share with you."

Lifting her eyebrow, she said, "I love what you share with me."

Barking out a laugh, he kissed her again, and said, "I'll come to your place when the cleanup is finished."

It took Madelyn a while to walk to her car and get out of town as the large crowds dispersed. The fundraising party was going to continue tomorrow night and end with fireworks seen from the town beach. Anxious to get home so she had some time to prepare for her meeting with Charles on Monday, she was glad to finally pull into the drive of her father's home.

Sitting in the car for a moment in the dark, she peered at the house, just visible in the moonlight. She had left a few lights on and was suddenly hit with a memory of coming home with her parents one night from the county fair. She had always loved the little house, her mother's flowers planted along the walk and the porch swing creaking in the breeze. Giving her head a little shake, she climbed out of the car and walked toward the front door.

A piece of paper was stuck to the door, partially hidden behind the screen. Curious, she pulled it down as she unlocked the door and walked inside. Tossing her keys to the small table she had left in the near empty house, she kicked off her boots before opening the folded paper.

Keep your mouth shut. I know who you're dating. If not, the next fire will be your house, not the shed.

Gasping, she dropped the paper onto the floor as she dug in her purse for her phone.

27

Driving up to Madelyn's father's house, rage firing through his blood, Zac's mood was similar to when he arrived when the shed was on fire. He had his phone on vibrate in his pocket and did not hear her call, so when Grant swung by the station to tell him about the 9-1-1 call she had made, fear gripped his heart.

Seeing several police and sheriff vehicles outside the house, he squealed to a stop, his tires kicking up gravel behind his truck. Jumping out, he raced to the door, slamming it open as he entered, seeing her sitting on the sofa. The almost bare room was filled with people.

Her pale face looked up, but she had barely stood before he advanced, his arms clasping her to his chest. Looking over her head toward the dining room where Colt and Mitch stood talking, he caught Mitch's eyes. Both men walked over, showing him the note which had been bagged for evidence.

"Why would they threaten me now?" Madelyn asked, leaning her head back to peer at the others in the room. "If I could identify them, wouldn't I have already done so?"

"I don't know," Mitch said, "but I've got the feeling that they laid low for a bit, wondering if you were going to identify them. Plus, you and Zac have now gone public with your relationship, so that might have brought out some fears. Now the desire to start another fire is growing, but with that desire, comes fear that they might be caught."

Rubbing her brow, she shook her head. "I'm so tired of having to leave this house." A nervous snort erupted, as she added, "I couldn't wait to get out of it and now that I'm being forced to, it pisses me off."

Colt said, "This escalates things, which means this person is getting desperate. I know it doesn't feel like a good thing, but desperate people make mistakes."

Looking down at her, Zac said, "Babe, go get your stuff. I've got you."

She nodded. "I can't believe I have to hide out in the Fire Station again." Quickly amending, she said, "Not that I don't want to be with you, but..." Sighing, she left the room and walked up the stairs."

"You got this?" Mitch asked.

"Got everyone on it now. I made a call as I was driving here. By the time we get there, at least the basics will be covered."

Mitch nodded as he walked over and placed a hand on Zac's shoulder. "We didn't even get a chance to congratulate you properly."

Hanging his head, he said, "She just found out that she got hired at the Eastern Shore Mental Health Group today also. I wanted to celebrate, not have to worry about some nut-job burning down the county or threatening my girlfriend."

"I'll have the officer on night patrol go by your place on a rotation," Mitch promised.

Colt jumped in, "And I'll have a sheriff car patrol by this place, even if she's not staying here."

Ginny walked in the room, clearing her throat, gaining their attention. With a head jerk, she indicated that Madelyn was walking back down the stairs.

As she entered the room, with her suitcases and a laptop bag slung over her shoulder, she said, "I'm ready."

He hated the defeat in her voice and vowed to make her feel safe.

Ten minutes later, they drove down a residential street in Baytown. He glanced to the side, but it appeared she did not notice where they were heading. He reached over and took her hand in his, giving it a little squeeze. He drove around two SUVs parked on the street and on to a short, concrete drive.

Madelyn's gaze drifted to the scene in front of her, seeing a small house, nestled behind a large tree in the front yard. Brogan and Aiden were coming out of the house, their faces matched in grimness.

"Stay here, sweetheart," Zac said before climbing out of the driver's side.

She watched as the three men stood on the front walk for a few minutes talking, angry air swirling around them. Katelyn and Belle walked out of the house and, with glances at the male trio, hurried over to the car. Opening her door, she barely had time to step out when Belle engulfed her in a hug, quickly followed by Katelyn.

"You poor thing," Belle gushed. "If you need anything, you call."

"Whose house is this?" she asked, just as Zac stalked over to her. She watched as both women offered him a smile before they, and Aiden and Brogan, moved to their vehicles. Her brow lined with concern as she turned back to him. "Zac?"

"Come on, let's get you inside," he said, ushering her up the front steps.

He led her into the open living room, furnished with only the old sofa, end table, and lamp from his firehouse apartment. A brick fireplace centered on one wall and the rest of the room was painted a pale bluish-grey. His flat-screen TV rested on a stand on the floor.

She turned to see a small, empty dining room on the other side of the hall. Lifting her eyes to his face, she caught the sheepish grin.

"Look, none of this is going the way I wanted it to," he confessed, tossing his hands out to the side.

"I don't understand," she said, but was interrupted before she had a chance to say anything else.

He slid his hands down her arms and took her cold fingers in his own. Leading her to the sofa, he sat, pulling her down next to him. "Okay, here's the deal. I've been thinking for a while that I wanted to get a place. Somehow the idea of continuing to live in the fire station apartment began feeling more like a place to crash and not any real home. So, I already had the idea of finding a place to rent on my mind, before I met you. Then, after we got together, the apartment seemed rather...dorm-like. Not the place I wanted to bring you to."

"But this? This is yours? Since when?" she asked, her voice filled with surprise.

"I actually signed the rental papers the other day and was going to get my stuff moved in and buy a few more things before I brought you here." Pulling her closer, he said, "I had the guys help move some things yesterday, but then when I got the call from Mitch, I knew I had to get you out of your dad's house immediately. So, I asked Brogan to grab the rest of my stuff and get it here. He got Aiden to help and Katelyn to go get some food."

Blinking, she said, "They dropped everything they were doing at the town fundraising festival to take care of this?"

A slow smile crept over his face as his hands cupped her cheeks. "Baby, you still don't get it, do you? This...this is what Baytown does. These are what our friends will do. And I know that when one of them needs us, we'll step in as well."

Kissing her lightly, he watched as concern moved through her eyes.

"Zac, this is wonderful for you, but please tell me you didn't do this just for me?"

"I didn't...not just for you. I did it for me, as well."

She bit her lip in uncertainty and dropped her eyes. "I know I need to stay here for protection right now, but I can't move in with you. Not permanently. We're too new. This is too fast. If I hadn't been threatened, I'd still be at my dad's place until it sold—"

"This is not me rushing you," he assured. "You're right...for now, you need to be here where you are more protected. There are neighbors on either side and right behind us, instead of out by yourself at your dad's isolated house. But, I promise, as glad as I am to have you here, I'm not rushing this relationship. I want it. I want you. But I want you to be comfortable with us as well. Okay?"

Seeing her lips curl into a slight smile, he kissed her lightly once more before saying, "Let me show you around and then I'll bring your things in."

Standing, he walked her down the hall to the kitchen. She viewed the large room filled with white cabinets and pale, yellow walls. He opened the refrigerator and she peered in, stunned at the food the girls had provided.

His bar stools had been placed at the breakfast bar, giving them a place to eat since there was no dining room furniture.

She peeked into the half bathroom and then into the laundry room.

"The backyard is through that door," he explained, pointing to the door at the back of the room. "There's a patio and small, fenced-in yard."

He walked back down the hall, his fingers linked with hers. Ascending the stairs, he said, "I think you'll really like this."

As they entered the upstairs bedroom, she gasped at the space. "Oh, my," she breathed. The room only held his bed, nightstand, and dresser, but it was so large, it could easily hold more. The ceiling was slightly sloped on the ends, but most of the room had full, high ceilings. She allowed him to pull her toward the bathroom, where she discovered a large, airy room, complete with a deep tub, separate shower, long counter with double sinks and a separate small room for the toilet.

"This is amazing," she said, her focus on the bathtub and the long soak to come.

"I can tell you need that tub more than anything. Come on, first things first." Walking back downstairs, he said, "Why don't you find something the girls brought over that just needs to be nuked to eat and I'll get your things from the car."

As he walked outside, she rummaged through the refrigerator and found that Katelyn had brought over some of the Guinness stew that the pub had been serving for the festival. Placing it in the microwave to heat, she observed as Zac easily carried her cases into the house, setting them on the floor. He stood, heaving a sigh as he walked over to her.

Cocking her head to the side, she asked, "Too heavy?"

Chuckling, he replied, "No, smartass." Sobering, he

said, "I had this all planned out in my mind how it was going to go. I wanted to get this place fixed up a little... buy some furniture...hang curtains." Seeing her lifted eyebrow, he corrected, "Okay, maybe not hang curtains since I have no clue what that would entail."

He caressed her cheek, adding, "But, I really did want to make it a bit more like a home. Then I planned on taking you to dinner, somewhere nice, before bringing you here to show you my new place. I thought it was too soon to have you move in with me, but I still hoped you would like it enough to want to spend time here. You know...someplace new and fresh. Not your dad's house. Not the fire station."

She smiled, her gaze holding his as she leaned her cheek into the palm of his hand. "A real home for you... something you haven't had since your mother died. Someplace we can start fresh in, making new memories that aren't tied into the past."

"Exactly!" Not surprised that Madelyn understood him completely, Zac leaned in for a kiss. Just as he was about to take it deeper, the timer sounded on the microwave.

Grinning, she said, "Dinner's ready."

Sneaking in another kiss, he said, "To be continued?"

"Absolutely," she grinned in return.

They drove by the ramshackle house, long empty with the roof partially caving in.

"Perfect." Their eyes stared at the drooping wooden porch. The window panes were broken in a few places. The abandoned house, eerie against the darkening sky, was just what they had been looking for. A slow smile broke over their face as they pulled into the woods nearby.

28

Madelyn's eyes blinked open, the darkness outside indicating it was still nighttime. She and Zac had held each other close after her long soak in his tub. Falling asleep in his arms, she had been jarred awake when his phone went off.

He had dressed quickly before bending over to place a kiss on her forehead. "Go back to sleep, baby. I'll be home as soon as I can."

Sitting up in bed, she realized he had been gone for hours and sighed, hoping he, and the other rescue team, were okay. *I wonder if the arsonist struck again.* After going to the bathroom, she crawled back into his bed, pulling the covers up. As she drifted back to sleep, the image of the two figures running away from her shed fire and the rear lights on their vehicle ran through her mind.

Zac, in full equipment, stepped into the now smoldering building, checking for live embers with two more from his crew. Anger flowed through his veins at the reckless destruction. From all outward appearances, this had to be the arsonist's work. Carefully stepping over the charred wood, he made his way toward the back.

Calling into the radio attached to his Bunker Coat, he cleared the room that had formerly been the kitchen. A strange sensation filled him at the realization that even though this house had been abandoned for years, it had at one time been someone's home. He stared at where the sink still stood amongst the charred cabinets and thought of a woman looking out the window at her kids playing in the back yard. His head was weighed down with the helmet over the Nomex hood, but it did not stop him from giving it a shake to dislodge the images in his mind.

His boots trod over the floor as he headed toward a back room, seeing Roger near the front. Stopping suddenly, his eyes landed on a lump underneath some of the wood. *Oh, fucking hell, no!*

Two hours later, the medical examiner had taken the body to the morgue after giving his immediate impressions. "It appears smoke inhalation would have killed him first, before the burning wood fell on him."

Colt, Mitch, Hannah, Roger, Greg, Zac, and other law enforcement stood outside along with the volunteers still hovering in shock. Colt turned to the gathering and said, "For all the volunteers here, you knew the deal when you signed up for duty. What you see stays confidential. Don't talk about this to the press, if you are asked. Keep everything you say through official channels. At this time, we have no identification and aren't going to make assumptions. I know this finding is upsetting…it is to all of us. But, you must maintain your professionalism. Everyone understand?"

With nods from all, the Fire Chiefs and Rescue Captains sent the volunteers home. Zac walked over to a visibly shaken Tad. "You okay?"

"No one's ever gotten hurt before," he said.

Nodding, Zac said, "This house was abandoned, so there's a good chance the person who died inside was homeless, just looking for a sheltered place to sleep." Tad had no response, so Zac continued. "You apply for the Chief's job, you gotta be able to handle things like this. It's not all just putting out the fires and working the traffic accidents, you know."

Tad rubbed his hand over his face, fatigue showing. "I know. I got this. Honest, I do. I've just never seen a burned body before…at least not in real life."

"Go on home. Get some rest. The mental health group will have some counselors come see us tomorrow. Be at the station by lunchtime."

Watching Tad walk away, he moved back over to the law enforcers and chiefs still present. "This ratchets up the game," he said.

Colt said, "State Police are already on their way and I just got a call from the FBI. They'll be investigating as well."

Mitch looked at the chiefs and asked, "You got any idea if it could be someone you know?"

"I've turned over some of our records for Baytown, North Heron, Cherrytown, and Easton to Harrison Investigations. I'll check with them to see if they've noted anything."

"Well, just to let you know, it's probably going to be taken out of our hands," Colt replied. "I'm sure the Feds will now be running the show."

Zac walked back to the ambulance and drove to Baytown. As he sat in the station, writing his report, he glanced toward the door that led to his old apartment. *Has it been less than twenty-four hours since I moved out?* The thought of Maddie in his new house, in his bed, had him hurrying through the last of the report. For once, he had someone to go home to.

Madelyn, sitting with a small group of volunteers at a table in the fire station, glanced to the other circle of chairs filling the space. There were members of four of the fire stations present, many she recognized even if she did not know their names.

She did not see Zac, but knew he must be around somewhere. When he had gotten home in the wee hours of the morning, he showered before crawling into bed. She had tried to talk to him, but he claimed he was exhausted and so she simply wrapped her arms around him from behind, lay her head against his back and listened as his breathing slowed before following him into sleep.

When she awoke, he was gone. Charles had called

her within the hour to tell her about the emergency counseling debriefing that was going to be happening at the Baytown Fire Department and asked if she would be available. Agreeing, she felt hurt that Zac had not told her what had happened. Thinking he was trying to keep her from worrying, she headed to the station, but it now became obvious to her that he was avoiding her presence.

Turning back to her group, she listened as they talked about their desire to become fire and rescue volunteers, the different calls they went on, and how, for most of them, this was the first burned body they had dealt with. Some had dealt with death before—several with car accidents or heart attack victims, and a few had seen a child die at the beach the summer before when he had a food allergy attack.

She listened, asked questions when appropriate, but mostly gave them a safe forum to talk about their feelings and fears. As the afternoon wore on, they slowly began to leave, many with hugs to each other and often hugs for her as well.

"Zac's a good man," one said to her, before introducing himself. "I'm Buster. I've been with the Cherrytown unit for a while. Zac patched me up when I got injured last month. I'm glad he's gonna be the new Rescue Captain and glad the State finally realized we need more help."

She nodded and made sure he knew she was available if he needed to talk more. Watching him walk away, she saw Sarah meet Tad with a hug and kiss before they walked out of the station. She viewed Roger and Greg leave as well. Emotionally exhausted, she made her way over to Charles and Bets, the part time counselor.

"I'm so sorry I had to call you," Charles said, looking at her. "You haven't even officially began working for us, but I knew we needed all the help we could get."

"It's no problem," she assured. "These types of trauma debriefings are always so difficult, but I know how important is it to get emotions dealt with early and to let them know we are here."

Looking around for Zac, she did not see him. "Zac left a little while ago," Bets said. "I didn't ask where he was going, but he looked like he needed some alone time."

With a smile that did not reach her eyes, she said, "Well, if that's all, I'll head out now." Agreeing to meet the next day at the clinic she walked out into the cloudy day, her mood as glum as the sky. Seeing Aiden walking toward her, she looked up in curiosity.

"Hey," she said softly.

He did not stop until his arms were wrapped around her and he kissed the top of her head. "How are you?"

Leaning back, her curiosity still piqued, she replied, "Been better."

"I'll bet." Aiden let go of her, allowing her to step back a foot, still peering up at him. "Listen, I wanted to see how you were, after the note, having to leave your dad's house, and now this."

"I'm okay," she said, dropping her gaze to the sidewalk.

He lifted her chin with his fingers and said, "Saw Zac head toward the pier...alone. I figured he might need you."

Tilting her head to the side, she narrowed her eyes. "Are you sure? Maybe he just really wants to be alone."

"I'm telling you that being alone is the last thing he needs." She remained silent, so Aiden continued. "He doesn't need time to get inside his head and start thinking that life is safer all alone. It wasn't easy for him to watch his dad fall apart after his mom died. So, to him, avoiding pain is to avoid love."

"Love?" she asked dubiously, her heart pounding.

"Madelyn, he and I've been best friends since we were babies. And I'm telling you, he's one hundred percent in love with you." Grinning, he added, "He might not be ready to acknowledge it yet, and it probably scares the shit out of him, but don't let him pull away."

Kissing the top of her head again, he gave her a nudge toward the pier. Offering him a little smile, she began walking down the street.

Aiden watched her, leaning against the brick fire station, a smile playing about his lips as well. As he pushed off and began walking toward the pub, he was suddenly surrounded by his siblings.

"Holy shit, if I hadn't heard it myself, I woulda never believed it," Brogan said. "Aiden MacFarlane, a romantic matchmaker."

Katelyn grinned, linking her arms with her brothers. "Awww, I think you're both cute!"

The trio laughed as they made their way toward Finn's.

Zac sat on the end of the town pier, slumped against one of the posts, the hard wood digging into his back. He rested his forearms on his bent knees, watching the gulls dip in and out of the water, calling to each other. The lump in his throat that had appeared as he moved through the station, seeing his brothers and sisters of the rescue services sitting with the counselors. Then his eyes had moved to Maddie and his heart ached that she had to be part of the group, knowing her own grief was still so fresh.

He knew he had to escape and the best place to try to wrap his mind around the swirling, tangled mess of thoughts in his head was the pier.

Madelyn walked down the long pier, with the gentle slapping of waves against the pylons, the gulls calling out over the water, and the distant shouts of children on the beach the only sounds heard. She did not see Zac and wondered if Aiden had been wrong. *Maybe he went home.* She continued until she was able to see to the very end and recognized him sitting with his back against one of the posts, his legs bent at the knees and his head bowed.

Suddenly unsure if she should approach, she stood still for a moment. Watching as he lifted his head, scrubbing his hand over his face, she began walking toward him once more. As she got closer, he turned his head toward her, his eyes filled with anguish.

Unheeding her concerns, she rushed forward, falling on her knees next to him, taking his face in her hands. "Oh, Zac, I'm so sorry for all you're going through."

He immediately curled her into his arms, pulling her body onto his lap. They sat in silence for a long time, each with their own thoughts, but hearts beating as one.

Zac finally pulled his head back from Madelyn's neck, and held her gaze. "Thanks for coming to find me."

"I thought you might want to be alone but Aiden told me I should make sure you didn't get inside your head."

Grunting, he acknowledged his friend certainly knew him well.

"Do you want to talk?"

"Are you being a counselor or my girlfriend?" he asked.

She thought before answering, "Both. I don't think I can separate the two."

"Fair enough," he nodded. Sighing heavily, he said, "It just brought back memories." When she stayed silent, he continued, "As I walked through the burned house, even though it was supposed to be abandoned, I couldn't help but think about a family living there at one time. A mom looking out at kids in the yard. A family sitting down to meals. When you see a house that has burned, it's a harsh reminder that it was once a home. A living, breathing home that you hope was filled with love, but is now just a charred shell. And, if I'm honest, it reminded me of my parents' home. When I was little, it was such a great place with Mom and Dad and me."

She shifted slightly to the side of his legs, making herself more comfortable, her gaze never leaving his. Nodding her encouragement for him to continue, she held his hands.

"Then when I found the body—"

She gasped, wide eyed. "You found the body last night?" At his sad nod, her eyes filled with tears. "Oh, sweetie, how horrible for you. Why didn't you tell me?"

"I wanted to spare you," he confessed. "You've had so much to deal with and I thought it was best to separate you from what I saw. I had no idea Charles was going to call you in today. So, of course, you found out all about it."

She squeezed his fingers, saying, "I always want to know what happens. I want to know what you're going through."

Sucking in a deep breath, he said, "I'm not used to this. And it scares the shit outta me." Seeing her head tilt in confusion, he added, "For the first time since my mom died when I was ten years old, I feel like I have a shot at happiness. With you. But, I know, so well, that life can change in an instant and everything I hold dear can be taken away. I thought I had a handle on that. Getting close to you, I knew I had to face that fear and I did. I thought I had it beat. It just kind of snuck back up on me."

"I can't give you any promises about tomorrow," she said. "Like you, I know how tentative life can be. But I can promise that, for as long as I can, I'll be by your side."

His heart pounded in his chest as her words seeped into the cold recesses of his being. "What are you saying?"

"I'm saying I love you, Zac Hamilton."

Crushing her to him, his lips landed on hers, pouring his soul into the kiss. Losing himself as he delved into her warmth, his tongue tangling with hers, he felt like a starving man desperate for a drop of her essence.

She mumbled against his lips, "Take me home."

As the word penetrated his lust-filled mind, he leaned back slightly to peer into her eyes. *Home. A home with her.* Grinning, he stood and lifted her into his arms with ease. Stalking back down the pier, he kissed her again. "Yeah, baby. Let's go home."

29

Zac walked into the police station, not surprised to see the entire force, along with Colt and Hannah, in attendance. As he made his way to an empty chair, Roger, Greg, and Adam walked in as well.

Colt nodded at everyone before beginning. "We have the preliminary findings from the medical examiner and the state forensic office. The body found was Sylvester Mangum. He's a longtime resident of the Eastern Shore and is well known among those who assist the homeless. I talked to them today and they said that he often would only stay a night or two in the shelters but would be gone for weeks before showing back up. It looks like he found an abandoned house to sleep in, and the arsonists never suspected someone was inside."

"State Police taking over now?" Lance asked.

Nodding, Colt said, "Yep, they're running the show

and the FBI will be investigating as well. We are stretched to our budget limits as it is."

"Good, then maybe the State will keep giving us the funds we need," Roger spouted.

As the others continued to comment on the budget, the legal jurisdictions, and the investigation, Zac sat quietly, his heart aching for the man who died, alone, and most certainly without even knowing what was happening around him. *So much like my dad.* Looking up, he caught Mitch and Grant staring at him, concern in their eyes. His mind told him to shoot them a carefree, half-grin, but his heart stuttered. Swallowing deeply, he looked down at his hands clenched together beneath the table.

Loud voices could be heard from outside the room and he sat up straight, ready to enter whatever battle was occurring.

"Fuck," Mitch breathed under his breath.

The door opened and in walked Corwin Banks and Silas Mills, with Mildred and Mable on their heels attempting to pull the men back.

"When are you going to learn, Corwin Banks, that you can't go pushing your way in to a closed meeting?" Mildred said, jerking on the sleeve of his coat.

Corwin blustered, his ruddy cheeks and jowls shaking with each word. "Chief Evans, I've got a crowd of people at the door of my office, wanting to know what we're doing about the dead man! A dead man! Why wasn't I told? I had to sneak out the back way to get here to avoid the mob that's threatening me, wanting to know why I haven't made a statement!"

"Not your statement to make," Mitch growled. "The fire occurred in the county, not in the town."

Corwin smiled widely, "Well, that's good, good."

"You fool," Mable said, giving his coat another tug. "Nothing's good about a lost life, no matter where it occurred."

Corwin had the good sense to blush under the glare of the two sisters. "That's not what I meant. It's just that it keeps it out of our town limits, so it makes it easier on us."

Mable's grey curls shook as she lifted her hand to him and pointed right at his chest. "Don't you forget an election year is coming up. You keep being a pompous ass and you might find yourself unemployed!"

Silas pushed out his chest, his eyes beady, and asked, "Who was the man killed? Someone that's going to get everyone upset?"

Mitch stood, his gaze nailing Silas, and said, "The body identified was Sylvester Magnum—"

"Who?"

"He was a longtime resident of the county, currently homeless—"

"A homeless man? If you ask me, we're better off without one more deadbeat in this area—"

Zac jumped to his feet, "Shut the fu—"

"Out!" Mitch roared toward the pair, cutting Zac off.

Corwin and Silas blanched in the face of his anger. "Well, I'm sure we respect all lives," Corwin began, as Mildred jerked hard enough on his coat to pull him backwards. "I'll give a statement to that effect and assure the public that our safety officers are doing all they can."

Silas' eyes narrowed as they swept the gathering, landing on Zac, whose rage was barely in check. A sneer curved his lips as he turned and walked out.

After the pair left, Mitch nodded toward Colt who concluded the meeting. As the others were filing out, Mitch and Grant stopped Zac before he could exit the room. Grant closed the door, effectively cutting off his exit.

Glaring at his friends, he said, "Not to be a dick, but I really don't want to talk right now."

"Just want to make sure you're all right," Grant said.

"This is hitting close to home for you," Mitch added, "and we just want to be here for you."

Scrubbing his hand over his face, he heaved a great sigh. Looking into the concerned faces of two of his oldest friends, he slowly shook his head. "Honestly? This case is pushing me to the edge, no doubt about it."

"You need help?"

He sucked in a cleansing breath and let it out slowly. "I've started talking to a counselor. I realized I had become numb to my dad's drinking…it just became the norm for my life back then. And when he died, I buried those feelings along with him. Went on with life. Navy. Firefighting. Rescue. This case has been bringing up some things that I'm getting help with."

"Glad to hear it," Grant said, his eyes warm on his friend.

"And Madelyn?" Mitch asked. "Her dad's death and then the fire at her place?"

Nodding, he said, "Gotta admit, becoming involved with her has probably had more effect on me than the case, but I think in a good way. Because of her, I've been getting a handle on what I need to face. Some things are just going to take longer than others." He turned his tired face to his friends, a small smile on his lips. "But, with her in my life now, it makes going home a lot less lonely, so I'll be okay."

His phone vibrated and he glanced at the screen. "Gotta go. Gareth wants to meet so I'm hoping he and Katelyn have had a chance to analyze our reports to see if they can spot any patterns.

A few minutes later he sat at the worktable at Harrison Investigations with Gareth and Katelyn, leaning forward in eager anticipation of what they had found.

"You were right," Gareth began. "I've gone through the reports and, while we can find some coincidences, there was nothing conclusive. This doesn't include all the applications that were turned down."

"I put the reports in a spreadsheet and then pulled data from that," Katelyn explained. She scooted papers toward him before continuing. "With your station, some of your volunteers arrived in their own vehicles, several of them making it to the fires before the trucks arrived. Tad, Joe, Connie, and Chuck were at the top of the list. With Cherrytown, they've got Cathy, Rick, and Buster at the top of the list for arriving first in their own vehicles. And with Easton, most of their volunteers arrive in their vehicles but, then, Easton is so small that it makes it simpler for them to do that."

He looked over the list, recognizing all the names as men and women he had met, many he had personally worked with over the years at fires or accidents.

"With North Heron, they've got more, of course, with a larger area to cover. Looks like the very top of the list is Helen, Stan, Lashawn, and Joseph."

Zac shook his head, amazed at what they had been able to discern, but frustrated at the lack of a clear-cut possibility.

Katelyn said, "Considering that the profile is generally white male, age seventeen to twenty-four, that narrows the list to Tad, Chuck, Stan, and Lashawn. Buster is right there, at twenty-five."

He slumped in his chair and said, "What sucks about this is that we could be looking for anyone. The only reason we're looking at this list is because they sort-of fit the profile. But it could be someone from Accawmacke County, somewhere else, or who the fuck knows?"

Katelyn leaned over, placing her hand on his arm. "I know how hard this is for you, Zac. I'm so sorry."

He offered a slight smile in appreciation of her concern. "I'm good…or as good as I can be." Standing, he said, "But, I'll be better when the bastard's caught." Collecting the papers, he thanked them both. "Send the bill and I'll get the payment for you."

With hugs goodbye, he headed back to the station, a strange sense of dread filling his mind.

Standing in the kitchen of her father's house, Madelyn signed the papers to list it.

"It looks nice and I think, at the reasonable price you're offering, we can make a good sale," the realtor said, her smile bright.

After the realtor left, she walked through the house once more, soaking in the memories, both good and bad. She had packed up the last of the furniture she was keeping, including the journals and scrapbooks, and had them placed in a storage facility on the outskirts of town. Standing in the doorway of her old bedroom, now void of any personality, she heard a knock on the front door. Thinking the realtor must have forgotten to have her sign something, she hurried down.

Coming to a halt, she observed her mother standing on the other side of the screen. Her breath caught in her throat as she approached slowly. Her mother, hair still the same dark color as always, was trimmed neatly in a shoulder length bob. Her face was still youthful, faint lines emanating from her eyes the only wrinkles visible. High cheekbones hinted at Native American blood, so resembling hers. Seeing her mother was like looking into a futuristic mirror.

Opening the screen door, she was able to see the concern in her mother's dark eyes and the nervous tick in her jaw.

"Mom," she greeted softly.

"I...I wanted to come...and...talk. Try to...well, just talk," her mother said, her voice filled with uncertainty.

Glancing behind her, she said, "There's no furniture

left. I've emptied the house and just signed the papers for the realtor to list it. But, you can come in if you like."

Nodding sharply, her mother stepped over the threshold, her face tight with pain. Her gaze drifted to the empty space and her chin quivered. "I never thought to be back here again," she said, barely above a whisper.

The anger Madelyn felt toward her mother melted slightly as she watched the evidence of pain on her face. "Mom, why don't we go somewhere else to talk."

Her mother dropped her chin to her chest as she dug out a tissue from her purse. Wiping her eyes, she said, "Maybe in a bit. But I think the first part of what I need to say needs to happen here. Here where it all started. And here where it all ended."

30

They walked into the kitchen, standing on either side of the counter. Madelyn watched as her mother lay her hands on the surface, almost reverently, touching it with her fingertips. Staying silent, she decided that this was her mother's show...her time.

Inhaling deeply and letting it out in one long sigh, her mother began. "I loved this house. Once. I still remember when your father and I saw it for the first time. We were newly married. Young. In love. Naïve. The realtor showed us around and we knew we could afford it...barely, but we were so excited, we would have given anything to own it.

"We painted each room and filled it with furniture. Lenny found great pieces at discount prices by searching yard sales and antique shops that had more than just expensive antiques. I thought he was the smartest man." She chuckled softly at the memory.

Looking at Madelyn, she said, "I knew he drank.

He celebrated most events by drinking a little too much, but I figured that's what some men did. My father did not drink alcohol at all, so I had no idea what was too much." Her gaze drifted around the kitchen again.

"I worked at the pharmacy as a cashier and your dad worked on some of the local farms. Money wasn't plentiful, but there was always enough to cover all our bills and save a little. I was frugal...it was my parents' teaching. Your father liked to spend money. He never had much growing up and with both of us working, it seemed like we hit the lottery."

Madelyn listened to her mother's recitation, realizing she never knew any of her parents' history, but then she supposed most children did not know what life was like for their parents' early in their marriage.

Her mother continued, "I don't know when I finally realized that things were getting worse. He celebrated the news of my pregnancy by going out with his friends and drinking. He also celebrated your birth by going out to a bar with his friends." Sighing again, she shook her head sadly. "But I loved him so. He was kind, caring. He loved you beyond reason and was such a good father. He worked hard, so I figured if he played hard, that wasn't bad. He wasn't a mean drunk. He wasn't abusive. He was just drunk. And that part of his life began to take over."

Madelyn's legs were tired from standing and she noticed the fatigue in her mother's stance. "Mom, you can't be comfortable. Would you like to sit down, or um...go somewhere else?"

Her mother glanced out the window. "How about we sit outside?"

Nodding, she opened the back door and they moved to the patio, where a few folding lawn chairs were propped against the wall. Setting them up, angled toward each other, they settled again.

Taking up her story, her mother said, "I suppose the first time I realized that we had a problem was when one of our checks bounced. I knew it had to be a mistake, but when I went into the bank, they showed me a series of withdrawals from our checking account. Fifty dollars. Twenty dollars. Seventy-five dollars. I was stunned. Our savings was intact, but our checking account was almost empty. I came home and confronted your father. He just laughed, told me that he had it covered. When I pressed him, he confessed that he had been buying antiques, searching for that one piece that would be worth thousands. That was our first big argument. He was spending money that was needed for necessities."

"How old was I then?"

Her mother thought, then said, "You were probably about seven or so."

Nodding, she said nothing, remembering that she was in elementary school before she ever heard her parents argue.

"I ended up taking a second job at the post office to help cover our expenses when he promised that he would not spend money without checking with me first." Shaking her head, her mother admitted, "I was resentful. I worked about sixty hours a week, made sure you were taken care of, did the housework, did the cooking, and began taking care of the yard. Your father was working his days at the Johnson's farm but spending his evenings drinking and his weekends out looking for furniture."

Rubbing her hand over her forehead as though to rub out the painful memories, she sucked in a shuddering breath. Madelyn, her heart aching, reached over to place her hand on her mother's knee.

"I'm sorry, I didn't know, Mom."

Jerking her head up, her mother landed her wide-eyed gaze on her. "Oh, sweetheart, I kept all that from you. I never wanted you to know. I might have resented your father, but he was so good with you, I didn't want to taint that." Sighing, she said, "Looking back, there are so many other things I should have done."

"What really happened, Mom?"

"Things kept getting worse. Your father lost his job because he showed up, more than once, intoxicated. I had to open up a separate bank account, in my name only, and started putting most of my paycheck in it, so that he couldn't get to it. Our relationship had deteriorated to arguments about his drinking and spending money he didn't have. I hated for you to hear it, but I was so tired. So very tired."

She heard the agony in her mother's voice, her heart aching for her parents' marriage dissolving even though they both had loved each other.

"One day, I went driving. I needed to get away. I had a rare day off, you were in school, and I just needed a break. I ended up in Accawmacke, at a coffeehouse near the water. I just sat, drinking tea, and looked out on the coast. The man who owned the shop came over, asking if I were okay." Giving a little chuckle, she admitted, "I had tears rolling down my cheeks and didn't even realize it. Anyway, he introduced himself and we began to talk. He was so kind. He listened as I poured my heart out to a perfect stranger."

"Saul," Madelyn said softly, understanding slowly coming over her.

Turning her sad eyes to her daughter, her mother nodded. "Yes. Saul." Looking back out over the yard, she continued, "I began to drive to his shop a few times a month, just to have a bit of peace. He was calm. Kind. A good listener. He was a little older than me and his wife had died years before from cancer. I never meant to fall in love with him. That's not an excuse. I was a married woman who was visiting another man, even if it was in public." Chuckling ruefully, she said, "We never even kissed after we knew we cared for each other."

"You told Tonya?"

"We were friends and she knew how bad things were at home. I told her about Saul and she was trying not to be judgmental, but she said I needed to end one relationship before starting another. In all honesty...she was right. As Lenny became less stable, and I realized he was an alcoholic, I tried so often to have him get help. He denied he had a problem and I felt trapped."

"What pushed you over the edge, Mom?"

Licking her lips, she said, "I came home one day from work and you weren't here. I was terrified until I heard the car careening into the driveway. Your dad was driving while intoxicated, with you in the car. I was livid. I waited until you went to bed and told him then that I was done. That I was taking you away until he got help. He just laughed and completely dismissed my threat. You were fourteen."

"I remember that," Madelyn breathed. "I called him because I had to stay after school to get some makeup work done and needed a ride home."

"Sweetie, it's not your fault. It wasn't your responsibility...that lay on his shoulders. So, I packed you up and we headed to North Carolina to where my parents were."

"And Saul?"

"He followed. He opened a shop in North Carolina, allowing his sister to take over the shop here." Piercing Madelyn with her gaze, she added, "I know you may not believe this, but I didn't sleep with Saul while still married to your father. I filed for divorce and yes, we dated while I was still separated, but it was not until the divorce became final that we consummated our relationship."

They sat quietly for several minutes, each lost to their own thoughts. Finally, she said, "You know, Mom, a lot of that makes sense. But when I think of the journals dad left me... He said that he got into AA and his counselor told him to journal his thoughts. So, he did that in the form of letters to me. He admitted he made mistakes. That he shouldn't have pushed me away when I came to see him. He admitted he drank too much, spent too much money. But, he also mentioned that he had been in contact with you and you intimated that we would be a family again. Then, there was the heartbreaking entry where he found out you were married again. Not to mention that you said I didn't want a relationship with him. How do you explain that?"

Blowing out a breath, her mother said, "I'm not perfect and, Lord knows, I made mistakes. Things that I now wish I had handled differently." Appearing to gather her thoughts, she said, "You begged me to see him again and it was right after he said he had joined AA. I thought it would be good. It would show me that he was trying to better himself and therefore I could at least allow you to have a relationship with him. Saul agreed and encouraged the trip. He said he wanted me to be sure that my feelings for Lenny had irrefutably changed. I didn't tell Lenny we were coming...I wanted us to see him without him being able to prepare ahead of time. I suppose it was me testing him." Ruefully snorting, she admitted, "That did not turn out well. He was off alcohol, but it was still hard. He was painfully thin and a little unkempt. He was embarrassed and we had surprised him so he said things that could be interpreted badly. I understood that, but you were so upset. So, I drove us straight back to North Carolina. The divorce went through the next year and I married Saul."

Leaning forward to take Madelyn's hand, she said, "I knew that I was no longer in love with Lenny. I would always have a place for him in my heart, but no longer wanted to be married to him. Life with Saul was good. He took care of us. Loved you like his own daughter."

"And me? I'm happy for you, Mom, truly, that you found love and you got out of a bad marriage. But what about me? You let your own anger get in the way and set Dad up to fail by not giving him a chance to prepare that day. You may not have been able to stop him drinking but you didn't have to ruin my chance at a relationship with him. If you knew why he was embarrassed and lashed out, why didn't you try to explain that to me? He was my father and you just decided that he wouldn't be anymore."

"I was only doing what I thought was best. He wasn't good for us anymore, Madelyn. The decisions he was making? Spending all our money, driving while drunk—and with you in the car! I told Saul how upset you were with what your dad said. We agreed that it was not in your best interest to see him again. At least, not for a while, not until you were older." Shrugging, she admitted, "I did not tell him that I was getting married. That was probably a mistake. He deserved to know."

"His journals said that you told him we could be a family again."

Shaking her head, she said, "Your father was always great at hearing what he wanted to hear...not always what was said. I told him that when he was completely sober, and you were older, then he could reach out and we would talk about when you could see him again. By then, you were almost sixteen years old and had joined some things in high school, finding new friends. We already had a life in North Carolina when I told him that I was married."

"How did he take that?"

Her mother looked over the backyard again, a wistful expression on her face. Madelyn watched her, realizing that the dissolution of a family was rarely an easy thing for any of the members, no matter what role they played in it. The toll on her mother showed in her face.

"Not well. Although, he didn't express anger...just sadness. He said he was so sorry to have not realized sooner that he had a problem. I told him that Saul was good to you, but that I felt that you would want to have a relationship with him. I don't know what he thought, Madelyn, but he didn't reach out to you. Maybe he thought it was going to come from you. Maybe he thought you were better off without him. Maybe he thought he didn't deserve you." Shrugging, she added, "I don't know and I didn't try to find out. I had my new life and it was a good one, so I let bygones be bygones."

"I'm going to be honest. I'm struggling with what you are telling me and what Dad said in his journals about wanting to see me. But actions speak louder than words, and neither one of you did the right thing where I was concerned. If Dad wanted to see me he should have made the effort. But you should have made the effort too—for me. I was the kid in all of this. You were the parent. And you let me stay angry for so long, when maybe I didn't have to be."

Taking a deep breath, she looked at her hands.

What else was there to say? It was too late to change anything now.

"When I came here, I was surprised when I walked in. The house could have been on Hoarders, with furniture piled to the ceiling in some rooms." She watched her mother's eyes widen, and said, "I met a nice antique dealer, who said he and Dad were friends and would go furniture shopping together. He's the one who placed a value on the contents and hauled them off for an auction. He came highly recommended, so I feel good about him taking care of that aspect of Dad's estate."

"And the funeral? I later felt guilty that you had to deal with it all alone."

"Baytown stepped up and helped. Jillian Evans, who married Grant Wilder, and Katelyn MacFarlane, who's now married also, got the American Legion and the Legion Auxiliary to take care of the service and reception. It seems Dad did get sober and actually made a life for himself...a simple life, but at least he had some friends." Seeing her mom nod, she continued, "He talked to Zac Hamilton about being in the Navy and Zac spoke at the service."

Her mom eyed her carefully, and said, "Is that the young man you're involved with?" As she nodded, her mom said, "I remember when Mary Hamilton died. Her husband took to the drink as well. Are you sure you're not involved with someone like your father—"

"No!" she bit out, suddenly angry. "Zac is nothing like his father or mine. He's a firefighter and EMT. In fact, he has been the Fire Chief. He's brave and kind and takes care of me. I won't allow you to insinuate that he is a drunk or that he will be. Don't cast theirs, or your, mistakes on me."

Sucking in her lips, her mother blushed. "I'm sorry. You're right."

They sat quietly, the silence broken by the crickets and occasional bird chirping.

"So, you're staying? Here in Baytown?"

"Mom, you know I was unhappy at the clinic with Julius as my boss. You and Saul have your own life, your own friends. I've made more friends and been accepted by more people here than I have in the past four years since grad school."

Her mother's eyes roamed over her, assessing, but warm. "I can see that. I confess that I also remember Baytown fondly, before things became untenable at home. I'll miss you, but am glad to see you really happy."

"You only live three hours away, Mom."

"So, you will still see me?"

Madelyn heard the fear in her mother's voice as they both stood. She wrapped her arms around her shoulders, saying, "Of course. You didn't always make the right choices, but neither did he. None of us do. I know you were trying to protect me. I now know that my dad loved me and never meant to reject me, even if I will never know why he stayed away. I wish I had the chance to know him when he became sober, but I can't go back and change the past. At least I have come to peace with what was and can move forward, taking the good memories with me and the journals, knowing that he cared."

"Maddie?"

She whipped her head around, seeing Zac walking around the corner of the house, his face full of concern.

Zac stared at the two women so alike in appearance that he instantly knew the older woman was Maddie's mother. His body tensed at the thought that Maddie would change her mind and decide to move back to North Carolina. His gaze, as well as his body, moved to her, assessing her mood. Reaching her, he relaxed slightly as her gentle smile met him.

"Zac, this is my mother, Gwen Bernstein. Mom, this is Zac Hamilton."

Taking Gwen's hand in his, he greeted her politely. "Nice to meet you, Mrs. Bernstein."

"Likewise," she said, smiling up at him, before turning to Madelyn. "I was just going, dear. Thank you for allowing me to explain, and for understanding. I hope you will bring Zac to visit soon. Saul would love to meet him."

Zac stood back, allowing her to offer her mother a deep hung. Pulling her back to him as they watched Gwen leave through the house, he looked down. "Babe, I got worried when you didn't come home."

"I'm sorry I didn't let you know I was still here. She showed up just as the realtor left."

He kissed the top of her head, his fears easing. "How are you?"

"I'm okay. She caught me by surprise with her visit, but we talked. She was honest and I have a better understanding of my parents. Both their relationship with each other and with me. I was angry with my dad for so long, I don't want to make the same mistake with my mom. It's all good. I understand and I love them both. Man, it feels so good to say that! Such a weight has been lifted."

"And you're staying?" he asked tentatively.

Smiling widely up at him, she wrapped her arms around his neck, pulling him down for a kiss. "There's no place on earth I'd rather be than in Baytown with you."

31

Light came through the window, but before she could blink her eyes open, Madelyn felt Zac's arms tighten around her, pulling her back against his chest. Grinning, she felt his erection pressing into her ass and wiggled slightly, causing a groan to slip from his lips.

Sliding his hand up to her breast, he kneaded the pliant flesh, tweaking her nipple. She shifted her leg as he reached around, sliding his finger into her channel, his thumb pressing on her clit. Desire pooled in her core and she began pressing harder against his erection. She reached back, her hand encircling his shaft.

He swiftly lifted her leg and guided his cock into her channel from behind, sliding deep into her warmth. It did not take long for them both to come, the explosion of his seed into her sex at the same time as her core tightened around him.

The groan ripped from deep within his chest tangled with the cry of his name on her lips. He lay, still deep inside of her, as their bodies cooled in the early morning. Lifting his hand to her cheek, he turned her gently as he leaned over to meet her lips. Kissing her, he muttered, "Good morning, babe."

Giggling, she shifted in the bed, hating to lose his cock, but wanting to see his face. Cupping his stubbled jaw, she whispered, "Good morning to you."

"Best way to wake up," he added. "Nowhere I'd rather be than in your arms."

The evening in the pub was calm and Madelyn enjoyed her fish and chips while sitting at the bar. Aiden's antics and Brogan's continual scowling at his brother had her laughing during her meal.

Katelyn plopped down on the seat next to her, saying, "Glad you're here. I know Zac gets nervous when you're not with someone."

Rolling her eyes, she said, "I didn't let him know where I was the other day and he got so nervous. I hate this, but don't know when it'll end."

"Probably not until they catch the asshole setting the fires."

"Did the FBI interview you?" Brogan asked.

Nodding, she stuffed another french fry into her mouth. "Oh yeah. The FBI and the State Police. They kept asking the same questions over and over again about the night of the fire in the shed, but I just don't remember anything other than what I told them."

"Why do they keep asking?" Aiden wondered aloud.

Katelyn replied, "People can suppress the tiniest of details that come back later. I guess they're hoping there's a distinguishing tidbit that Madelyn might remember."

"Well, unfortunately, I haven't remembered anything new."

Her phone vibrated and she picked it up. "Zac says he's still at the station." Looking up, she explained, "They were having another emergency meeting. I think the area law enforcement and Fire Chiefs were meeting tonight." Finished with her meal, she said, "I think I'll walk up the street and meet him there."

"Not alone," Brogan said. "Hang on a minute and I'll go with you. I can pick up Ginny at the same time."

Smiling, she accepted his offer, knowing Zac would rest easier if she were escorted. Sending a text back, she let him know she was coming to him and Brogan would walk with her.

The sun had just dipped below the horizon and the town's street lamps glowed against the darkening sky. As they reached the block where the fire station was located, she was amazed at the number of vehicles. "Wow, how many people are here?"

"I guess between Baytown, Easton, Cherrytown, North Heron, and who knows who else is here, there might be about thirty or so people at the meeting. It doesn't include the volunteers, but the police, sheriff, deputies, as well as fire and rescue are all here for it."

As they approached the building, Brogan said, "We can go in here and wait."

Nodding, her eyes moved to a white, panel van, idling down the block. Walking through the open bay door, she watched as Brogan moved to talk to a few of the volunteers that were milling about near the fire trucks.

Standing to the side, she smiled at a few of the people she knew. Tad walked over, greeting her.

"Hey, Madelyn. How are you doing?"

She smiled and replied, "I'm fine."

"I heard you were interviewed by the big dogs."

Chuckling, she said, "I guess you could say that. The FBI and State Police wanted to grill me about the shed fire."

"You remember anything specific?" he asked, his eyes boring into hers.

"Not anything more than I'd already told them. Two figures...but I don't know if they were male or female." Shrugging, she said, "I'll be so glad when it's all over. I'm terrified they will strike a building that someone else is in again."

Nodding, he grunted before lifting his hand in a wave and moved back to the others. Her phone vibrated and she moved to the door to answer the call. A short conversation with her mother ensued and she disconnected, glad to have salvaged the relationship. Standing in the doorway, her eyes drifted to the van still idling. The left, red taillight flickered continually. Staring at the back of the vehicle, a tickling of a memory edged into her mind as she watched the fluttering light.

Pushing off the wall, she moved toward the van, curious as to who was inside. The door opened and she recognized Nola from the picnic. "Oh, hello," she said. "I was just looking at your van."

"Why?" the young woman asked, her face hard.

"It seemed...uh..." her words floated off as the flickering light held her attention, a memory of the flickering taillight solidifying in her mind. The lights on the vehicle as it left her property. What she assumed was braking was instead just like the faulty bulb she was staring at.

Turning to hurry back to the station, she felt an intense pain in the back of her head before blackness descended.

32

Sarah raced into the fire station, skidding to a stop in front of Tad, Brogan, and the others, screaming, "Madelyn! They got Madelyn."

The gathering looked at her, their faces slack with confusion. Tad grabbed his girlfriend by the shoulders, holding her in place. "What? Who's got Madelyn?"

"Nola. I saw Nola. She hit Madelyn and put her in the back of their van!"

Brogan rushed outside, just in time to see the white van disappearing down the street. "Fuck! My truck is at the pub!"

Tad yelled for Zac, who came out of the meeting room, the other emergency response members piling out with him. Tad's gaze landed on Roger and his eyes narrowed.

"Sarah saw Nola hit Madelyn and take off with her."

Roger started to move, but Grant and Ginny immediately moved to either side of him, with Burt right behind.

Zac, fear clawing at his throat as the news hit him, ran to his truck. Brogan grabbed the keys from his hand and climbed into the passenger side. Mitch, Colt, and the other law enforcement personnel raced outside, their sirens blaring as they fell in line behind Zac's truck.

Madelyn blinked her eyes open as she rolled to the side on a hard surface. Her memory returning, she leaned her head back to see that she was in the back of the van, Nola at the wheel. She was not restrained, but hesitated to sit up, afraid to let Nola see her awake. Something rolled into her leg and she looked down, observing empty bottles. Two red plastic cans for gasoline were sitting nearby, with a pile of rags to the side. *The accelerants the arsonists used. Nola? Roger?*

Hearing sirens in the background, she knew the police must be close. Suddenly Nola took a turn too fast and Madelyn rolled to the side again, slamming against the metal door. Her head ached, her heart pounded, and she prayed Zac and the others would get to her before Nola got away.

The radio in Zac's truck blared with the warning Mitch

was spouting. “Brogan, move to the side. Let us pass. State Police and North Heron Sheriff are in pursuit.”

“Don’t listen to him,” Zac ordered, his hands gripping the dashboard.

“Fuck, man, you know I gotta.” Brogan slowed the truck down slightly, moving toward the right shoulder so that the law enforcement vehicles could pass before he moved back. “Call your people,” he ordered.

Zac knew if Nola wrecked, the fire trucks and ambulances would be needed, but before he could react, the dispatcher let him know they were on their way. *Thank God, Tad must have taken over.*

Dark had descended fully now and his eyes were trained on the line of red taillights and flashing emergency lights from the vehicles in front of them. Praying it was not too late, he held on tighter as Brogan turned sharply to the right onto a smaller road, following the caravan of police.

Sitting up, Madelyn caught Nola’s eyes in the rearview mirror. “Pull over, Nola. You can’t escape.”

“I didn’t want to do this. I never wanted to do any of this.”

Hoping to make some kind of connection with the wild-eyed woman, she said, “Roger. It was all him, wasn’t it?”

“Yes!” Nola bit out. “I told him it was a mistake. But he said it was the only way.”

Bouncing off the side of the van again as Nola took

another curve, she said, "Let's slow down and you can tell them. You can tell them it was him. His idea. His doing."

"I'll be just as guilty." Nola wiped her face, her eyes once more landing on Madelyn's in the back. Twisting her head around, she ordered, "Sit down. Stop moving."

Looking out the windshield, she saw a dead end ahead, a large tree directly in front of them. "Look out!" she screamed as Nola swung her head toward the front, stomping on the brakes.

The van went into a skid, careening wildly from side to side as the back fishtailed. With nothing to grab on to, Madelyn threw her hands over her head the instant before the van slammed its side into the tree. Hurling against the metal door again, she screamed out in pain as her arm took the brunt of the fall and her head bounced on the floor. The vehicle rocked to a stop at a precarious angle, listing to the side. The canisters had landed on top of Madelyn, gasoline spilling out.

"Shit!" she cursed, kicking the cans away from her body. Twisting, she got to her knees and looked at the driver's seat. Nola was slumped over, her body held in place by the seatbelt, the deflated airbag in her lap.

Crawling toward her, her right arm almost useless, she managed to peer out of the passenger window, seeing the ground close, and knew it would be impossible to escape that way. Standing on the console, she tried to open the driver's door, but did not have the strength to push it upward. Glancing down, she observed blood drops on the unconscious Nola, then realized they came from her. Wiping her cheek, her fingers were coated in red.

The sirens were now close and the flashing red and blue lights from the various emergency vehicles were all around the outside of the van.

"Maddie! Maddie!" she heard Zac yell.

Banging on the back of the van drew her attention and she watched as Zac's face peered through the window.

"Maddie. Can you get to the door? Can you unlock it?"

She skidded across the metal floor toward the door, but was unable to see how to unlock it. "I can't see anything," she yelled. Looking down at her soaked pants, she yelled, "There's gasoline in here...and rags! It's spilled all over me. Nola's unconscious in the driver's seat."

"Fuck!" came the expletive. "Are you hurt?"

"My arm might be broken."

Zac, his heart in his throat, turned as the other rescue members encircled the van. He looked at Greg, Adam, and Terry, followed closely by the many volunteers. "She's in the back. Gasoline from canisters has leaked. We can't use the jaws to get her out without the possibility of sparking a fire. Go through the driver's door. Nola's unconscious. Maddie's injured."

The others quickly stepped in as he turned back to the door. Tad led the firefighters as he made his way to extract Nola through her door.

Knowing he needed to let them work the accident, he placed his hands on the window as he willed his heartbeat to slow. "Get some light here," he called out to the others.

Bright spotlights were immediately focused on the van, allowing him to peer in. Madelyn's pale face stared back at him, her eyes wide with fright, blood running down her chin. "Babe, I've got you. They're going to open her door and pull her out. Does this light allow you to see the locking mechanism?"

With the interior now illuminated, Madelyn blinked while swiping her hair from her face. She heard the driver's door opening and the van rocked slightly as someone was working on Nola.

"Babe. Maddie," Zac called. "I need you to focus, sweetheart. Look at this door."

She turned back and, with more light inside now, spied a metal handle on the side. Reaching out with her left hand, she flipped it with some difficulty. She had barely lifted her hand off the lever before the door was jerked open.

Zac's arms reached in and gathered her, lifting her in his arms.

Protesting, she cried, "No, no, I've got gasoline all over me."

"Doesn't matter, baby," he said softly, hustling her away from the van. The gathering parted for him to move, some of the volunteers following closely. Mitch, Grant, Brogan, and Ginny hustled along with him to the back of one of the ambulances. "Give us some privacy," he barked and his friends quickly formed a blockade as they held up blankets. Ginny stepped in with Zac, assisting in pulling Madelyn's clothes off.

They were careful of her arm, which Zac splinted as soon as it was free from her gasoline sprinkled shirt.

Ginny slid Madelyn's pants down her legs, which were soaked at the bottom, and then looked up at Zac. "Her panties are fine."

Nodding, he said, "Thanks. Let's get her wrapped." Lifting her gently, he placed her on the stretcher as Ginny covered her with a blanket.

"Officer MacFarlane, I'll take it from here," Ann called from the ambulance door. Ginny smiled at the efficient woman and hopped down, allowing the EMT to assist Zac.

The vision of the van slamming into the tree, almost turning over on its side, filled his mind. Trying to force himself to work on autopilot, Ann elbowed him in the side.

"Zac," she said softly, "let me do the work and you just focus on being the boyfriend."

Nodding numbly, he leaned over, cupping Madelyn's cheek. Kissing her hair, he said, "I'm here, baby. I love you, I'm here."

"Stay with me," she whispered, her eyes dark in her pale face.

"Always," he said, his lips still pressed against her head.

33

Zac stood at the two-way mirror watching as Roger, with his public defender present, was interrogated by Colt. The State Police were also with Colt, but Mitch was standing with Zac in the observation room.

"We were something, weren't we?" Roger asked, a smile playing about his lips.

"Something?" Colt prodded.

"Yeah. They had a name for us. For me. The Ghost Arsonist. And we did it. We got this place on the map. Got the FBI looking into us, the State Police. Hell, no one could figure out who we were. I saw the excitement on the faces of the ones I worked with. They'd come driving up to the fire and I could see the glow in their eyes."

"Did you set all of the fires?"

Shifting in his seat, Roger shook his head. "She needed an outlet. Nola gets bored easily and I wanted to make sure she stayed with me." His hands shook as he lifted one to rub over his short hair. "She liked fire... always did. Been around her when we were kids and knew she liked to play with fire. As she grew up and held my interest, I knew I needed to keep her. Do something big to keep a woman like that."

"A woman like that?"

"You know. Beautiful. Hell, I ain't nothin' to look at, but when she agreed to go out with me, I knew right then that there was nothin' I wouldn't do to keep her."

"And the fires?"

Chuckling, Roger said, "She got excited when we'd go out and light a fire. Afterwards, the...um...well, the sex was good. Better than good. I knew I'd found a way to keep her."

"What was the first fire you set?"

"We used to just go somewhere and set a small fire, like in a camp pit. Then we got to talking about how she'd like to see something big on fire so she could see me work." Shrugging, he continued, "So we went out and set the old Culler shed on fire...back off Marker's Lane. It went up quick and we just stood there, watching the flames shoot into the air. As soon as we heard the trucks coming, we ran off, but she was fascinated with watching the fire fighters working. She loved it. Best sex I ever had was that night."

In the observation room, Zac breathed, "What the fuck?"

Mitch nodded slowly, his voice low as well. "What some people will do for love...or their version of love."

Still listening, they heard Colt ask, "And the times you were at the fire as Chief?"

Grinning, Roger replied, "That gave her a real thrill. But, I gotta admit, I started getting a thrill too. We got a name. We got notoriety. And then we got you guys. We were in the national news and finally we were highlighting that we needed more help, more equipment." Leaning back in his metal chair, Roger smiled. "Don't you see the help we were giving to the counties here?"

"And the man killed in one of your fires?"

The smile slid from Roger's face as a cloud passed through his eyes. "That wasn't supposed to happen." He appeared to be struggling with himself for a moment before lifting his eyes to Colt, then sliding them over to the mirror. "But, sometimes there are causalities in war."

Zac, thinking how close Madelyn came to losing her childhood home to the fire and her life in the accident, growled, "I've heard enough." Turning, he stalked out of the room and out of the station. Once in the sunlight, he slid his sunglasses on his face and climbed into his truck. *Time to go home...home to Maddie.*

Two days later, sitting on the sofa in Zac's house, Madelyn swung her legs to the floor in an effort to get more comfortable. Her arm, in a cast, was propped up on a pillow in her lap. The front door had become a revolving door of friends and well-wishers coming through. Zac had hovered over her, fretting in a way that was both endearing and confining. Their refrigerator was well-stocked with casseroles, salads, and desserts.

He walked in from the kitchen and his brow lowered. "What are you doing? You shouldn't get up."

"Zac, my ass will grow to this sofa if I don't move," she complained, standing to stretch her legs. "I'm fine... you know that."

"A broken arm and a concussion is not fine," he argued, stepping closer to place his hands on her shoulders. "You need to rest."

"Yes, and I've done that for the past two days." Lifting on her toes, she kissed the underside of his jaw. "I want to know."

He looked down at her and nodded. Taking her hand, he walked her back to the sofa, this time settling first before easing her into his lap, careful of her injured arm. "Roger and Nola were arrested the night of the accident. Roger, at the station, and Nola, at the hospital. To be honest, we're all stunned. Here we were, looking at the volunteer lists, the rejected applications, and anyone else we could think of, but never looked to the Chiefs."

"You can't blame yourself," she admonished. "Chiefs aren't usually the arsonists. It's the wanna-be firefighters."

Nodding, he agreed. "I know, but the idea of how many times Roger and I worked together when both our stations would respond to an emergency..."

"Have they said anything?"

Heaving a great sigh, he said, "It appears Nola's been a firestarter since she was a kid. It was, like you described, an addiction for her. When she met Roger, she was thrilled to be with a fireman. And he made Chief last year, but the money was never as good as they would have liked. He said he wanted to keep her interest, so he was willing to do whatever it took."

"And the man who was killed?"

"He said they had no idea he was there. I think it scared the hell outta Roger, but he seemed to be willing to keep going for her."

"She was the strong one," she stated.

His gaze jumped to hers, his brows lifted. "Yeah."

"I've seen it before...a strong woman leading a weaker man. He may have presented the strength needed to be a Chief, but in reality, it was all for show... for her. That's why she went after me."

"You were suddenly there, too close to discovering what was in the van. She panicked. Hit you, pushed you into the van and just took off, with no real plan in mind."

"As soon as I saw the flickering taillight, it came back to me. I can't believe that I had suppressed that memory all the times I went over that night in my mind. Even when the FBI interviewed me. I never thought of the light that flickered. But when I saw it the other night, the memory slammed into me."

"Jesus, when I think what could have happened," Zac said, his shoulders slumping, fatigue hitting him.

She lifted her hand, cupping his cheek. "Sweetheart, you have hardly slept in the past couple of days. Why don't you go lie down? I'm fine. We're fine. They've been caught and more will come out about their activities and motives, so we've still got a long way to go before this case is over. At least now no one has to fear sunsets anymore."

He kissed her forehead, pulling her close to his chest. She tucked her face into his neck, relaxing in his arms.

A knock on the door interrupted their moment. She lifted her head and, staring into his face, she laughed as he rolled his eyes. "I guess you had better get that."

"Any chance we can pretend we're not here?"

"Let us in," they heard Katelyn call.

"It's unlocked," he called, then watched as Katelyn, Jillian, Jade, Tori, Ginny, and Belle walked in.

"The men are coming right behind," Katelyn announced, her arms full of grocery bags. "We're bringing the party to you all."

Grant, Brogan, Lance, Mitch, Gareth, and Aiden followed, their arms full of more bags and cases of beer.

Lifting his eyebrow, he stared at the group filling his living room. "Impromptu party?"

Clapping him on the back, Aiden kissed Madelyn's cheek. "Figure we can celebrate the two of you, buddy."

Grinning in return, Zac winked at her. "Best reason to celebrate, isn't it, babe?"

Her smile was his answer as they settled back to enjoy their friends.

Three Months Later

The sky was streaked with yellow and orange as the sun settled lower on the horizon. The flame colors danced and morphed against the water, as Madelyn sat in the car, the final journal in her hand. She had read the words so many times, but knew that today she would want to read them again.

Dear Maddie,

It's been a couple of years since I wrote in this journal. I don't go to counseling anymore, but I have stayed active with AA. I kept up with you, mostly on Facebook, following you and watching your life in posts and pictures. Your mother used to accuse me of hearing only what I wanted to hear and after all these years, I think she was right. If I had been more open to what she was trying to tell me all along, we might could have salvaged our family.

I decided years ago to make peace with your mother's leaving, subsequent marriage, and did not try to contact you. A difficult decision, but from all evidence, you are living a happy life.

I have decided to leave my humble estate to you, in the hopes that when you return one day to Baytown, you will remember the good times spent here.

I joined the American Legion and had the opportunity to speak one evening with a wonderful young man, who had also served in the Navy. We spoke at great length about our experiences and I could not help but think that he was the type of young man any father would be proud to see their daughter be with.

I realize that by the time you read these entries, I will

most likely be gone, but it still gives me pleasure to have you know that you will be back in Baytown, even for a little while. If you get the chance to look up Zac Hamilton, please let him know that I appreciated our talks.

Take care, my dearest Maddie, and know that while your father was not perfect, he loves you very much.

Forever,

Your dad

Madelyn closed the journal, her hands resting on the worn cover. Saul looked at her, his smile warm, and asked, "Are you ready, sweetheart?"

Nodding, she swiped at the tears that threatened to fall. "I'm ready," she declared and lay the journal onto the seat.

As Madelyn walked down the makeshift aisle, her arm on Saul's, she smiled at the many residents of Baytown she now knew and called dear friends. The women from the Auxiliary and the co-workers from the clinic. Her eyes fell over the women standing near the front...Jillian, Katelyn, Tori, Jade, and Belle. Their smiles soothed her nerves as she focused on the man at the front, surrounded by his friends. Mitch, Grant, Aiden, Brogan, Callan. Others filled the chairs in the sand.

Zac's gaze never left her from the moment she alighted from the vehicle, approaching him now. Taking her hand, he bent to kiss her cheek as she stood in front of him.

The minister's service was short and soon their

vows were spoken, all underneath the ever-changing sunset sky.

Hours later, the reception was in full swing at Finn's Pub. Some couples danced as others sat at the bar and tables, laughter filling the air.

Zac, one hand clasping Madelyn's against his chest, the other resting on the small of her back, barely swayed to the music, lost in her eyes. "I love you, Mrs. Hamilton," he whispered, his nose nuzzling hers.

Her smile beaming up at him, she said, "I love you, too, Mr. Hamilton."

A call for another toast had them dragging their eyes from each other to turn, facing their friends. A moment later, Belle approached, regret in her eyes.

"I'm so sorry, but I have an early shift at the nursing home tomorrow, so I need to leave."

Madelyn hugged her tightly, saying, "I'm so glad you were part of my day...and part of my life."

Belle smiled, her gaze shifting to Zac before coming back to Madelyn. "You two are perfect together."

Hugging her again, she whispered in Belle's ear, "When you least expect it, it'll happen for you too."

A wistful smile slipped over Belle's lips as she waved goodbye to their friends and walked out the door.

A few minutes later, the door to Finn's opened and the gathering turned to see a huge man walk in. Long hair, built like a mountain, his piercing eyes roamed over the heads of the others in the room, landing first on Jason before settling on Zac.

"Hunter!" Zac called out, snagging Jason's attention, both men smiling as they stalked over to the newcomer.

Shaking hands and black slaps ensued as they greeted their friend. Zac grinned when Madelyn moved to his side.

"Hunter, you've come at a great time. This is my wife, Madelyn. Baby, this is an old Navy buddy that I reached out to about moving to Baytown. Like Jason, it looks like he's taken me up on the offer."

Hunter's eyes moved over her, his gaze obviously taking in her wedding dress. "Pleased to meet you. Seems like I came at a bad time."

"No, no," she rushed. "Any friend of Zac's is more than welcome. Come on in, there's plenty of food and drinks."

Zac made the introductions to the others, especially the men in the American Legion. As the men talked for a few minutes, Jillian sidled up to Madelyn.

"He doesn't say much, does he?" Jillian commented.

"And he's huge," Jade added.

Just then the women heard Zac ask, "Do you have a place to stay?"

"Gotta camper."

"And what about a job?" Zac continued.

"Handyman. At the nursing home. Start next week."

That tidbit of information had the women grinning as they turned away, moving back to the bar. Soon, Hunter left, eschewing the reception, and the men returned to claim their women for more dances.

The next morning, she awoke as the sun was just rising in the horizon, casting the faintest light into their room. She felt Zac's arm tighten around her middle and smiled.

"Whatcha thinking?" he asked, his voice gruff against her neck.

"I was just thinking about our wedding last night, on the beach at sunset."

He stayed silent, waiting for her to continue. She twisted in the bed so that she was now facing him, his arm now resting on her hip.

"I've now decided that my favorite time of day is sunset...it will always remind me of us."

Grinning against her lips, he kissed her, gently at first before taking it deeper. As the sun rose in the sky, they stayed entwined, their hearts beating as one.

Don't miss any news about new releases! Sign up for my Newsletter

If you liked Sunset Flames, check out the other book in the Baytown Boys Series

Baytown Boys (small town, military romantic suspense)

Coming Home

Just One More Chance

Clues of the Heart

Finding Peace

Picking Up the Pieces

Sunset Flames

Saint's Protection & Investigations (Military Romantic Suspense)
Serial Love
Healing Love
Seeing Love
Honor Love
Sacrifice Love
Remember Love
Discover Love
Surviving Love
Celebrating Love
Searching Love (coming 2018)

Heroes at Heart (Military Romance)
Zander
Rafe
Cael
Alvarez Security (military romantic suspense)
Gabe
Tony
Vinny
Jobe
Sleeper SEAL
Thin Ice
Letters From Home (military romance)
Class of Love
Freedom of Love
Bond of Love
The Love's Series (detectives)
Love's Taming

Love's Tempting

Love's Trusting

The Fairfield Series (small town detectives)

Emma's Home

Laurie's Time

Carol's Image

Fireworks Over Fairfield

Please take the time to leave a review of this book. Feel free to contact me, especially if you enjoyed my book. I love to hear from readers!

Facebook

Email

Website

Made in the USA
Lexington, KY
09 February 2019